THE TESTIMONIAL

by Ira S. Hubbard

DORRANCE
PUBLISHING CO
EST. 1920
PITTSBURGH, PENNSYLVANIA 15222

The contents of this work, including, but not limited to, the accuracy of events, people, and places depicted; opinions expressed; permission to use previously published materials included; and any advice given or actions advocated are solely the responsibility of the author, who assumes all liability for said work and indemnifies the publisher against any claims stemming from publication of the work.

Dorrance Publishing Co
701 Smithfield Street
Pittsburgh, PA 15222
Visit our website at *www.dorrancebookstore.com*

ISBN: 978-1-4809-1192-5
eISBN 978-1-4809-1514-5

ACKNOWLEDGMENTS

I never knew if I would actually write a book. It was a lifelong goal, and it was also a difficult one to realize. This work was something I greatly enjoyed.

I would like to thank Daisie Redden, who was the first person to read a complete, rough draft of the book. She gave me the valuable feedback and insight into the story I was trying to tell.

I would like to thank Bethany Wood, who also took the time to read a rough draft of the book and who gave me thoughts and ideas for the story.

I would also like to thank my big "sis," Loretta Faye Ventro, who also took her time to read a rough draft of the book, all while working a full-time job and attending college. I am very grateful to all three people for their time and feedback. There are specific parts of this book that were influenced by each of these ladies.

I want to thank my parents, who both, in their own way, have greatly influenced me. My father taught me the importance of hard work and who, I am glad to say, gave me a solid work ethic. My mother always taught me to believe in myself.

I would also like to thank my wife, Amanda Hubbard, who was the inspiration for the book. My wife gave her heart to God last year. When I decided to write a book, I had several ideas in my head. Watching my wife go through the journey from a sinner to a Christian, however, inspired me to pursue the ideas I had for the story of this book. Like everything in my life, my wife is my inspiration and my best friend.

PROLOGUE
NORTH KOREA

He sat in a meditation pose, his legs crossed, and his open palms facing upward. His back was covered with tattoos and drawings. In the center of his back was a picture of Jesus on the cross, blood flowing from his palms and feet, the crown of thorns on his head, blood coming down his face. The cross went horizontally across his back, just below the shoulders and vertically up his back, from the bottom of his back to the top of his neck. One of their finest hours, he had always told himself. He always found comfort in that moment before the resurrection; the moment that it all seemed to be coming together for them. Then it was all taken away. For over two thousand years, they had waited; waited for their chance. A chance that some said would never come. He took in a deep breath of air. He loved coming here. It was one of the most reclusive places on the planet. The fact that it was a communist country was the largest appeal for him. He loved being in places where the rule of the leading party was absolute and there were no Christians to be seen. He had earned this vacation; beaches, sand, and sun never held the appeal for him that it seemed to for others. Incense burned around the room, and the open windows allowed a slight breeze to enter, which made the many burning candles flicker. He had meditated and prayed for days. He was closer to his master now than he had ever been. Something was coming, he could feel it. He didn't know what, but his master had been telling him this for the last few days. His phone began to ring. He took in another deep breath and slowly opened his eyes before answering it. He pushed a button and slowly raised the phone to his ear. "Cain?"

The voice on the phone said, "Yes. We need you in America; the United States."

Cain was silent for a moment. Then he said, "I don't go to America. There is nothing there that concerns me."

The voice said, "It's in the open. We have confirmed it. It's in the U.S."

Cain pondered this for a long moment and then said, "Do you know where?"

"Not yet," was the reply. "We have someone on the inside; a traitor. He is feeding us a steady stream of information; he wants to betray the Christians."

Cain looked up, closed his eyes, took another deep breath, and said, "Our master has been telling me something has been coming for days. This is it. This is the beginning of the end. I'll be there." Without another word, he hung up the phone and tossed it on the floor in front of him. He raised his arms upward and said aloud, "It's time, master. Use me as a tool. Work through me, and I will kill them all!"

With this a hard wind blew through the room, and the entire room shook as the candles blew out. As the room shook in what looked like an earthquake, Cain repeated in a louder voice, "I will kill them all in your honor, master!"

CHAPTER 1

He awoke to the sun in his face. He had been meaning to buy shades for a long time. He always hated the way the sun would ruin his late morning sleep. Today, though, nothing would bother him. He was too excited. He went to make his coffee. He usually loved mornings. He loved the way the day was beginning fresh and all the possibilities it could bring. Today was a special morning. His kitchen was plain. It was very small with no decoration. He ate his breakfast on an old metal kitchen table that looked like something someone had thrown it out. The red on top was faded, and the legs were rusted. He drank from a plain, ceramic mug and ate from one of only two plates that he owned. If he ever had company, he could not accommodate more than one other person without having to break out the Styrofoam plates and cups. He went to get ready. His bathroom was as plain as his kitchen. No decoration, not even a clock. The faded, flowered wallpaper, which was starting to peel, was an off-yellow, or at least he thought that was supposed to be the color. After his shower, he meticulously groomed himself and paid particular attention to his hair. He checked the reflection looking back at him. His black hair was perfectly combed. His dark eyes looked into the mirror at his dark complexion. At six feet tall, he had an Italian look about him, or at least that's what he was sometimes told. At other times, people would walk up to him and begin to speak Spanish, thinking he had to be Hispanic. In truth, he was not sure where he actually came from. His mother knew little of her heritage, and he never knew his father. He checked his nose for those darn hairs that constantly seemed to creep up on him. He was wearing his best suit. His tie was tied perfectly, and his shirt was pressed. He checked his shoes. If he shined them one more time, he was afraid that he may wear a hole in them. He could not find anything else to do. He put some hair gel in his hair. Today was going to be one of the most important days in his life. "Well, that's about as good as it gets," he said aloud to himself.

At twenty-nine, he looked young and energetic. He was beginning to feel his age. He didn't seem to show it, but, he was watching for the signs. He didn't personally care, but he knew his age would be closely scrutinized. In the business world, they don't promote old people. They wanted young people with lots of years ahead of them to work. Being one year away from thirty, he was already starting to worry he may be too old for a promotion. Whatever his heritage, he assumed he must have descended from people who aged well. He thought about that for a minute. He had lived his twenties as a workaholic. He had saved, saved, and saved some more. He had worked more hours than anyone he knew. He had lived and breathed his job. He had become one of the most knowledgeable employees at his company. He had stayed away from women, alcohol, and drugs; things that a lot of his colleagues indulged in often. It wasn't that he didn't drink—he actually enjoyed it in those rare times he had indulged himself. It wasn't that he didn't like women. He never had the desire to try drugs. Anytime he was around them, it was as if something kept him from trying them. It was just that he was determined he would not end up a nobody. No matter what else he did or didn't do, he would make his mark in the world. At a young age, he had made a commitment to himself that he would work the hours no one else would work and he would make the sacrifices that others would not. Ultimately, he saw himself as a very wealthy, middle-aged man, coaching other young executives on the merits of hard work. He had never let anyone distract him from his goals. There had been women— lots of women, actually. But he never let them get close. He always kept them at arm's length. It had been lonely at times, but today was the day it would all pay off. As he walked back through his bedroom, the sunlight hit him in the face again. If today goes well, I think I may buy some blinds to celebrate, he thought to himself. Then his face lit up as he exited his small apartment. If today goes well, I can get a whole new apartment, he thought.

As he waited by the bus stop, he recited his lines. He thought of what he would say. He had a couple of jokes to soften them up. He was just trying to decide who he would speak to first. He knew that Mr. Trenton was the most important man in the room, but the other executives would have input on the final decision. Would he make small talk first or just get right to his presentation? Small talk was always his weakness. He always preferred to get right to business. His supervisor had told him more than once that he would have to master the art or he may never get promoted. He had watched others pass him by, but today was his day, today was his chance. He had finally gotten a chance to interview for a corporate position.

As the bus pulled up, he felt people bunching in around him, all looking for their chance to get on the bus. Normally this didn't bother him. He decided years ago that he wouldn't think of getting a car until he became a junior executive. It was a commitment to which he had stuck. Besides, who would want to own a car in this city? Today was the first day he could remember wondering if he should have given in and let himself have a vehicle. Even if he didn't drive it every day, he could use it on days like this. The bus was very crowded. He noticed an open seat to the outside. A large man had the window seat. He jumped in the aisle seat, thinking at least he would not have to bunch into a seat with someone else. As the last of the people got on the bus, a lady came down the aisle. She had long, graying hair. Her head was covered with a dirty scarf. She wore a long, green, faded dress. Either she had owned it all her life or she had gotten it at a charity store. Everyone else had managed to find a seat. She was the only one left in the isle. As she shuffled down the aisle, she looked for a seat. Each person she came by looked at her in disgust. She seemed unfazed by their stares. She slowly looked each one in the eye, with the unspoken question, "May I have a seat?" Each time their look told her she was not welcome. He had become accustomed to this. She was probably homeless. Most people had put up an unconscious wall to these people. Even though he was raised in a city, he could not build such a wall, as hard as he tried. He had to give his mother credit for that, he supposed. She had always taught him to see all people as people. There were no real differences. She always wanted him to see them for who they were on the inside, not the outside. Most people only saw the outside. Most people could walk right past them or ignore them without a second thought. There were times he wanted to resent them and what they were to society but, in the end, he always felt sympathy for them. He could pass on luxuries for himself without a second thought, but he was always a sucker for those people with the cans in their hands who he would pass on the sidewalk. He rarely went by one without dropping something in.

The seat in front of him was open. There was a well-dressed woman in a business suit who was sitting in the middle, with a smaller, young man occupying the window seat. Everyone knew these seats could hold three people. He was sure she would be able to sit there. She slowly approached the woman. The woman, busy on her phone, didn't look up. The older lady stood there, watching patiently. The bus driver looked annoyed, waiting for her to be seated. The woman finally looked up from her phone. She studied the older lady for a moment. Then, as everyone stared, she slowly slid herself to the edge of the seat, ensuring the unspoken message was conveyed to the woman: "You're not welcome here." The older lady didn't seem to mind. She just began to move to the next row of seats back…his seat. He was so frustrated. With everything else he had today, he didn't need distractions. He could feel his anger building. She would have to find somewhere else to sit. Not today, today's too important, he told himself. By this time, she was standing over him. He would not be like everyone else. He would look her in the eye and tell her to find another place. Couldn't she see he was busy? He looked up and then...he saw the softness in her eyes; the gentle stare. She would move on, if he really wanted her to. He stared for a moment, and then he slowly slid over into the large man who was almost asleep. He felt his right elbow push into him as he slid over. The man, not seeming to care, adjusted himself and then began to pursue his nap. The bus slowly began to lurch forward.

He was so aggravated. I'll just look down, he thought. She would have to see that he was busy and just sit silently through the bus ride. He began rehearsing his lines again. He had to be perfect; he could not make a mistake. He had to look them each in the eye. "So, what's your name?" she said in a heavy British accent.

This was totally blowing his concentration. British? he thought. A homeless British person in America? He didn't want to ask. He didn't want to hear her story. He didn't have time. Not today.

"Your name?" she said again.

He responded without looking at her. "David."

"Oh, what a grand name; a good Christian name," she said. He didn't respond. "Did you know that name came from the Bible?"

"Yes," he replied, the frustration evident in his voice.

She continued, not seeming to notice. "David was a great king, a giant killer, a warrior. One of God's finest." He had heard all this before. His mother used to tell him often of the stories. He knew who David was, or he knew the story. He never understood his mother. How she could believe in something so faithfully? Something that never gave her anything back? Something that wasn't true? He always felt he must have taken after his father. He never shared his mother's beliefs. He never understood her devotion. The old lady spoke again, "Did your mother name you after the David in the Bible, or was it another David?"

Obviously she was trying to make small talk. He really didn't care to engage in small talk today, with so much at stake. "No, it was the David in the Bible and, yes, I know the history of the name," he replied, barely masking his annoyance with her.

She continued, "It was always one of my favorite stories. The boy who slayed the giant and later became the king." He continued to stare down. "It must give you comfort," she stated simply.

While he found the statement a little presumptuous, he had to ask, "Comfort?"

"Yes," she replied, "knowing you were named after someone of such importance."

"I really don't believe in any of that," he replied.

"Any of that? You mean the story of King David, or the Bible?" she asked.

4

"Well...both," he replied flatly. "I think it is simply a very well written book." There, he thought, that will have to shut her up. He began to rehearse his presentation again in his head.

The bus slowly came to a stop. The old lady slowly lifted up out of her seat. The old lady spoke, without looking at him, "Well, it doesn't really matter." Then she stared down at him and spoke softly, "It...He is real. Whether you believe in him or not, it doesn't make him any less real."

He looked up again, his eyes meeting hers. He saw it there. She believed with everything inside of her. While he didn't possess it, he could recognize it in others. As he grew up, he was around many people who believed; he could always see it in the eyes. Regardless of what they said, one look in the eyes and he always felt that he could tell if they were sincere.

"Oh, well," the old lady sighed as she turned away. "He is patient, and you are still young; we won't give up on you just yet." She proceeded down the aisle. As she walked away, she said, "Goodbye, David; may God bless you."

He watched her get off the bus. He found her annoying, but he also could not stop looking at her. As the bus pulled away, he watched her slowly limp down the street. "What a fruit cake," the man beside him said as he turned to get more comfortable for his nap. He didn't respond; he just continued to stare as the bus drove by her on the street. He considered their conversation for a moment then, looking at his watch, he began to work on his presentation again.

The bus pulled to the corner of Fifth and E Streets. He got off. At least the weather was cooperating; it was a beautiful day. He had to walk the last block. He never got off the bus in front of the building. He never wanted anyone in his office to know he didn't own a car. He always told fellow employees that he lived close, loved to walk, hated to drive, or whatever else kept them from asking too many questions about how he got to work.

He was maneuvering through the crowded street when his phone rang. It was Rus. Rus was his supervisor. He was the senior director on his floor. He had been with the company for almost twenty years. He was well-connected and seemed to know everyone. Rus had been his supervisor for almost his entire ten years at the company. Everyone called him Rus. No one really knew why. There had been an office pool going for years now about his name. If anyone could find out why he went by Rus, the entire office would chip in for a vacation to Hawaii. Many had tried to crack the mystery. Some had even tried to spy a glimpse of his file from H.R. One particularly aggressive employee actually got into the file cabinet a few years back, only to find he wasn't in the regular employee files. All members of management in the company had their first name, last name, and title on their doors, but his door simply said, "Rus, Senior Director." The theory was that his legal name was Russell or Rusty, and Rus was short for that. It seemed simple enough. David always smiled when he thought about this. His secret was that he was probably the only one in the company who knew the truth. A few years back at a Christmas party, Rus had gotten too drunk to drive. David drove him home in his car and got him to divulge the truth on the way. As a boy, he was a chronic bed wetter. His mother, who had to wash his sheets daily, joked that the cast iron bed he slept in was going to rust and fall apart. She called him her little Rusty. The name stuck. His entire family started calling him Rusty. When he became a teenager, it shortened to Rus. David had initially planned to cash in his discovery for the free trip at the team's expense but, in the end, he liked Rus so much he could not deprive him of the fun he got from the whole thing.

The phone was on the third ring now; he thought he had better answer before Rus had a meltdown. He clicked the answer button, and before he could speak, he heard, "Morning! Are you ready?" Rus was always like a cheerleader.

"As ready as I'm going to get," David said.

"Listen, don't worry too much; it will just make you start sweating, and they will throw you out of the room!"

David appreciated the poor attempt at humor. "Is this my pep talk?" David asked.

"More like your pre-interview before the interview," Rus said. "Listen, I want a few minutes with you before you go in with them. Go straight to the top floor; I'll be there waiting."

David absorbed that for a moment. He had had his talk with Rus yesterday before he went home. He had gone over his presentation, his answers, and his back-up plans if they threw him a curve in the interview. There was really nothing more to talk about. He was a little puzzled what Rus could want. "Okay, I guess I'll see you then," he said awkwardly.

"Great. Oh, one more thing: use the restroom before you get up here. It may be your last chance for a couple of hours," Rus said, laughing.

"Wow, you really do think of everything. I'll see you in a few minutes." David hung up the phone. He was a little worried that Rus wanted to see him. Was something wrong? Did Rus have some last-minute concerns? He had to admit, the bathroom thing was a good idea. He had been so focused on rehearsing his answers that he would have forgotten and may have had to get up in the middle of the interview. He increased his stride now. He was early, but he didn't want to have to be in a rush. He had allowed himself time to sit in the waiting room and work on his prep. The restrooms would be crowded this time of morning; he wanted to get in and out quickly. A few minutes later, he arrived at the building. It was one of the tallest in the city. He looked up. Going all the way to the top floor today, he thought to himself. The lobby was very crowded. It was a mixture of employees and clients, all moving in for meetings. He stepped out of the restroom and strode toward the elevators. The line was long, and it stretched all the way out into the lobby. He checked his watch; he still had plenty of time. He looked up for a moment; the lobby was beautiful. He saw it every day, but he never got tired of looking at it. The walls had mirrored panels that extended up beyond view. There was a fountain in the center that had water slowly streaming down that went up for at least one hundred feet. In the center, where the fountain met the floor, was a seating area. Some clients liked to sit here and review their material or talk on their phone. Some employees liked to have their lunch there. David never found the time. His lunches were always at his desk, working on a report or replying to e-mails. As he scanned the seating area, his gaze stopped at a lady looking at him. As their eyes met, she quickly looked away. He, too, looked away. Was she looking at him? He thought she was, but maybe he was mistaken. He slowly looked back in her direction. She now looked engrossed in her cell phone. He had to admit she was beautiful. She had black hair, pulled tightly back. She was wearing an all-black business suit. She was trim, her long legs were crossed. Her thigh-high skirt came down almost to her knees. He could not make out her complexion from this distance, but her form was stunning. The glimpse he caught of her face was of high cheek bones and full lips. He couldn't help but stare. Maybe she wasn't looking at him. For a second, he thought she was looking at him first. Now he wasn't sure. He looked for a second longer, but she didn't look up again.

He heard someone make a throat-clearing noise behind him. He looked forward, and the line was moving. He looked back at the people behind him. He made a quick apology and moved forward. Just as he was moving out of sight of the woman, he looked back. She was gone. He scanned the area, but he could not find her. She was lost in the crowd now. The elevator was very crowded. He really was starting to sweat. The ride up took a long time. People got on and off. Buttons were pushed, but the elevator kept moving up. After what seemed like an eternity, he got to the top floor. As the elevator came to a stop, it hit him that he had never been on the top floor before. He could not believe that he had not thought about that before; ten years and never a trip to the executive floor. As the doors opened, he slowly walked off. A middle-aged, red-haired woman was sitting behind a very nice, black, sleek desk. Her glasses were pressed hard against her face. She gave him a look as if to say, *What is your business here?* After a moment, David said, "I'm here to see Mr. Trenton. My name is—"

"David," she interrupted. "You are a little early, but Rus wants to see you. He is waiting for you in Conference Room B. When you are done, you can proceed to Conference Room A for your interview." She looked down at her keyboard as if dismissing him. He wasn't sure where conference room A or B was located. He got the impression that he shouldn't ask, so he just started walking down the hall behind the desk. As he walked past her, she said, "Don't be late for your meeting," without looking up. He assumed this was her way of trying to be nice.

He said, "Thank you." She didn't reply. He walked slowly down the hall. Rus, he thought. She had said 'Rus is waiting on you.' Rus really did know everyone, he thought. As he walked slowly down the hall, he looked in the offices. They were amazing! The offices were large, posh, and elegant. They all had leather furniture, huge, high-backed chairs, and stunning views of the city, even from the hallway. As he moved down the hall, most of the offices were still empty. A couple of the offices had executives in them, sipping coffee and reading e-mails, starting their days. He felt like a tourist. Could one of these offices be his someday?

"You look like a tourist," came Rus' voice, laughing.

Slightly embarrassed, David looked around to see if anyone else was around. He looked back at Rus. "I guess this is the door to Conference Room B."

"Yes, unless you would like to finish the tour first," laughed Rus.

"No," David said. "We need to hurry; I've already been warned not to be late."

CHAPTER 2

The room had a long, mahogany table. High back, soft-rolling chairs with arm rests were all the way down and around it. There were drink stands and places to plug iPads or laptops at each seating. They really didn't spare any expense in this room, David thought.

"Sit down," said Rus, motioning to the nearest chair.

"What's this all about? I thought we covered everything yesterday evening," David said.

"Look, there was something I should have said." He sat down. "I just wanted to take a minute to let you know that you are ready. You have done all the things necessary to be in that room. You need to hold your head up and be proud. I have taught you everything that I know. You have worked the hours, learned the processes, and have all the necessary experiences to go to the next level."

David absorbed that for a moment. Inside, he had to admit, he had always resented Rus a little. Rus could have recommended him for this a few years back. He felt he was ready three or four years ago. Rus insisted that he was not. Rus had an incredible reputation. He was one of the most respected directors in the company. His team always ranked in the top 10 percent of the company, and Rus was a great talent developer. Many of his team members were recommended for other assignments, usually with more pay and responsibility. Rus stuck to one motto when it came to his people: Never promote someone till they are ready. He never waived from that. Rus would make you jump through the hoops; put in the hours and he would give you tough feedback when you were wrong. Sometimes he would push you so hard you would want to walk out. In the end, you found yourself wanting to stay on his team for one reason: He was genuine. He may not always tell you what you wanted to hear, but he always treated you with respect. He really cared for his team. While he, at times, resented that Rus had made him wait for this opportunity, he was aware of the fact that when Rus told his superiors someone was ready, they knew they were. He often wondered if he could have successfully taken on more responsibility three or four years ago. He didn't know, but he would like to have had the opportunity to find out. In the end, he considered Rus a friend. He didn't have to agree with him on everything, and he never took it personally. He appreciated that this very busy man had taken the time to speak with him before his interview. He looked up at Rus and smiled. "Thank you, I really appreciate the support. I'll try not to make you look bad in there." Rus smiled. David, smiling back, said, "You know, if I get into the program, you could be working for me one day."

"Believe me, I know. Why do you think I have put all this time into you? When you get up here, I plan to have you loan me the corporate jet the next time my family wants to go to Disney World."

David had often wondered why Rus didn't move up himself. "You know, I have to tell you, I have always wondered why you don't move up," David confessed.

Rus looked at him for a long moment, as if wondering if he would respond to this. Then he said, "My daddy told me to 'stay with what you are good at and don't get in over your head.' My mother always told me to know the value of family. She always said that when you have a good thing, don't do anything to ruin it." Rus often spoke of his parents. Anyone could tell he loved them deeply. David always liked this about him. He always felt that Rus embodied the best qualities of both his parents. David didn't have kids, but if he ever did, he hoped they would have the best of him and their mother. Rus continued, "I have a great house, a beautiful wife, and three, great, trouble-finding kids. I have a career that lets me provide for them, and we pretty much get to do anything we want. I have a job that I love and that I am good at. I'm living the dream. When you are this fortunate, why mess with it? I wouldn't take another position if they begged me."

David smiled. "Thanks again for coming up here; I won't forget it."

Rus put a hand on his shoulder. "I'm going to wait down by the elevator for you. I'll walk you back to your office, and you can tell me how it goes." David headed for the door. Rus called out, "Remember, they put their pants on one leg at a time, just like you."

David smiled, as he appreciated the support. He retorted, "You have never seen me put on my pants."

David entered Conference Room A. He was about five minutes early, but he wanted it that way. The thing he learned about the difference between Conference Room A and Conference Room B was that there was no difference. They seemed to be identical in every detail; except this room was occupied by the three, most powerful men in the company. Mr. Trenton was with two other men. David had met all three men before, but only briefly at the national meeting they have every year. Since the company went international a few years back, it had since been called the international meeting.

Mr. Trenton looked up from their conversation on the other side of the room. "David, come, let me introduce you." David walked nervously across the room. Mr. Trenton called him by his name. He didn't even know that he knew who he was, outside of the interview today. He could feel his palms sweating. He started to panic. He tried to casually rub his right hand against his slacks as he walked across the long conference room. Mr. Trenton placed a hand on the back of his shoulder. "David, this is Dick Pittsinburger, Chief Operating Officer."

David extended his hand. Dick said simply, "Pleasure to meet you." Dick was a tall man. He was in his fifties. He had reddish, brown hair and a thick mustache. He gave David a cordial hand shake and a friendly smile. David had heard of Dick. He had been with the company since he got out of college. He had thirty-plus years with the company, and David had always heard that no one was more knowledgeable about every single division in the company than Mr. Pittsinburger.

Next Mr. Trenton introduced him to Bob Kearn, Chief Financial Officer. Bob was a very thin man; about five feet, five inches tall. He appeared to be in his thirties, but had one of those faces that he could also be in his late twenties to early forties. He wore a three-piece suit and had a very pale, thin face. He wore glasses with circular lenses, which actually helped his appearance. He had brown hair that looked as if it were thinning. David couldn't help but think he looked every bit the part of the traditional bean counter. Bob had been brought in from outside the company last year. He was a very intelligent man who had a reputation of being exceptional with numbers. He also had developed the reputation of not being good with people in his time with the company. He was more at home with his spread sheets and computers than with flesh and blood people. Bob extended a cold, sweaty hand and said, "Good morning," in a mousy, quiet voice. David returned the gesture. He was actually a little relieved that he was not the only one in the room with sweaty palms.

Mr. Trenton gestured to a chair on the other side of the table that was already pulled out. "David, please have a seat." David thought it was odd that Mr. Trenton did not shake his hand or formally introduce himself. He had been very casual with him. He wondered if he wanted his two subordinates to think he knew the rank and file better than he actually did. Mr. Trenton was an imposing man. He stood well over six feet, with a barrel chest and a large mid-section. He looked more husky and muscular than an overweight, middle-aged man. He kept his head shaved, which seemed to accentuate his strong forehead. He always wore the finest suits. Today was no exception. He wore a dark brown suit that looked tailor made. He was from Texas, but his accent wasn't usually heard when he spoke. He was a millionaire, one who was working on being a billionaire before he retired. He had a reputation for working hard and playing hard. His parties were legendary, but so was his wrath if you disappointed him. He was in his sixties but could easily pass for late forties. David wasn't sure if he had had work done or just took good care of himself.

David sat down. Mr. Trenton started, "Well, David, you are the last interview. Rus has had a lot of great things to say about you. He tells us you are ready for more responsibility. What do you think?"

David was ready for this; he had very good responses for a lot of the questions he expected, and this was one of them. He cleared his throat, "I am, Mr. Trenton." David knew not to use his first name. He learned long ago that the upper management liked to use first names with their employees to appear closer to them, but they did not like you using theirs. David continued, "I have ten years with the company, and in that time—"

"Yes, I am aware of your service," Mr. Trenton interrupted. "David, let me tell you something about myself. I can feel a person out in just a few minutes; have to in my line of work. Now H.R. says that we have to use the same interview on every candidate we promote; keeps us from getting sued by some less-deserving person who does not get a position they think they are entitled to. So Bob here is going to ask you some questions, but before he does, I just have a few things that I want to cover."

"Yes, Mr. Trenton," David said. An awkward silence set in for a moment. He wasn't sure if he was supposed to say more.

Then Mr. Trenton spoke again. "David, what do you think that we are looking for in a field director?"

This was another question that David was ready for. "Sir, in my time with the company, I have learned that people make this company. They are the driving force behind everything we do. We are nothing without the successful teams we have built. As a field director—"

Mr. Trenton interrupted him again. "Yes, yes, we have great, successful teams. I helped build them." David was beginning to worry that he was not getting off to a very good start. "David, do you know how much profit we made last year?"

David was ready for this one, too. He spoke almost robotically, reciting numbers he had rehearsed for days now. "Yes, sir, last year's net profit was $2.73 billion, with $1.9 billion coming from our domestic operations and—"

Mr. Trenton interrupted again. "Yes, that's accurate. Now when I think of this company, I think of a company that makes billions of dollars—billions of dollars." He paused a moment for effect. "That's nine zeroes, son," he said, and for the first time, David could hear the Texas drawl in his voice. He was clearly getting excited. He spoke again, "Now, when I think of a field director, I think of someone who can understand that this company is about making money. We are in the business of making money. People and effective teams are a tool we use to do that. They are one of many tools we use to do that. The field director I promote..." He paused, suddenly remembering he was not alone in the room with David. "The field director we promote will understand that and will move forward with the understanding that all our focus is on *profit*." He accentuated the last word. David was a little surprised by this. He had been in the company for a decade now, and this is something that he never heard before. In all his time here, he had heard how the company prides itself on its effective teams. David had helped build some of them. Now to hear how little they meant was like getting punched in the stomach.

David tried to mask his surprise. He looked Mr. Trenton in the eye and said, "Yes, sir, if I am given the chance, I can be that man for you and this company." Mr. Trenton gave him a long stare in the eye. David looked back. Was he supposed to speak? He then realized that Mr. Trenton was looking him in the eye for sincerity. He stared back. He felt like he was in middle school again and was playing that game to see who blinks first. He had waited too long and worked too hard to get here; he would feel his eyes go dry before he would blink. As they stared at each other, David wondered about what he had said. Could he really be that man? He had said it because it was expected, but in reality, he didn't know. He knew that he wanted the chance to find out.

Finally, as David was about to blink, Mr. Trenton sat back in his chair and smiled. "Well, that's about all the questions I have. Bob, why don't you start the interview now?"

Bob coughed quietly and then made a throat clearing sound. "Yes, Mr. Trenton." He pulled his chair up closer to the table and spoke in his low, mousy voice, "David, tell me about a time when you—"

Then there was a knock at the door. The door slowly opened. It was the receptionist from down the hall. She said, "Excuse me, gentlemen," with her gaze going across all three executives. Then she looked at Mr. Trenton. "Sir, there is someone here asking to see David. He was sent up from the twenty-ninth floor." Mr. Trenton started to speak, but before he could, she continued, "He is a police officer."

A police officer? David thought to himself. Why would a police officer be here to see me? Mr. Trenton and the other executives stared at David, as if he now needed to explain this. David was speechless; he didn't know what to say.

Finally, Mr. Trenton spoke up, "Do you have any idea why a police officer would want to speak with you?"

"No, sir, I have no idea," David replied. For a moment all three men stared at David, as if questioning his answer. David had no idea what kind of expression was on his face now. He couldn't imagine what this was about, and today of all days!

After an awkward silence, both Mr. Pittsinburger and Mr. Kearn moved their gaze to Mr. Trenton, as if to see how he wanted to proceed. He was clearly not expecting an interruption. He finally spoke in a low, serious voice. "David, you had better go and see what this is all about. This interview is important, but there is a police officer on our property, and he is asking for one of my employees. I think you should go and speak with him."

David got to his feet, his knees were weak. He tried to steady himself as he stood, but he knew he appeared shaken. He had to put a firm hand on the table to steady himself. Did this just destroy his chances? Was the interview over? He felt he had to do something, but he wasn't sure what to say. Finally, he had to regain some momentum for this interview; this may be his only chance. He cleared his throat and spoke in his most confident voice, "Mr. Trenton, I'm sure this is nothing. I can't imagine why a police officer would want to speak with me. David is a common name," he said with a smile, "so this man has probably confused me with someone else."

None of the three men smiled back. All looked at him stone-faced. David now felt foolish, smiling like an idiot. Then Mr. Trenton spoke again, "Just go and see what this is about, and we will either meet with you or re-schedule, if we can."

If we can? David thought to himself. No, he wasn't going to let this opportunity slip away. He replied, speaking a little more quickly now, "Yes, sir, I'm sure this will only take a moment, and I will be right back."

He walked into the hallway. The receptionist was waiting, and she introduced him to the police officer. She looked at David and said, "This is Detective Simms." David reached out a hand. Simms appeared to be in his mid-to-late- forties. He had a small chest and a large waist. His large belly flopped out over a belt that was pulled very tightly around his waist. His hair was almost gone, but he had one of the most obvious comb-overs that David had ever seen. Even the hair combed over was not enough to cover his scalp. He wore a cheap, poorly fitted suit. David thought that he must have spent a long time tied to a desk or was one of those serious doughnut-eating cops you always hear about. Simms gave him a firm hand shake.

He said, "I am sorry to have to bother you. I verified with your H.R. department downstairs that you are who I am looking for. Do you know how many different David's there are in this building?"

"No," David replied flatly.

"Neither do I," he said, laughing. "The lady was still trying to count them all."

"What is this all about?" David asked.

"Can we go somewhere to speak?" asked Simms.

The receptionist spoke up, looking at David, "Conference room B is empty, and you can take him in there."

"Thank you," was all David could manage.

They turned, and David proceeded back to Conference Room B. When they entered the room, David gestured to a chair, and they sat. Simms fell back into the chair as if he didn't have the energy to slowly set down. The chair creaked under his girth. He reached into his pocket and retrieved a small notepad. David let out a low chuckle. "Is something funny?" Simms asked seriously.

"No," David replied. "It's just that I can't believe you guys are not carrying an iPad or data phone or something. I just can't believe you guys are still using pocket notebooks."

"Oh," Simms said, his guard dropping, realizing it was a trivial laugh. "We have a tight budget, and they are always looking for ways to cut it. I'm honestly still surprised they pay for these notebooks."

Simms leaned forward with a pen now in hand and his notebook open on the table. "Mr.—"

"David, call me David," David interrupted. "What is this all about, Mr. Simms"

"Detective Simms," Simms corrected him.

David, now frustrated and wanting to get back to the interview, said, "Okay, what's this about, Detective Simms?"

"It's about your brother." David looked at him incredulously. "Tim? You pulled me out of this meeting to discuss Tim?"

"Yes," Simms responded, seeming to ignore David's obvious frustration. "Your brother has gone missing." David looked at him, as if waiting to hear more. Simms returned his gaze as if wanting to hear David's response before he offered him more.

Finally David broke the silence, "My brother is a religious fanatic. You should start there."

"It was the 'fanatics' you refer to who reported him missing. When is the last time you saw him?" Simms asked.

David, looking at the floor, gave him an unemotional response, "March eighteenth of last year."

"Interesting," Simms replied, making some notes in his notebook.

"What's interesting about it?" David asked.

"Well, if I hadn't seen my brother in over a year, I might reply that I hadn't seen him since last spring or even last March. But to know the exact date is a little...well, interesting." Simms stopped, again waiting for David to offer more.

David leveled his gaze at him with a hard stare but spoke in a low, somber voice. "It's the day we buried our mother."

Simms expression showed he didn't expect this answer. He replied, "I'm sorry. I was not aware she had passed away. I am only asking because it may become relevant as my investigation progresses. How did she pass?"

"Cancer," David interrupted. Simms waited for more, but there was no more. David had said all he was going to say.

After a long pause, Simms made some more notes in his notebook and repeated quietly, "I'm sorry." He then proceeded with what seemed like some routine questions. "Who is older, you or Timothy?"

"Tim. Don't you know this? You said you confirmed me with H.R.?"

"They only confirmed your identity; I didn't get to look at your file," Simms stated. "Do you know of any favorite hangouts, places he may go?"

David stared at him for a moment and then responded, "Mr. Simms..."

"*Detective* Simms," Simms interrupted.

David realized that this was a serious breach of protocol; this man was obviously very proud of his position and didn't appreciate his title not being utilized. David made a mental note to not repeat the mistake a third time. "Detective Simms, I feel I should try to save us both some time. My brother and I are not close. We haven't been for years. I do not know anything about his life. I do not know where he hangs out. I don't even know where he lives. I have no phone number for him. I only know that he ran off with a bunch of religious freaks, and he has decided to devote his life to them. I really can't help you."

Simms stared at him a long moment, as if considering what he had said. Then he responded, "The people that reported your brother missing feel he could be in grave danger." He let that statement sit with David for a moment. David did not respond; he just stared back at him. Simms spoke again, "You are the only lead I have in finding your brother. The people that he has been living with stated that you were his only family."

He again paused for David to speak. This time David did respond, "We have no family. Our father died when we were very young. Our mother never re-married, and we never had any other family that I ever met. It was just me, my mother, and my brother."

"How long has he been involved with the 'fanatics...'" He paused in mid-sentence, as if re-thinking the phrasing of his question, "group you referred to?"

David had to think about that question for a moment. "I'm not totally sure. I would say around twelve years. He started in the whole religion thing right out of high school. It seemed to get worse the last four or five years. I thought he was going to be a priest or a preacher or something, but he decided to join that cult."

"Cult?" Simms responded.

"It's a church or something," Simms stated. "It's some kind of cult; Tim began thinking he was saving the world or something. He believes in that stuff so totally they brainwashed him, and we couldn't get him back."

"We?" asked Simms.

"My mother and I tried a couple of times to get him to come back to earth, but he was convinced in his calling and his mission."

Simms made some more notes and then looked back up at David. "I take it you don't share his views?"

"No," David replied flatly. Again Simms seemed to want more, and again, David didn't offer any more. David looked at his watch and then back at Simms. "Do you have any more questions for me? You pulled me out of a very important meeting." Simms stared at him for a long moment. David felt he could read his mind. He felt that he was amazed he didn't care more for his brother. The truth was that he couldn't forgive his brother for abandoning his mother in her time of need. It was him that was at her side until the end. Tim was nowhere to be found. When she finally died, David didn't even know how to reach him. He didn't even bother to show up for her funeral. He made a brief appearance at the burial and that was it. That day David felt he was done with him. He had tried to tolerate his cult and his beliefs. David had heard all his talk about how he wanted to be a better person, how he wanted to make a difference in people's lives. He wanted to serve God. When the chips were down, when his family needed him, he couldn't even be there for his mother. She wanted him there, she needed him there. Her final thoughts were of him—*him*—even as David was holding her hand.

David looked at Simms. He had been lost in thought for a moment, and Simms seemed to be letting him have that moment, maybe hoping he might recall something of benefit. David looked back at him now. "I have one more question. If he contacts you or you remember something that could help, will you call me immediately?"

"Yes, but he won't, and I won't," David replied flatly.

Simms studied him again, as if wanting to say something else but then changed his mind. He jotted down his name and number on a sheet out of his pocket notebook, tore it off, and handed it to David. "Call me day or night if I can help."

David looked at the paper and then at Simms and said, "So, you don't have a card?"

"No, those budget cuts." Simms said with a groan as he got up out of the chair. David rose and was expecting a hand shake, but Simms just looked at him and said, "Thank you for meeting with me. I hope it was not too big of an inconvenience for you."

David ignored this and said simply, "I guess you know the way out." Simms left the room. David took a moment to compose himself. He needed to focus right now. He could not think about this. This was one of the most important days in his career; one of the most important days of his life. He needed to prepare himself mentally and get back into the other conference room. He stood up, tucked his shirt, adjusted his tie, and headed into the hallway.

Rus was in the hallway. David slowed his walk and spoke to him, with the intention of walking past him. "I don't have time to talk right now; I have to get back in there."

Rus put a hand on him. "David, they're gone."

"Gone?" David asked.

"Yes, they had a flight to China. You know how important China is right now." David did. The company went into China eighteen months ago. After about six months, the company learned that doing business with China was not all that they had thought it would be; all those people, all that potential for profit. The Chinese government had proven to be very difficult to work with. They had also proven to be very unforgiving of mistakes. Upper management had put a lot of work into China. It was no secret that they spent most of their time and energy in the last year getting the Chinese operation off the ground. Rus continued, "They had a flight booked and had to go. They couldn't wait."

"Rus, the company owns the plane. They could have waited if they wanted to."

Rus took a deep breath. "They were very concerned that a police officer wanted to speak with you. They wanted to look at...rescheduling the interview. They wanted me to find out what this was all about. He was down at H.R. looking for you, asking to see your file. This doesn't look good." Rus paused for a moment and then he started again. "Why did the police officer want to meet with you?"

David now took a long breath of his own. "It was about Tim."

"Timothy, your brother?" Rus said.

"Yeah, he's gone missing. Those fanatics that he hangs out with reported it to the police. The detective thought I might know something." Rus stared but didn't speak. He appeared to be waiting for more. David continued, "I don't know anything. I told him I would be the last person Tim would come to. It's hard to tell where he might be.

Rus considered this for a long moment and then asked, "Is there anything I...we can do?" This got David's attention. He was in his supervisor/H.R. mode. David had long ago learned that when Rus was in his personal, friend mode, he would use words like me or I. When he was in work mode, he would use words like us or we.

David was unsure why he was going into that mode now, but he responded, "No."

Rus then put his hand gently on David's shoulder. "Listen, I'm going to call Trenton tomorrow. I'm going to explain this and try to get you another interview, but you need to know that you may have to wait until next time."

David couldn't believe this. "Next time? What do you mean next time?"

Rus took another deep breath and then spoke softly, "David, you got a visit from the police—the *police*. It could not have happened at a worse time. The reality is that this is a very competitive position. They are interviewing qualified candidates from all over the world. When you interview for something like this, you don't always get a second chance. You might have to wait for something to come up in the future."

David looked at him, incredulously. "The future?" David's voice began to rise. "I have given ten years to this company! Ten years! Do I have to wait another ten for them to give me another interview? This is ridiculous! I demand—"

"Demand?" Rus interrupted. "David, you don't demand anything from these people. They are millionaires, and they could care less what you demand. I know that you are devastated." Rus leaned in, looked him directly in the eye, and lowered his voice as if he was afraid someone would hear. "No one can know how hard you worked for this but me. I have been with you the entire time. I know how much you have put into this, what it means to you."

David could not believe it. The biggest day of his life, destroyed because of his brother. He sighed, "I just want to get back to work now."

He started to walk away. Rus spoke in a firm voice now. "No, you are not going to work."

David turned to face him again. "What do you mean?"

Rus straightened, as if to say that he was back in his H.R. mode once again and said, "David, you are no good to me like this. You won't be able to focus, and you won't be able to concentrate. You have tons of vacation. I have allowed you not to take it, but I think now I'm going to insist. Starting now you are on vacation. When—if we get the interview rescheduled, I will call you immediately." There was a long pause between them. "I want you to take at least a week off. I will call you in a week and, if we agree you're ready, you can come back if you want."

David felt deflated; he didn't even know how to argue with him at this point. He just couldn't believe the way the day had gone. Ten years of hard work, for what? he thought to himself. He simply mumbled, "Okay."

David started walking to the elevator. Rus called out, "Call me if you want to talk." David didn't stop or acknowledge him; he just kept walking. He got off at the lobby. He felt numb. He was in a daze. He didn't know what to do or where to go. He went to the coffee shop in the lobby and ordered a small coffee. He went to the large fountain. He needed some time to reflect, to think. As he sipped the hot coffee, he began to slowly look around. Then he noticed the woman again. For a second he thought she was looking at him. Now she was clearly looking away. He got a better look at her this time. Her deep-set, dark eyes had a penetrating look to them. Her complexion was dark, but not tan. She had a dark, natural color to her. He tried to look away, but he couldn't seem to take his gaze from her. He watched as she looked absorbed in something, but he could not figure out what. He wondered if she liked to come to the fountain. Maybe that was why she was here. A large group of people walked in front of her. He waited for the crowd to clear, but when it did, she was gone.

CHAPTER 3

"Hold my hand!" the voice cried out.

David jumped up, felt himself coming awake in a haze. Then suddenly he remembered where he was. He grabbed his mother's hand. She gripped it tightly and cried out in agony. He hadn't slept in over two days. He knew he needed to, but he couldn't leave her; not now. The hospice nurse was in the other room, but she had already told him that there was nothing more she could do. His mother was nearing the end. The doctors had told her she didn't need to come back anymore. She had refused all medication for the pain. She wanted to go out on her own terms, in her right mind, for as long as possible. David had tried to find his brother; he had looked everywhere, left messages. He even went to see the people in the "church." He was beginning to believe that they were just a bunch of fanatics. It looked more like a country church with few members in the outskirts of the city. David was beginning to think it was some kind of cult that had sucked his brother in. He just couldn't think of another explanation. Why else would he give so much of his life for these people? They had told him they didn't know exactly where he was, that he was "on assignment." David had rolled his eyes at this. It was like he was an investigative reporter or something. He was probably selling Bibles, and they were down on their quota for the month. He couldn't believe that his brother was not here. Even Tim wasn't this low.

The pain was receding again. His mother was starting to lie back down. The grip on his hand was beginning to ease. Her sheets were soaked with perspiration. Her long, black hair was wet, like she had just showered. It was very difficult for him to see his mom like this. He asked if she wanted water, but she shook her head no. She sucked in a deep breath and began to speak. "David, I don't know how long I have left, but it's not long now. God is calling me home." She waited for him to respond, but he could only nod his head. He had a look on his face like a small child who was getting ready to be left somewhere he didn't want to be. Then it hit him: he was being left; his mother was going to leave him soon. Leave him all alone. She was going to cease to exist. He knew death was the end, that there was nothing beyond, but he had never had to face it with someone he loved. He knew she believed she was going somewhere, to some make-believe place where everything was perfect. He knew it was a lie, but he wanted her to go out as happy as she possibly could. He felt a tear come down his cheek. He wasn't crying, but he couldn't stop them; they had been coming sporadically now. She looked at him with that understanding gaze that you can only get from your mother. She put a weak hand on his cheek and wiped away a tear. She took another labored breath and then began to speak again, "There are some things I want to say before I go." David's head continued to nod in agreement, and more tears were coming now. "It's about Tim. I know you two have always been very different men. He has more of me in him. You have more of your father."

She never spoke of their father. Neither he nor his brother had any memories of him. He left when they were very young. They had heard that he died soon afterward. Their mother refused to talk about him. They did not attend his funeral, and she didn't keep a single photo of him after he left. Neither of her boys ever knew what their father even looked like. Now, as she approached the end of her life, she seemed to finally want to talk about him. "Your father loved you and your brother very much. He loved me very much. He was a soldier. He was so handsome when we met. I fell in love instantly." She giggled. Remembering this was giving her some pleasure.

David didn't care to discuss his father; Tim was the one always asking questions about him. David was fine with knowing he had a mother who loved him. He had had questions as a boy, but as he matured, he learned to live without him; and for him, that was that. Tim was different. It was like a hole in his life he could never fill. David knew Tim was like their mom. He had often wondered if he was so drawn to their dad because she was drawn to him at one time. He didn't know and anymore, didn't care. But if pretending to care and letting her talk about him gave her some peace—some pleasure—he would do anything. He nodded and managed to conjure up a half smile.

She continued, "I always understood your brother. I always knew how he felt. When I look at you, I always think of him. I want you to know that he was a good man; conflicted, but good. I always saw the good in him that others could not. There may come a time when you will have to face your hatred of him. There may come a time you will have to let it go and be strong." Her hand, still on his cheek, began to squeeze. Then suddenly her nails cut into his cheek, and she let out another shrill scream. She sat straight up, her arms flapping about this time. David wrestled her right arm down, holding that hand tightly in his own. He wanted her to know she was not alone. He would be here until the very end.

After a couple of minutes, she started to lay down again, the pain easing off. She fell totally silent. She glanced at him and then at the ceiling. She began to force herself to take long, labored breaths. Tears came down his face again and something else. He reached his hand to his cheek. It was bleeding. He now had tears and blood coming down. He didn't care. He just continued to focus on her now, for the last time in both of their lives. After a few minutes, she looked back at him. Her right hand was still in his. He had never let go. She squeezed it again; just a gentle squeeze this time. She stared into his eyes. It was becoming difficult to speak now.

"Your brother...he is a soldier. He is off fighting for us. He's not like his father, but he is a soldier." David gulped, tried to smile. Her mind was going now. She and he both knew that Tim had run off with the church. He was some kind of missionary or something; but soldier he was not. She continued, "I still don't know what path you will choose. I want to see you again. I want to spend eternity with you. You are my son, and I love you so much. Don't turn your back on God. Think about your salvation. Think about what your life will be."

David knew this was a debate they had had many times. He said, "I've never seen any proof of a God, Mom. Look at you, where you are. Where is God now? No one is with you but me."

She said, "David, God has a plan; we can't question it. I've kept God's word in front of you. He is all around you, and you have to take the time to see it. Promise me I will see you again."

Tears began to come down her face now. "You will, Mom." He knew it was a lie. He knew it was only a fantasy, but it was what she needed to hear.

She looked up at the ceiling again. She took several, deep, labored breaths, and looked back at him. "David, I need you to promise me you will not abandon your brother. He is all you have now. You are all he has now. As time goes by, you will need each other."

David looked at the floor. He couldn't believe it. Here she was at the end; he had abandoned her, and all she could think of was his well-being. The gentle squeeze became more now. She was squeezing harder now. Her voice found strength; she raised her head off the pillow. "Look at me! Promise me! I want your word that you won't abandon your brother! That you will always look out for him!"

David hesitated. He would do anything for her. They both knew that. He just couldn't believe that this was how she was going out. He was the younger brother. Wasn't the older brother supposed to be the one looking after the younger brother? Her chest started heaving. Her breaths became very rapid. Her chest kept rising and falling quickly. She was going. The tears came again. Then he realized he hadn't responded to her. He said, "I promise,

Mom, I promise!" The heaving stopped. She looked into his eyes and then smiled. Then her eyes lost all life, and a fixed stare took over. It was as if she was looking past him at something so beautiful she couldn't take her eyes off it, so transfixed that nothing else mattered, except what was beyond him. He buried his head into her chest and, in the last moment, the one he had been preparing for, the one that he had decided he would have to be strong for, he lost all control. He started sobbing uncontrollably. "Don't go, Mom! Please, don't leave me! I love you, Mom!"

He sat straight up in his bed. He looked around, taking in his surroundings. The whiskey bottle lay on the floor, by the bed. He had drunk almost all of it. He ran his hand through his hair. It was wet with sweat. The dream was so real. But it wasn't a dream, really; it was a memory. One he had tried to block out. He had promised his mother. It was her final wish. He looked at the clock: 4:24 A.M. He slowly lay back down. He knew now what he had to do.

He was up early. He called a cab, went down to the street, and climbed inside. It was a long ride to the place he was going. He sat in the cab, staring out the window, and began to think. He thought about his mother, he thought about his brother. He thought about everything. Images poured through his mind. He never understood how his mother and his brother could believe in something so absolutely. He knew the Bible. He had read it. He knew the books. His mother saw to that. His mother had raised him in church. He always felt that he was the only one who understood it. It was a two-thousand-year-old book full of fairy tales and mythical people who lived for hundreds of years. It was an accomplishment, to be sure, but that was all. His mother and brother believed it was all true: that people used to live hundreds of years; that there were miracles just because someone prayed; that there was a being who created us and that we all get to go to a fairy tale place some day and live together forever. He always felt it took courage to see the truth. He always felt he could face it where they couldn't. A person gets to live around seventy-five years. The lucky ones live longer; the unlucky ones do not live as long. When a person dies, that's it. You're gone. All you leave behind are your children, if you have any, and your accomplishments. He always felt that it was just hard for a lot of people to accept. He was always very tolerant, very respectful. Some people needed to believe that there was more. It got them through the day. In some cases, it got them through life. His brother had dedicated his life to a lie; a lie that had been told for thousands of years now. He believed it so completely; he gave up everything to chase it. He couldn't even get away long enough to be with his own mother when she needed him most. He had always thought of himself as an atheist or an agnostic; he never was sure which. The truth was that he really didn't care. He knew that whatever he was, he had clarity. He had a goal for his life. He wasn't going to spend his life chasing fairy tales.

He was so deep in thought that he was surprised to hear the cab driver asking for his fare. They were here. David gave him a fifty dollar bill and asked him to wait. "No problem, the meter will be running though," was the response. David didn't reply as he got out.

He looked around, took in his surroundings. He had only been here once before, last spring, to tell his brother that he was needed at home. The church was white. It looked as if it had been built over a century ago. It was small, complete with a steeple, like we all hear about as a child. It was in disrepair. It badly needed an update, a re-model. The paint was visibly worn, chipped, and faded. The only positive was the landscaping. The bushes were immaculate. The sidewalk, while old, was neat and clean, and the yard around the church was well-manicured. David proceeded inside. As old and small as it was, he expected it to be locked, but the door opened. Inside David saw old, wooden pews. He saw dark paneling with windows that were painted with pictures of Jesus and other ones that were decorated with angels. A small, black sign at the front of the church was filled with removable letters and numbers. It boasted a membership of twenty-seven on the previous Sunday and a Sunday school class with a whopping five kids.

David looked around, saw no one, and then called out, "Is anyone here?"

A few moments later, an old man yelled back, "Just a minute, I'm trying to get this bulb in."

David looked around and didn't see anyone. He made his way through the church. In the back, behind the pulpit, there was a door. David peered inside. The door led to a hallway that appeared to lead to an area in the back of the church. There was an older man on a chair, changing a light bulb in the hall. He spoke without looking at David, "These new bulbs are supposed to last a year, but I think it's some kind of rip-off. I feel like I just had to change this a few weeks ago. The ladies of the church say we have to be green, whatever that means." He completed his task and then, with a groan, stepped heavily off the chair and turned to face him. He introduced himself. "My name is Isaac. What can I do for you?"

He was a short man. He had an average build, with a small, rounding belly. He had all gray hair, but no white. He appeared to be in his mid- to late-sixties. He had piercing, green eyes that had a sharpness to them. He was dressed simply, in a pair of slacks, with a black, button-down shirt.

David opened his mouth and began to speak, but he was interrupted. "I remember you; you are Mr..."

"David," he said quickly.

"David," Isaac repeated. David knew of the church formalities of Mr. and Mrs. or brother and sister. He didn't want any part of that. He only wanted some answers. Isaac looked him over for a moment then said, "Okay. What can I do for you, David?"

"It's about my brother. I'm looking for him," David said.

"Well, it looks as if we have something in common. We are looking for him, too," said Isaac.

"When is the last time you saw him?"

Isaac seemed to consider this for a moment. "It's been over a week. He came back from a...business trip and then went out one evening and never returned."

David wasn't sure what to say next. He spoke again, "So, you called the police?"

"We didn't have much choice. We didn't know what else to do. We looked everywhere we could for him. We felt that the authorities should be informed."

"As his next of kin, you should have called me first," David remarked.

Isaac stroked his chin and then looked up at David. "Well, I suppose you're right. We could have called you, but since you are here, I'm guessing you don't have any idea where he is either."

David felt himself beginning to get frustrated. "What function did my brother perform here? What was his job?"

Isaac looked skeptical at that question. "I don't think that is something he would want me to go into with you. I will tell you that your brother is a good, good man."

David felt his frustration increasing. "Look, all I want to know is what he does here."

While David seemed to be getting frustrated, Isaac remained calm as he responded, "David, you are asking questions that I feel Tim should be responding to, not me. If you can help us at all in locating him, I would be very grateful."

David's frustration was now turning to anger. "Look, the police came to my work! You are refusing to answer questions, simple questions, about my brother. It's clear to me that you know more than you are saying. Let's just cut the crap. You and I both know that I know what you guys are all about. I am not as easily fooled as my brother. Either you start answering my questions, or I will be back with the police." Isaac just stared at David. David continued, "Did you or one of your people do something to him? Did you? If I find out you caused him harm I'll..."

Isaac reached out and put a firm hand on David's shoulder. The grip was so powerful that it caused David to pause. David tensed; he actually thought they may fight for a minute. Isaac finally spoke, "David, you clearly love your brother. You may not believe this, but I love him, too. He is one of my closest friends. I am the one who called the police. I have cooperated fully with them. I will answer any questions that I can, but I will not betray your brother's privacy, unless I am convinced it would help to bring him back to us."

To us? David thought. Like they were his family. While he disagreed with his brother's lifestyle, he could tell that this man was trying to protect his brother. David felt his pulse start to slow, his breathing start to slow. He felt a little silly. He had come to ask questions, not to argue. He didn't care for this man and what he had done to his brother, but he didn't mean to disrespect him or the church. He again found himself unsure what to say.

Isaac broke the silence. "You should go home. We have done all that can be done. The police are doing all they can do."

David could see this was going nowhere. He reached up and pulled the hand from his shoulder. "Thank you for your time. I'm not sure what happened here. I'm not sure where my brother is or if you had anything to do with his disappearance. The one thing that I want you to know is that I won't stop looking for him. I will keep looking until I find him and find who is responsible for all this."

Isaac stared into his eyes for a long moment, sensing his determination. He wanted to say something to stop him, something to make him go home. Stay home. When he opened his mouth he simply said, "God bless you, David. I pray he keeps you safe."

David rolled his eyes at this and then he turned away and quietly left the church. After David was gone, a woman came down the hallway from the back of the church. She was petite. Her long, black hair hung down her back, reaching the small of her back. She was dressed very conservatively, with a black blouse and a skirt that came to her ankles. She could see Isaac deep in thought, still staring at the door David had just left through. "What was that all about?" she asked.

"A complication," Isaac responded without looking at her.

"What are your instructions?" she asked.

Isaac spoke again without looking at her, still staring at the door. "Keep following him. Stay with him. I fear his safety is our responsibility now."

David got to the club about 11:00 P.M. He didn't want to get there too early. He had heard that these downtown clubs didn't really get started until 11:00 P.M. or midnight on most nights. He hated to admit it, but he was desperate. He felt he had to try something to find his brother. He had promised his mother that he would do all he could. He was hoping to get some clues from the church, but all he did was waste his time there. He had thought all afternoon what he could do next, then he thought of this place. Once, at Christmas a few years back, he was telling Tim a story about this intern who had said what a cool place this was and kept trying to get him to go. Tim mentioned that he knew the place and suggested that David stay away. When David asked, incredulous, how he would know such a place, Tim became elusive. David got the impression that he had slipped, let his guard down, and said something that he shouldn't have. Tim seemed very concerned that he admitted knowing the place. He finally told David that he had went there to witness to people. David thought that maybe he had come here more often than his friends at the church knew about. Maybe he was doing more than just witnessing. It was a long shot, but it was all David had left.

David stood in a long line to get inside. After nearly an hour, he finally entered the club just before midnight. The music was deafening. The lights were everywhere. There was a hard, bass beat to the music that rattled his core. You didn't have to listen to the music; you could feel it in your body. The dance floor was packed. People were dancing and groping one another. David could tell he was not dressed appropriately. He had on a simple tee shirt, jeans, and tennis shoes. Most people there were dressed in a variety of wild clothes. He wasn't sure where to start. He noticed a very crowded bar. The bartender seemed to be pouring drinks in bulk. A lady was lining up glasses, and he seemed to be just filling them as fast as she could set them up. David thought this was a good place to start.

He stood at the bar for some time, trying to get the man's attention. Finally, a woman asked, "What's your poison?"

Even though she screamed it, David could barely hear her with all the noise. David shook his head no and then motioned for her to come closer. She seemed frustrated but leaned her head in. Even though he was now only a foot from her, he still felt the need to yell. "I'm looking for someone." She pulled her head away, looked at him for a moment, and then just walked away, without a word. If at first you don't succeed, David thought.

He spent the better part of the next thirty minutes trying to get the bartender to come over. Finally, after repeated motions, the bartender came over. He was a large, bald man. He looked like he worked out, but not for a few years. He had that look of someone who used to work out, but now had the middle-age spread and was making the transition from buff to husky. "Do I know you?"

"No," David yelled back.

The bartender seemed frustrated now. "What do you want?"

"I'm looking for someone." The bartender just looked at him. David continued, in his loudest voice, "I'm trying to find someone. If you can help me, I can make it worth your while."

The bartender stared at him for another moment and then slowly held up his left hand, palm open. David understood this, so he put a twenty dollar bill in his hand. The man shot him a look that said, *Really? Twenty dollars?* David pulled out a fifty dollar bill next. He slowly placed it in the man's hand. David leaned in. "I'm looking for someone who may come in here from time to time."

The man slowly put the bills in his pocket, looked around, began to laugh, and then slowly walked away. He moved back to the assembly line and began pouring shots again. David wondered if he wasn't offering enough money or if he was just out of his league. He left the bar and began working the floor. He went to different tables, talking with spike-haired women—at least he thought they were women. He talked with women with colored hair and women who were old enough to be his mother, but dressed like they could have been his daughter. He tried talking with some of the men, but the straight ones were annoyed with his questions. The gay ones tried to pick him up. He tried talking with some couples, but he ultimately found out nothing. Either no one knew Tim or no one wanted to give him any information.

Disgusted with his lack of progress, he finally found a small table near the corner of the building, sat down, and ordered himself a drink. While he waited for it, he tried to think. He didn't know what else to do. He didn't want to quit, but he was running out of options. Then he felt a light hand on his back. He turned to see a man. He was clean cut, in his twenties. He had light brown hair, combed back and to the left. He had brown eyes, with a smile that looked like it belonged on one of those teeth whitening commercials. He had on a white shirt with a pair of khakis. "I hear you are asking some questions about Tim."

"Yes," David answered, feeling some relief that he was finally getting somewhere. "Do you know him?"

"Not here," the man replied. "I may be able to help, but we can't talk here. Come with me." The man turned and began to walk through the crowded dance floor, with David following close behind. The man clearly knew this place well. He moved through the crowded dance floor with ease. David felt himself bumping into people, and he kept repeating, "Sorry, excuse me, sorry," as they made their way to the other side of the club. They went through a door and then proceeded down a long, dark hallway. David could hear noises on the other side of some of the doors. It was difficult to make out, but he was sure it was illegal activity; probably prostitution, drugs, or both. He could still hear the thump, thump of the club music. They continued through another door. David followed him through.

Suddenly David found himself outside, in a dark alley. The man turned. David immediately felt himself tense. He started to panic. He was about to get mugged. He turned and tried to open the now closed door. It wouldn't open. He turned back around and there were two other men now. He could feel his adrenaline pumping through him. He knew he was in trouble. David asked, trying to sound unafraid, "What's this all about?" The men ignored him and began to close in.

David felt his feet come together. That was the first thing he had learned in martial arts training. When you are on the defensive, you start with your feet together to ensure your balance. You make sure your footing is solid. His brother was the expert. His mother had pushed them both into karate, jujitsu, and anything else she could find. She always felt the boys needed the training, the discipline. David never had the enthusiasm for it; his brother did. They both were in karate the longest, mostly because there were karate classes on their block they could easily get to. Tim earned a second degree black belt. David never made it past a brown belt. He still practiced at home occasionally, but he never actually used any of it. He knew he would need all the training he had now.

The men began to close in tighter around him. The panic was extreme now. David felt he had to do something. Finally he decided to act. He pushed his back against the wall. He wanted to know that one area around him was secure. He tried to look as scared as he could. In truth it wasn't very hard. Right now he was more panicked than afraid. The men seemed to be buying it. One began to smile as he moved in closer. David then looked at the man on his right, and then he kicked the man to his left. The heel of his shoe caught the man perfectly in the jaw. He went back with a groan. David then threw a punch with his left to the man on his right. By this time, the element of surprise was gone. The man easily blocked the punch and countered with a body blow into David's mid-section. David felt himself go to the ground in pain, his ribs aching from the blow. The man now stood over him. He slowly pulled a knife from his pocket. The man who had led David out here seemed to be looking down the alley, ensuring no one was near. David was down, but not out yet. While the third man was slowly trying to get back to his feet, David sprang up with an upper cut. This time the man was caught completely off guard. David felt his fist crash into the man's face, and the man fell back, the knife falling somewhere to the ground in the dark.

David stood up and began to run as fast as he could. He ran down the alley as fast as his legs would carry him. He thought he might yet make it out of this. Suddenly he ran out of alley and ran right into a dead end. He turned to see the man who had first approached him in the bar close in. The other two were a few steps behind. David, still moving quickly, felt he had to act, his life depended on it. He turned and charged the man. The man clearly wasn't ready for this. Realizing he was ahead of the other two, he backed up a little when he saw David coming at him. This emboldened David. He charged head long at the man. David threw a kick that the man easily dodged, but he staggered back as he did. David threw a second, round house kick that caught him squarely in the chest. The man fell back, straight on his back, with the wind knocked out of him.

One of the other men was there now, the first one David had kicked, and he punched at David. David tried to dodge the blow, but what would have been a cross to the face became a cross to the side of his head. The punch caught David in his left temple. David felt the blow, and he was knocked sideways. He tried to stay on his feet, but he staggered sideways and fell.

The man, now looking confident again, slowly closed in on him. Looking down, as David fell, the man spotted an old piece of pipe on the ground and picked it up. David looked up and saw the man coming at him, the pipe now overhead. The man prepared to swing the pipe at David. David put his hands up, felt himself panicking. The pipe suddenly came out of the man's hands and fell to the ground somewhere behind him. He looked incredulous, and he staggered backward, as if someone knocked him back a couple of steps. He looked at David with shock in his eyes. How had the pipe come out of his hands? David looked equally shocked. He again took advantage of the temporary situation and rolled toward the man, coming to his feet near him. David was able to take another step and then kick the man back. He staggered and fell back. With his adrenaline still coursing through his veins, David decided to get on top of him. He knew he couldn't keep this up for long. He had to even the odds; it was three on one, and they would eventually get the best of him.

He climbed on top of the man, pinning him to the ground. David intended to knock him out, but then he felt a blow to the back of his head. One of the others had picked up the pipe and clubbed him. David fell to the ground and felt himself getting dizzy. It was over, they had him now. The man who approached him in the club was there now. He leaned over David. He looked David in the eye as he spoke to the two men behind him. "That did it. He's not going anywhere now. Kill him and then get rid of the body."

The man stood up, ran his hands through his thick hair, and started tucking his shirt back into his pants. Then he paused, as if just realizing something was extending out of his torso. He slowly looked down to see what looked like a knife or sword coming out of his chest. Someone had stabbed him in the back, and it was protruding from his chest. He looked incredulously at David and then fell to the ground. The other two men were fighting a small man, dressed all in black. The man was incredibly quick; the other two men didn't seem to be able to keep up with him. David saw him still fighting the other two men as his eyes started to close, and then everything went black.

CHAPTER 4

David awoke with the sun in his eyes again. He was home. His head pounded. He could not remember ever having a headache this bad. He sat up in the bed. This made his head hurt worse, so he lay back down. He tried to open his eyes, but it was difficult, and the pain shooting through his head was intense. He squinted, and then he heard a voice. "I see you are awake. Good. Good. When you are ready there is some Tylenol by your bed with some water. I think you will need it."

David sat up again. He tried to ignore the intense pain in his head. "How did you get into my house?" The voice chuckled. David forced his eyes to open. Then he realized he wasn't home. He was in a sparsely decorated room. The room had no wall decoration, other than a crucifix. There were no pictures. There was only one window, and it had no curtains or shades. The sun was shining directly on the bed where he had been sleeping under what looked like a handmade quilt. With pain still shooting through his head, he squinted to see who was talking to him. It was Isaac. Isaac pulled up a small, plain, wooden chair next to the bed and sat down.

"You are not home. They must have hit your head pretty hard."

"Where am I?" David asked.

"You are in my home. One of our people brought you here last night."

The pain in his head was too excruciating, David had to lie back down. As he did, he spoke, "I remember…the man. I saw him fighting them. Did he get hurt?"

Isaac was slow to respond. "The person you are speaking of is fine. Do you have any idea why those men would want to kill you?"

"No, I was asking about Tim; trying to find out something about where he might be," David replied, holding his head.

"What made you think to look in that place?"

David was unsure if he should answer this. He was worried he might get Tim in trouble. He clearly wasn't supposed to know that place had any connection to them. "Tim told me he witnessed to people there a few years ago. I thought someone there might remember him."

"We had already explored the options there," Isaac said flatly. "David, get some sleep; we will talk more after you rest."

David sat up again, the pain radiating through his head. "No, I want to go home now!" He could only sit up for a few seconds. The pain was too great; he had to lie back down.

He had both hands on his head as Isaac spoke. "We will take you home. I just want you to rest. You are safe here. When you feel up to it, you can go, or we will take you home, but you are in no condition to travel now. Please, rest a little more, give the medicine time to work, and then you can do whatever you want."

David wanted to argue, but he knew Isaac was right. He agreed and started to drift off to sleep again. Isaac slowly got out of the chair, pulled the quilt up, over David's chest, and then left the room. He walked into a small kitchen, where the long, black haired woman was sitting. She had just poured herself some coffee. Isaac came in and sat down across the table from her. "I see you're up. Were you able to get some sleep?"

"Not much," replied the woman. Isaac knew why she always had trouble sleeping after a tough night.

"You said last night three men jumped him. How many did you have to kill?"

She sipped her coffee for a moment. Then she stared straight ahead as she answered him, "Two for sure. I'm not sure about the third; he might have made it. It depends on how quickly someone found him."

Isaac nodded. Then he said, "You had no choice. They would have killed him. You were doing your job." She nodded, sipped her coffee again, and stared straight ahead, as if in a daze. Isaac knew how skilled she was; he knew what they did was not easy and she was one of the best he had ever seen. She still struggled with taking lives. It was not as easy for her as it should be— as it needed to be in her position.

She turned her gaze to him. "What are we going to do with him now?"

Isaac considered this and then he responded, "He has definitely made a bad situation worse. He doesn't seem to know anything. With any luck, he will go back to his company and chase his promotion."

"And if he doesn't?" she asked.

Isaac just stared back at her. After a long pause, he finally spoke. "Let's pray about it. Let's see what thus sayeth the Lord."

Istanbul, Turkey

The priest ran down the street, his heart pounding. He arrived at an intersection that led to several, different streets. He chose the street that led to the waterway. He ran for several yards and then ducked behind an indention in the street; he thought he had lost him. He tried to breathe deeply, quietly. His heart was pounding so hard he thought the man could hear it. He heard footsteps slowly approaching. The walk was brisk, steady, but not a run. He heard them getting closer; closer. Then they stopped. For a few moments there was an eerie silence. The priest closed his eyes tightly. The man was probably standing in the intersection, and he had a one in four chance that the man could go in the wrong direction. Who was this man? He could not figure out who he was or why he wanted to kill him. He had narrowly escaped, and now he had been running for his life. He was not a fighter; he was a man of God. He couldn't understand why this man would want to harm him. He tried to be patient, but he couldn't hear footsteps, and he didn't know where the man was. He was sweating profusely. He wiped sweat out of his eyes. His heart was still racing. He felt himself start to panic. He couldn't just stay here; he had to keep moving.

He exploded back into the street. He ran for a good minute and then stopped to look back. The man was still at the intersection. All he could see was a silhouette. He tried not to move. Maybe the man hadn't seen him. He couldn't tell what direction the figure was facing. Then the figure started walking briskly toward him. He felt panic flood his body. He ran as hard as he could. As he turned a corner, the uneven, rocky sidewalk caused him to trip. He fell flat on his belly. He got up as quickly as he could; he was out of breath. His ankle had been twisted in the fall.

He was limping now, limping quickly. He was on a street that was parallel to the water now. He hoped maybe someone would see him, maybe a boat would be out this time of night to see the city; maybe a tourist, but there was no one. He continued to hobble along, but his body was giving out. He was not in the best of shape, and he could tell the man behind him was. He had to do something, but he didn't know what to do. He noticed a long stick on the ground. It looked like a walking stick. He thought maybe a tourist had discarded it. There were always things lying around. This was, after all, a major tourist destination. He picked it up and moved into a doorway of a business that was closed. He could hear the footsteps getting closer. As they continued to close in on him, he felt his heart pound even harder. He would only have this one chance. The footsteps were so loud now. He thought the man might walk right by him. He waited until the last possible second. The swing would have to be perfect. Just as he thought the man was on top of him, he came out and swung the stick with all his might. The man caught it in his hand. The man backhanded him, and he fell to the ground. The priest looked up at the man. He was very clean cut. He was roughly six feet tall, with blondish brown hair. He had his hair combed straight back on his head. He had on a white, button-up shirt with a light sports coat, trousers, and boots. The man calmly reached into the inside of his coat and retrieved a gun with a silencer on the end. The man had a cold look in his eyes; they looked emotionless.

The man spoke, "If you wish to pray first, I will give you sixty seconds."

English, the priest thought; he spoke English. The priest had learned English. He had a severe accent, or so he had been told, but he knew the language. The man's English was so good that he could not be from Turkey. The priest looked at him; a tear began to roll down his face. He didn't want to die like this. He spoke to the man and said, "Are you going to kill me?"

The man, looking stone-faced, nodded. The priest couldn't believe it; he didn't know this man. Why would he want to kill him? The priest looked back up at the man and said, "In the name of God, why?"

The man pointed the gun at his head and said coldly, "He's not MY God." Then he pulled the trigger, and the priest's body went limp. The man grabbed him by his arm, dragged him over to the sidewalk, and dropped him by the edge, near the water. Then he took his foot and kicked him over the side and watched his body fall into the water. He stared for a moment, watched the body slowly roll, and then settle in the water, face down. He took a cell phone from his jacket and punched in a number. The voice on the other side answered. "It's done," the man remarked into the phone.

"Good, very good," the voice told him. "We have a new assignment for you. You are going to America."

America? the man thought. He hadn't been to the states in years. Why would they want him to go back there? The man replied, "I'll be on the next flight out. Exactly where in America am I going?"

David woke up again. This time his head didn't hurt as much. He felt better than before. He could tell it was later in the day. Afternoon, he guessed. He had slept in his clothes. His shoes were beside the bed. He put them on. He opened his door and went into a dimly lit hallway. He wasn't sure which direction to go. He could see a light on down the hallway, to his right. He proceeded down the hall. It led to a small, simple kitchen. The long table in the center of the room and the extra chairs stacked in the corner told him that this was not a private residence. Isaac was making a sandwich. He motioned to David. "Please, sit." David silently complied. Isaac didn't speak for a few moments. He placed a sandwich in front of David. Then he went to make himself one. David wanted to decline the food, but he was really hungry. The sandwich looked great. David picked it up and began to eat it. Isaac returned with his own sandwich, smiling. "I never was much of a cook, but I have been told that I make a mean sandwich," he said, laughing. Isaac laid his sandwich on the table and then returned with two cups of coffee. "I hope you drink coffee. Unfortunately, I don't drink much else. I'm afraid it's either this or water."

"Coffee is fine," David mumbled as he munched on his sandwich.

"Good," Isaac replied. "I hope you like it black; I never go for all those fancy creams everybody seems to be using these days."

David gulped down a drink of the black coffee and then looked at Isaac. David asked, "Where am I?"

Isaac, beginning to chew his first bite of sandwich, had to gulp it down to reply. "You are at my church." David didn't respond; he considered this. Isaac spoke again. "You were brought here last night. You were very fortunate; you would have been killed, had we not intervened."

David was unsure what to say now. He felt he should be asking questions, but he wasn't sure what questions to ask. He picked up the sandwich and began to munch on it again.

As David was considering what he should say, Isaac said, "David, I hope that you will return home and forget all this. The best people are trying to find your brother. Everything that can be done is being done. I know you want to help, but you are only making things more difficult. For your own safety, I suggest you return to work. You will have my personal guarantee that I will keep you informed of any progress."

David looked at him curiously and then said, "You seem eager for me to go home. I gave my mother my word, on her death bed, that I would not abandon my brother. I appreciate the kindness that you have shown me. I know that I could be dead now if it was not for your efforts, but there is no way that I am going to stop looking for him."

Isaac stared at him for a long moment and then said, "What will you do now?"

David wasn't prepared to answer this. He blurted out, "I'm going back to that club. I will be more careful this time. If they didn't know anything, they wouldn't have tried to kill me."

Isaac looked down at the table and spoke softly, "They will kill you; don't you see that? You are not trained for this kind of thing."

David stared at him defiantly and said, "I'm not leaving my brother's fate to you and your...group."

Isaac sighed. There was a long moment of silence between them. David was preparing to get up when Isaac spoke. "I'm going to tell you some things that I would rather not." He hesitated. He slowly looked back up at David and then said, "I feel partially responsible for your involvement in all this. I see now that it was a mistake to involve the police. I should have anticipated they would come to you." He hesitated again and then said, "I didn't foresee your...response to all this. I'm going to give you a glimpse into your brother's life. Please understand that I am only doing this because you have left me no other choice. I cannot make you stay away, and I am worried we may not be able to protect you again, if you choose to pursue this. Once you start down this path, I am worried your life may never be the same. "Before I start, I want you to understand that there are limits to what I am willing to tell you." David just looked at him blankly. What could he possibly be going to tell him? Then Isaac continued. "Your brother is...working for us." This was not news to David. He knew that he had sworn his life to these people or something. "David, what do you think that it is we do here?"

"Well, it's a church. I get the general concept. People come, and you preach to them. They pay tithes, and you believe that you will help them all get to heaven. From the looks of the numbers you have posted, I don't think you guys are doing very well."

Isaac spoke again. "David, there is a war out there. It has been fought for two thousand years now. There are people outside these walls who would like to see people like us go away. This church is a small part of something much bigger, and so is your brother." There was a long silence between them again. Isaac looked as if he was thinking, pondering what he would say next. Then he took a deep breath and spoke again. "You are on the fringe of something you don't understand. You are dealing with people who are very powerful and have tremendous resources. I have placed you under the church's protection, but there are limits to what we can do. If you insist on this course, I fear you will die."

David considered this. He looked into Isaac's eyes. They looked soft. David said, "Look, I'm sure in your own way you are trying to help, but I really don't believe in all this stuff. It sounds like you have a little cloak and dagger going on within the church or something. I don't want any part of your war, if that is what you are calling it. I just want to find my brother."

Isaac looked surprised. He said, "You don't believe in this stuff"? I knew that you were not saved, but are you telling me that you are an atheist?"

David shrugged and said, "I'm not sure what you should call me, but I know enough to know that most of what you believe in here is about as real as a sci-fi movie."

Isaac seemed genuinely shocked. "I had no idea," he said, as his mouth hung slightly open.

David got up. "Look, I really do appreciate what you have done for me. I'm going home now. Please tell that man I am very appreciative of what he did, and I hope he is okay. If I find out anything, I will let you know. I hope you will do the same for me."

Isaac looked like he was in daze and just nodded slowly. David turned to leave. As he was walking out the door, Isaac spoke again. "David, just because you don't believe in this *stuff* doesn't make it any less real."

David stopped but didn't turn around. Then, after a pause, he walked out of the room.

Isaac sat there for a few minutes and then the woman came in again. Before she could say anything, Isaac asked, "Did you know he was a non-believer?"

She looked puzzled and said, "Tim said he wasn't in church."

"No," Isaac said flatly, "he's an atheist."

She just stared at him. "Do you know what this means?" Isaac said. Ruth just stared at him. He continued, "It means that Tim didn't want us to know. If he was dishonest about this, then maybe he didn't just disappear. Maybe this disappearance was his idea."

She sat down next to him and then said, "Just because Tim didn't want us to know about David doesn't mean he has betrayed us."

"You don't know that for certain," Isaac said.

She knew he was right. She asked, "What are we going to do now?"

Isaac, staring straight ahead, answered, "I don't know. I need to call command to see what they want us to do."

"In the meantime, why don't you let me pay him a visit, introduce myself, and take another try at him?"

Isaac considered this and then said, "What will you tell him?"

She replied, "Nothing that will place his life in more danger than it is already in. He could be dead in twenty-four hours if we do not figure out a way to get him to back off."

Isaac knew she was right. He said, "Go. Until I get directions from command, I want you to continue to watch over him." She began to rise, but Isaac grabbed her arm firmly. "Be careful, this is becoming very unpredictable. You may encounter more than imps next time."

She placed her hand on his hand and gave it a light pat. "I will."

The plane landed in the airport in New York City. The man got off and proceeded through the terminal. He got his luggage from the baggage area. There was an area where men and women were holding signs with names on them. The well-dressed man proceeded to one of them that said simply said, "Judas." The man looked at the sign wordlessly and nodded. The driver grasped his bags and escorted him to a waiting limousine. The man got inside and had a seat. The limo was fully equipped with all the extras, including a full bar. Judas loved to drink. He tried to be careful about when and how much. It was his biggest indulgence. He knew that he should not be drinking today, but he could not resist. They never brought him in like this. He had wondered through the entire flight what was going on. He hadn't been back in America in a long time. The fight had shifted away from the states years ago. There were always altercations in America, but the world was the battlefield, and he had been on the front lines. The Christians were trying to penetrate the safe zones in the Middle East, China, and Southeast Asia. For all their efforts elsewhere, they were losing America, and both sides knew it. There were always the occasional missions in Europe, South America, and Africa, but not North America. Why would they bother? Things there had been going well for decades now. He enjoyed his travels. He knew his role, and it wasn't here. Whatever was going on, he knew it was big. They would not have called him halfway around the world if it wasn't.

He finished his drink just as they arrived. The limo pulled up in front of a sleek skyscraper. He was told it was one of the tallest in the city. The front for this particular company was one that brought in millions of dollars of revenue. He was greeted by an Asian assistant, dressed in all white. He looked her over and smiled. She returned his smile and simply said, "Come with me."

He thought to himself that she was a typical employee to expect. Buddhists and Muslims were a favorite for the companies they used. Their beliefs in Mohammad or Buddha made them ideal employee material. In America, they liked the diversity; it worked to their advantage in some areas. They even got tax breaks for it.

He got off the elevator on the top floor. The lady took him into a large, posh office. He was brought into a room with several, well-dressed people. A man came over to shake his hand. He was middle-aged, but young-looking. His blond hair looked tightly cropped, and he had a face that looked like it had been pulled back at least once. There were a number of other people in the room; they stayed away. The man smiled like a politician and said, "Judas, welcome. We're so glad you're here. Come, sit."

Judas sat; he was visibly uncomfortable. He didn't like these people. He didn't trust them. He liked what he did. He served in his own way. When he was not on assignment, he enjoyed a very high-end lifestyle. These people had an agenda; they always wanted something. He knew they were in charge, but he liked to keep them at a distance. The man never introduced himself formally. They had met once before and he had video-conferenced with him a few times. The man wanted to make him more at ease, so he said, "Nice job in Turkey. That priest had become a serious concern. He had stuck his nose in too many times. Glad to have him out of the picture."

Judas forced a smile and said, "Thank you."

The man motioned for the other nameless leaders to come sit with them. He said, "You must be wondering why you are here."

Judas didn't respond immediately; he thought he should consider everything he said before he said it. Finally, he said, "I haven't been to America in a long time."

The man said, "Yes, I know. We usually keep our best people on the front lines."

"Usually?" Judas asked.

"Yes, usually, but now we have a special situation." Judas could not think what would be so special here. The man continued, "We have been monitoring a situation here. It seems that the Christians have lost one of their people." He paused. Judas didn't speak, so he continued, "There is an outsider involved. We tried to have him taken out, but there was a soldier protecting him. She took out the team we had instructed to kill him."

Judas nodded thoughtfully. He felt uneasy about the way everyone was looking at him. He felt he was expected to say something, but he didn't know what to say. He finally asked, "A soldier? How many of our soldiers did this person kill?"

"Not soldiers, imps. We had three assigned. The soldier killed two and left the third for dead. We found him some time later, and we killed him for his failure."

Judas again nodded. He tried to look thoughtful, but he didn't understand why they needed him. This sounded pretty simple. He asked, "What do you want me to do?"

The man smiled. "Direct. I like that. You are to find the man in question. His name is Timothy. We will provide you with a full workup on him. Kill anyone that gets in your way."

Judas nodded in agreement. He felt himself feeling frustrated. This seemed like such a simple job, and surely they had people for this. He finally spoke, "It seems that this is a pretty simple matter..." He hesitated and then continued, "...to bring me here to handle."

That statement hung in the air for a moment and then a lady at the table spoke. "We think there may be a defector." This stunned him. A defector? he thought. He had not seen a defector in a long time. He had heard stories of Christian soldiers trying to cross over to their side, but they were all years ago.

The man spoke again. "We are using a lot of resources on this one. We have a team of imps in the area planning a strike on the brother. They are going to make one more effort before you are on the ground there. Once you are on the ground, you are to find the missing Christian."

Judas didn't understand. Why were they so interested in one missing Christian soldier? The man continued, "There is one more thing: we are using Cain on this one." Judas was surprised. Cain. He had heard of him; everyone had heard of him. He was ruthless; he was one of their best. He had been rumored to possess special powers and was believed by some to be closer to their master than anyone. He was always on the hard assignments. While they had never met, he was sure that they had heard of each other.

Judas asked, "Will we be working together?"

"No," the man answered, "we want you to work independently of each other. We will be monitoring the situation and will be giving each of you directions. This is very important to us." Obviously, Judas thought.

"We will provide you with any resources you need. Just call us. We want this resolved quickly."

Judas could tell this was important to them, but he still didn't understand why. The man said, "If the imps fail, Cain will find the brother and eliminate him. He will kill the soldier protecting him. While he takes care of that, you will make contact with an informant we have been working with and then report to us once you have assessed the situation. Remember, the most important information we need from him is anything that will help us find the soldier, Timothy."

He started to rise when the woman spoke again. "You must be cautious and report everything to us."

Judas looked puzzled, he always reported everything. He didn't understand what all the urgency was for. He said, "Don't worry, as I eliminate the Christians that get in my way, I will find out where the soldier is."

CHAPTER 5

David was tired. He wasn't sure why. He had slept a lot during the day today before he came home. He had a lot to reflect on. He had made himself a cup of cocoa and was just settling down in front of his nineteen-inch television to watch something while he enjoyed his cocoa when the doorbell rang. David proceeded to the door. He couldn't imagine who would be calling at this hour. He looked through the peephole. There was a woman, with her long hair pulled tightly back. She was dressed in a black, leather outfit. He thought she must have ridden a motorcycle. Her black leather jacket was the type you see on bikers. David thought for a moment. She looked so familiar. David opened the door. Before he could speak, he realized who she was. This was the woman by the fountain at work! The shock washed over him, and he found himself speechless. The woman waited patiently for him to speak. When he could not, she finally said, "Can I come in?"

David, wordlessly, stepped aside she walked past him, and he shut the door. He finally found his voice and said, "Hi." He felt silly as soon as the word was out. Hi; smooth, real smooth, he thought.

She smiled at this. She couldn't help herself. She had been watching him for over a week now, but this was the first time she had gotten this close to him. She was amazed at how attractive he was. His tall frame, dark eyes, and full lips reminded her of a male model. She thought he should be on one of those posters you see at the mall or in the airports, modeling suits or a watch. She wasn't sure what was wrong with him. He seemed to be having trouble talking to her. Maybe she had awakened him. She had thought about what she would say, but she felt she should identify herself first. She said, "I work with Isaac."

David's expression went from a blank stare to a confused look. He said, "Isaac? I saw you at my work."

"Yes," she replied, "I have been watching you for over a week now. We were concerned for you, and I was instructed to keep an eye on you."

David began to realize that this woman, while incredibly attractive, was working with the fanatics. His expression began to harden. "I don't appreciate you following me. I didn't ask for your protection. I certainly didn't ask for you to come to my home, late at night. What do you want?"

She said, "I would like to talk with you."

"So talk," David replied.

She responded, "Can we sit down?" David wordlessly walked by her and led her into a small kitchen. "May I sit?" she asked. David wordlessly motioned to a chair in his small kitchen. She saw a cup of what looked like coffee. She smiled and said, "Coffee? Do you have a pot made?"

David shook his head and then said, "No, it's cocoa." David thought he would be a little embarrassed a few minutes ago, but now he didn't care that he was a grown man drinking cocoa alone, late at night.

She continued smiling and said, "I would love a cup if you have any more." David wordlessly retrieved a cup from the cabinet, filled the cup with water, put it in his microwave, and stood in front of it. When it was done, he turned, set it in front of her, and laid a pack of powder beside it with a spoon. He sat across the table from her. She ignored his obvious annoyance with her. As she poured the powder in the cup and began to stir it, she said, "David, I know that you spoke with Isaac earlier today. I would like to try to explain some things to you."

"What things?" David asked.

She took a long breath and said, "I am very worried for your safety. I know you don't think you are in danger. Due to the fact that your brother is one of us, I am going to do something that I rarely do." She let that statement hang there for a moment. Then she continued, "I'm going to tell you who we are and what we do, and it is my hope that you will forget this and let us take care of your brother."

David sat back in his chair, crossed his arms, and stared at her for a long moment. He considered just asking her to leave. He really didn't feel that he needed to hear what she had to say. He really didn't care who she was or what she did. But, in spite of himself, he was curious. Tim had always acted like he was in the CIA or something. If nothing else came out of this, maybe he could learn a little more about what his brother does. "Okay," David responded, "go ahead, tell me who you are."

She sipped her cocoa, trying to think of how best to explain it to him. "We are...protectors of Christians."

"Protectors?" David asked sarcastically. "From whom: Democrats?" He rolled his eyes.

"David, Christians have been persecuted for centuries. I work with a group of people who have dedicated their lives to keeping them safe and protecting the Christian way of life."

David leaned his chair back as she spoke. He set it back on the floor, leaned in, and said, "Okay. I'll bite. Who is it that you protect them from?"

She waited a long moment and then sipped her cocoa again. She looked him in the eye; her voice was low, almost a whisper as she set her cup down. "Satanists."

David chuckled. He repeated in a much louder voice, "Satanists?" and laughed out loud. These people really were fanatics. He couldn't believe he had let her in. He stood up. "All right, let's go, you're leaving!"

The doorbell rang again. David was really getting upset now. "So how many people came with you tonight?"

She stood up and said softly, "Just me."

David spoke as he walked to the door. "I'm going to see who this is and then I want you gone." He looked through the peephole again. There was a man outside who David didn't recognize. He was dressed in simple jeans and a tee shirt. He was heavy set and had long, shaggy hair. David asked, "What can I do for you?"

The man said, "May I come in? I would like to speak to you."

"About what?" David asked.

Just then the woman was behind him. "You don't know this man?"

"No, and I can't imagine what he would want at this hour."

She gently pushed him aside. "Let me take a look." After she removed her eye from the peephole, she said, "Stall him; I need a minute."

David felt silly; he was probably a bum or a drug addict. He could even be a neighbor; he had so many, and it was hard to keep up. "What do you want?" he asked.

"I have some information for you, about your brother."

As David was asking this, the woman moved across the room and looked out the window. She saw several cars in the street that were not there a few minutes ago, when she arrived. She looked back toward David, and in a firm voice said, "Do not open the door!"

The way she said it caught David by surprise. He was trying to process all of this. He spoke through the door. "How did you know my brother?"

The man in the hall didn't answer. He looked to his left and said, "He's not gonna let me in." David felt his pulse quicken. There were other people with him. His mind started racing; he didn't even own a gun.

The woman was back at his side now. "We have to get out of here. Do you have a back entrance, fire escape, or something?" David stared at her; this was all happening so fast. Then there was a loud thump on the door. Someone was trying to break it down. "Get back!" she shouted. She reached inside her jacket and pulled out a long blade. It looked similar to a machete; too short to be a sword, but too long to be a knife. She had the blade in her right hand, she pushed him away with her left hand, and then the door busted open.

The first man through ran right at her. She cut him across his chest, and he fell to the floor, screaming. The second man stopped. He had a gun in his hand and had it pointed at David. But upon seeing his partner on the ground, he started moving it in her direction. Before he could point it at her, she moved with lightning speed and cut his hand from his arm. It fell to the ground. He screamed, but he barely got out a scream before she cut his head off. David staggered back in shock. More men were coming through the door; he couldn't tell how many. She was fighting them all. She was moving with an amazing speed, and they were falling to the ground around her. David felt panic coursing through him. He ran back into the kitchen. He frantically tried to find something to defend himself. He picked up a simple kitchen knife, put it in his back pocket, and then opened a drawer and picked up a frying pan. He came running out with the frying pan held over his head. When he returned to the living room, there were a number of men and women lying on the ground. Blood was everywhere. The woman even had it on her. She looked at him with his frying pan. He thought how silly he must look.

She looked at him expressionless and said simply, "Imps."

David just looked at her. He said, "You killed them."

She replied, "Had I not been here, they would have killed you. There may be more; let's go."

"Shouldn't we call the police?" David asked.

"No, we have to go now!" David felt he couldn't argue. "Stay close to me," she said. David walked out the door behind her. There were more of them coming up the hall. David felt his pulse quicken. The woman walked confidently toward them, with the long knife held behind her right arm. She walked up to them; before any of them could react, she cut them down.

David was in a full panic now. He had never seen anything like this before. Behind them, down the opposite side of the hall, more imps came. The woman reached inside her jacket with her left hand and retrieved a gun. She fired a few, random shots in their direction. This scattered them. David followed her into the stairwell. They had to go down three stories to get to the bottom. As they got to the second story, David heard the door open above them. They were right behind them. Then they heard the door at the bottom of the stairs also open; they were trapped.

"What are we going to do now?" David asked.

"No choice; stay behind me, and if I go down, run!" she said.

Several men poured through the door. She fired a few shots with her pistol, but it didn't scatter them this time. They were armed and returned her fire. They were pinned on the second floor with people closing in from above and below. She moved down the stairs, toward the first floor, crouching low and hugging the wall as she went. David crouched and, staying behind her, felt the panic swell through him. There was no way they were going to get through them.

As they approached the first floor area, by the door, the area was full of men and some women. They were all armed and ready. The woman crouched in the corner and looked up. She said "Father, please, we need help. We are in your hands, O'Lord. Amen." Then she saw that the entire, dimly lit area was lit with high-hanging fluorescent lamps. Several were burned out, hence the dim lighting. She took out her pistol and fired several shots. From where she was, she was able to take out the lights on the first and second floors. The darkness worked to her advantage. There was still light coming from the two, upper floors. She moved back up, toward the second floor. She came under fire but was able to get off a couple of shots. It was enough to kill the lights on the third floor stairwell. Now the only lights came from high above, from the fourth floor. The bottom floor was now in almost total darkness.

As she came back down the steps, she grabbed David's arm. He was shocked at her strength. She spoke in a low voice. "Stay close to me!" She then moved past him and down toward the bottom floor. There were voices, confusion; the door to the street came open. David could see light pouring in from the street light outside. A couple of them went back outside. Time was short. She picked up her pace as she reached the bottom floor. She let out a scream and jumped with her oversized knife. The combination of the darkness and her scream threw them off balance enough for her to take out several of them. David felt like a small child; he didn't know what to do. He felt his fists ball up.

It was then that he realized he still held the frying pan in his hand. He thought he would try to clear a path and help them get out the door. All attention was on the woman; no one was looking at him. It was very hard to see anything in the darkness. He could hear the others coming down the stairs. He ran forward and swung the frying pan with all his might at the nearest one. David caught him completely off guard. The thump actually gave David a sick feeling in the pit of his stomach. The man fell to the ground without even a groan. David then moved toward the door. The next person in his way was a woman; she had a gun in her hand, but it was at her side. The darkness had been their only ally. David was able to swing the frying pan at her. This time it was just a glancing blow, but it was enough to knock her off her feet. She went to the ground, screaming obscenities. David could see the door. He knew what he would do now. He would open it and then scream for the woman to come running. With her speed, she could get away, and they could run down the street.

As he approached the door, he felt his feet being knocked from under him. The darkness worked both ways. One of them had caught David off guard, and he hadn't seen it coming. He fell hard to the concrete floor, felt the wind get knocked out of him, and the frying pan went tumbling into the darkness. He rolled over to his back, but the man was too quick. He was on top of David. He punched David hard, directly in the face several times. David felt his nose start to bleed. The pain from it shot up into his head. He grabbed his face with his hands. The man then reached into his jacket, for what David assumed was either a gun or a knife. David remembered the knife in his back pocket; he had to act quickly. He wasn't even sure if it was still there. He quickly reached back and found that it was. He pulled it and swung upward with all his might. Just as the man pulled a pistol from his jacket, the knife found its way into the side of his neck. David looked as shocked as he did. The man stared at David for a moment. In the darkness, David couldn't tell if he was bleeding. But then a few seconds later, he felt something warm coming down on him; he knew it was blood. Then the man slowly fell sideways off David. David had never killed anyone before. He sat up. He knew he should run, but he was in shock. He used his legs to push his back up against the wall. He sat there, not knowing how to get up. In the dark, he could make out the woman. Somehow she was still on her feet, but the odds were wearing her down. She was fighting off several of them at once when another approached her from behind. David wondered why no one was trying to shoot her, but he assumed they were afraid to fire a gun in the darkness, for fear of hitting one of their own.

A woman with a knife had managed to get behind. She pulled it back, ready to stab the woman who was protecting him in the back. He held out his hand and cried out, "No!" The knife suddenly flew to the side and out of the woman's hand. She cursed, fell to the ground, and began to look for it. The woman heard her swear and spun around and kicked her. This movement allowed the ones in front of her to get her. David could not see how, but she fell to the ground, and they were on her. She was probably dead now.

The others were arriving from upstairs. They had them now. David just sat there, stunned. The door opened beside him, and he felt a hard hand grab him and pull him up. The strong hands pulled him through the door and then threw him onto the street outside. It was a man. In the dark, David could not see him very well. He turned, without speaking, pulled a semi-automatic weapon, and opened fire. David could hear the bullets spraying and hitting metal inside. The man fired for what seemed to be a long time. Then he moved inside, the door closing behind him.

A few moments later, he came out with the woman. She seemed to be okay. She had tears on her clothes. She had clearly been beaten, but she was on her feet. The man wordlessly picked David up, pulled him to his feet, and pushed him in the direction they were running. The woman took David by the arm and pulled him with her across the street. Her motorcycle was parked there. The man was moving with them. He turned and started running backward, trying to see if anyone was following them. As he did this, he ejected and re-inserted a clip into what looked like an oversized pistol. From the way it fired, David guessed it must be an automatic pistol of some kind. The woman climbed onto the motorcycle. She jumped hard on the starter, and it fired up. She motioned for David to get on behind her. He felt like he was in a daze. He climbed on.

The woman now spoke to the man. "Thanks, are you okay?"

"Fine," he replied. "Just go."

"What about you?" she asked.

"I'm fine. I got this."

She didn't argue. She put the motorcycle into gear and said to David, "Hold on!" David gently put his hands around her waist. He still felt like he was in a daze. He was watching the man who helped them run back across the street and then disappear around the corner. She grabbed his hands firmly, pulled them together at her stomach, and pushed them together. "I said hold on!"

David firmed up his grip around her waist, and the motorcycle roared as they took off down the street.

David found himself back at the church, in the kitchen. Isaac set a cup of coffee in front of him. David just stared forward, a blank look on his face. Isaac sat across from him, but didn't speak. After a while, David said, "Who are you people?"

Isaac seemed to consider the question, but he didn't say anything.

"You're...the woman you sent told me that you were some kind of bodyguards for Christians. She said that you fight Satanists. The whole thing sounds like some kind of fiction to me."

Isaac looked at him for a long moment and then said, "What is it you want to know about us?"

The truth was that David wasn't sure. He had all kinds of questions in his mind, but wasn't sure where to start. He finally said, "How did you guys get into all this? I mean, how long have people like you been around?"

To David's surprise, Isaac smiled and said, "Our group has been in existence for almost two thousand years. We trace our beginnings back to a Roman convert who knew Apostle Paul."

"Apostle Paul?" David asked.

"Yes," Isaac continued, "our founder was a man named Marcus. He was a Roman general in Israel. He knew of Jesus. He had heard Jesus speak and was touched by him. He was present for his crucifixion. Not long after, he sought out the apostles. He had questions. He eventually was converted to Christianity by

Apostle Paul. The Romans were never aware of his conversion. He continued to operate as a Roman general. He was also present for Apostle Paul's execution. He wrote very fondly of him. He came to despise the persecution of the Christian's by the Romans. He felt that the Christians needed to do something to fight back. It was very obvious that there was no way they could rise up and expel the Romans; not during his lifetime anyway. So he founded a secret organization. He didn't give it a name, but he found men who were willing to learn to fight.

"As a Roman general, he was well-trained. He passed this training on to other Christians and began a kind of guerrilla warfare, designed to protect Christians from persecution and keep them safe. His people were loyal and had to swear their loyalty to the Christian cause. Much like priests and nuns, he required the people he recruited to give up personal possessions and relationships. They had to be totally loyal to the cause. Many Christians were saved. Marcus oversaw the organization until his death. Upon his death, we began a succession of leaders. Over the centuries, we have refined our training, our methods. All through modern history, we have been there, just under the surface, just out of the eye of history."

David absorbed this. With his mind still racing, he asked, "Do you consider yourself apostles"

Isaac said, "We consider ourselves protectors; however, our leaders call themselves apostles, and each country has ruling body. We call it the Apostolate."

David said, "My understanding is that the qualification to be an apostle was to see Jesus. How is it you feel you can call yourselves apostles?"

Isaac said, "We call ourselves apostles to honor our founder, to honor the apostles. They were the inspiration for our creation."

David gave him a skeptical look and then asked, "How is it that I have never heard of you? That there is not a single mention of you in any history book that I have ever heard of?"

"David, you must understand that we are bigger than any one nation, any one time period, and any war. We are protectors. That is our mandate. We have to be disciplined. We have to follow our protocols. Much like spies you see in the movies, we have to do whatever is necessary to keep our actions secret. There is a saying that we have: 'We are here to protect Christianity. We don't always get to practice it'. We feel that we have a higher calling. Our people have to blend in to society, whatever society we put them in. That means that we have to dress, behave, and even say things that keep us from suspicion. When we are out of the public eye, we try to dress and act according to our beliefs. These things are necessary for us to do the work we do."

"You said that your founder founded this...group to keep your people from being persecuted by Romans. Last I heard they haven't been around for a while. How did you get the idea that you fight Satanists?" David asked.

"Our group is designed to protect Christians around the world from anyone. Up until around one thousand, it was more from different dictatorships and monarchies; different leaders that didn't embrace Christianity, that saw it as a threat to their reign. Our group was still small and somewhat unrefined during that time. What is not commonly known is that the dark ages were darker than our history books tell us.

"During the dark ages, the witch trials were close to bringing the true threat to the surface. Like us, the Satanists keep themselves just under the radar of history. Many of the witch stories you hear about during the dark ages and even among the first American settlers were actually converts to Satanism. Many of these people were discovered and ultimately brought to the public's attention by our people. It was during this time that we realized that they were the true enemy. We do not know when they started. Many believe they have always been there or at least, like us, have been there for a very long time. Tell me, David, what do you know of Satanists?"

David considered this. "Nothing, really; they do something that has to do with goats, drink blood, things like that."

"No," Isaac said firmly, "that is not correct. They are extremely well-financed. They are very modernized, and they only truly convert a choice, few people."

David frowned. "They seemed to have a lot more than a few of them tonight."

"You mean imps," Isaac corrected him. "Imps are not Satanists. Not really. They are fighting for them. They think they are believers, but they are really tools and sometimes cannon fodder. Imps are low-level, low-risk recruits. They usually seduce them with promises of alcohol, money, sex, or drugs. Drugs are the most common. Their addictive nature makes these people dependent on them. True Satanists are as well-trained as our own soldiers. They believe their master is the real God and that their job is to win as many souls for their master as possible."

David tried to process all this. After a long silence between them, David asked, "If you have been at war with them for so long, why hasn't one side tried to wipe the other out?"

"There have been attempts over the centuries. Not in my lifetime, but our history has recordings of it. Both sides have made attempts at different times. We have stations all over the world; so do they. It is virtually impossible to know where they all are." Isaac sighed and then continued, "Besides, they have found another way of attacking us and taking souls for their master. I don't think they see us as much of a threat as they used to."

"What do you mean?" David asked.

Isaac seemed to be thinking for a long moment. David wanted to say something else, but he sensed that Isaac was looking for a way to say whatever else he wanted to. He waited patiently and then Isaac finally spoke. "David, I am only answering your questions. It is not my intention to influence you. You must first understand this." David nodded, and Isaac continued, "I only say this because you told me the last time we were together that you didn't believe in all this 'stuff.'"

He took a long, deep breath and then continued, "It all started in 1945. Well, it started before, but 1945 was when we understood the threat; the threat that has continued since and has taken many souls from our Father."

1945? David thought. What in the world does that have to do with a holy war?

As if reading his mind, Isaac said, "1945 was the year that the Second World War ended. Our history texts record this year as the beginning of a new era. Unfortunately, it seems to have been the beginning of an era that has seen the Satanists gain a significant amount of ground, especially in America. Since then they have slowly, methodically improved their penetration into society. We have seen less and less of the Christian population that we had taken for granted prior to that time. It was a fundamental shift in the way they worked. It has paid off greatly for them."

"What are you talking about?" David asked.

Isaac again paused; he seemed to be really thinking hard about how he wanted to answer. Finally he said, "Atheism." David didn't understand. He felt his mouth come open, but he didn't know exactly what to ask. Isaac continued, "It started on the world stage with the old Soviet Union." Isaac leaned in and spoke slowly. "You have to understand the beginnings of the communist movement. The founder of the Soviet Union, a man named Lenin, based the structure of their government on the teachings of a man named Karl Marx. Marx was a nineteenth century philosopher."

David looked confused. He asked, "So Marx was a Satanist"

"No," Isaac answered quickly, "Marx was an atheist. He called Christianity the 'Opiate of the masses.' When the Soviet Union was founded, this was an integral part of who they were. They believed that the belief in any God was counterproductive to society. Isaac sat back, took another long breath, and said, "We are not in a holy war. We are fighting for the rights of our Christian brothers and sisters. David, I know you were raised in church. I also know that you don't believe in this 'stuff.' I would like to ask you to indulge me. Theoretically, if the Bible is fact and not fiction, as you believe it to be, what would happen to a non-believer when they die?"

David started to put it together in his mind. Isaac could see David processing this; now it was Isaac who waited for David to speak. David finally said, "So they began to push atheism instead of Satanism?"

Isaac nodded and then he said, "The Soviet Union was the first major nation in recorded history to push the belief in no gods. Up until that time, every nation believed in something. But for the first time, here was a nation that was encouraging people to believe in nothing. During the Second World War, our people were heavily engaged in saving Christians in Europe. We saved many Jews from the concentration camps."

"Jews?" David asked.

"Yes," Isaac replied.

"I thought you only protected Christians."

"David, the Jews are God's people. We protect them all. We are not here to judge. As I said, we are protectors. There are many faiths around the world. We believe only God can judge the righteousness of them. Our goal is to keep them all safe from persecution and Satanists. As I was saying, initially, we saw the Allied victory as a great triumph. It wasn't long afterward, when the Cold War started, that we began to realize that things were changing. By embracing atheism, the Satanists began a new strategy of winning—by not losing. An atheist goes to hell and gives up their soul, just like a sinner does at death. Our Father doesn't make distinctions. Over the years, atheism has increased worldwide. The Soviet Union has been gone for over three decades now, but the atheist movement continues to grow worldwide. Both sides are constantly working hard to keep track of the other. We know they still like to keep a large presence in any communist country; presumably because they feel safe there. Atheism has become their greatest weapon."

Another long silence settled between them. Finally Isaac spoke again. "David, the things we have discussed tonight are things that I never tell an outsider. There is a very specific reason that I have told them to you." David stared, as if waiting for the rest. Isaac said, "You know something. I don't know what you know, but you have knowledge that can help us."

"Why would you think that?" David asked.

"They have made two attempts on your life in the last twenty-four hours. They attacked your home tonight with a considerable force of imps. Remember what I told you. These people are very intelligent, very calculating. They are not reckless. Every move they make has been methodically planned. They have a very good reason for wanting you dead. Do you know what that reason is?"

"No," David replied sincerely. The disappointment in Isaac's face was apparent. David began to understand. Isaac had told him all this, hoping to convince him to give up some critical piece of information that he didn't have.

Isaac said, "Regardless, I hope that by telling you this, you will understand what we are up against and let us protect you." David slowly nodded his head up and down in a slow yes motion. Isaac said, "The room that you were in earlier is still available for you. You are safe here. Get some sleep. We'll talk again in the morning."

David slowly stood up and walked toward the door. Just as he was about to leave the room, he turned and said, "I don't think I have taken the time to thank you. You and your people have gone to great lengths to keep me alive. Regardless of the reasons, I am grateful. Whether I believe this or not, I would be dead if it weren't for you. I just want you to know that I am sincerely thankful."

Isaac smiled and nodded. Then he said, "David, I have prayed a great deal about you and this situation. The decision to place you under our protection was not mine. It was God's. If you really want to express gratitude, consider that as you go to sleep tonight."

David stared at him for a long moment and then slowly turned and walked out of the room.

Isaac waited on the door to David's room to close. Then he went down the hall, past the room David was in, and down another corridor. Then he opened a door that led to a basement. The basement was dark and damp. Isaac could see a light on behind a door on the far side. He opened it, and there were his two soldiers. They were talking as he entered the room. As he entered, they stopped their conversation. He sat down and motioned for them to do the same. As they were sitting down, Isaac spoke, "I told him to get some sleep. Either he doesn't know anything or he is unwilling to tell us what he knows."

"He has to know something." This comment came from Ezekiel. Ezekiel was a large man. He had a large frame and was built like a tank. He was a former Marine. He kept his head shaved smooth. He towered over most people at six feet, five inches tall. The only thing on him that didn't look rock hard was his stomach. He had a gut that didn't seem to go with the rest of his body; the result of a diet heavy in red meat and breads, lots of them. Everyone called him Zeek, except for Isaac, who always insisted on using his full name, as it was intended. Ezekiel had been with them for years. He was recruited by someone in another area. After his training was complete, he was assigned here. He frequently disagreed with his fellow soldiers but always took Isaac's orders without question. Most people found him intimidating, but Isaac always saw the conflict in him, the effort he constantly made to be a better man. The two men had grown close over the years, and Isaac trusted him with his life. "What do you mean, Ezekiel?" the female soldier asked.

Zeek looked over at her as he spoke, clearly indicating to Isaac that they were having yet another disagreement. "They don't send that type of a force and use that kind of power if they are not sure he knows something."

Isaac wordlessly turned his gaze to his other soldier; she understood he was waiting to hear her thoughts. "They may just want him out of the way. He seems clueless to all this."

Isaac nodded; that much seemed obvious to him. "What did you tell him?" Zeek asked.

"Nothing, really; just gave him a history lesson." Isaac responded, "I think I told him enough to keep him here, at least for a while."

"I think we should interrogate him," Zeek said.

"That's ridiculous," she said. "Look, there is more going on here than we know. Tim's gone, the Satanists are trying to kill his brother, and if I had not been there tonight, you would have been killed."

She knew he was right. They were in the dark, and she would have been killed if he hadn't intervened. She sat silently. Isaac spoke next. "We have to find out more. We need to get out there and get answers. I need options. Do either of you have any additional information?" Both people looked at Zeek.

While she had been protecting David, Zeek had been working the streets. "Yeah, I have two things. First I found out that Tim was recently in the inner city, in the old industrial section." Both of them knew this section. The area was full of homeless people. Why Tim would be there was anyone's guess. "I also found out that he may have visited a church in the Mission District." A silence settled in. Isaac seemed to be considering the information he had just heard. Then Zeek spoke again. "What did command say about the brother?"

"Nothing," Isaac replied flatly. Then he said, "I haven't called them yet." Both soldiers tried to hide their shocked expressions, but they failed. Isaac said, "For some reason, I find myself praying and seeking guidance. I don't feel ready to call just yet. I think we need a little more information."

"I would like to go meet with the priest who Tim met with. I have met him before," Zeek said.

Isaac nodded and then said, "That means you will go to the old industrial section."

Zeek spoke again. "There's something else." He hesitated, looked at each of them, and then said, "I think there is a traitor among us." This shocked both of them. Zeek continued, "Someone is feeding information to them. I don't know who, but I think it's someone close to us."

Isaac said, "We depend on a lot of people in the community to sustain us. All the civilians we use, regardless of their faith, undergo extensive background checks. You both know how thorough our people are." A silence settled among them for a moment. Isaac said, "I will have to contact command and inform Moses of this. I will do it, first thing in the morning. In the meantime, both of you be careful and pray before you leave tomorrow. Now, more than ever, we need God's hand guiding us."

Zeek looked at Isaac with an intense stare. He said, "I will find the traitor; you have my word."

At this Isaac gave a thin smile. He looked at Zeek and said, "Just be careful; this is escalating. Don't trust anyone. The three of us need to confide only in each other till we can figure out who it is."

Both of them rose and began to leave the room. Zeek walked past Isaac and out first. As she walked by him, without looking up, Isaac said, "Take David with you in the morning." She stopped and stared at the back of his head for a long moment. She never questioned orders, but this was highly unusual. As if understanding her concern, Isaac spoke again without looking back at her. "Ezekiel is right; they seem to have the advantage right now. He may see something we could miss. They did grow up together, and he knows him as well as we do, for the most part. We need every advantage right now. Keep him close and continue to protect him. They won't expect him to be out with you."

She nodded and then said, "What if they discover he is with me? It will be harder to protect a civilian in a place like that."

"One thing at a time; they will not expect us to use him like this." After a moment of silence, Isaac said, "There is something about him. I didn't expect to see so much of his mother in him."

He walked into the bar. At this time in the morning, there was virtually no activity. A man sat at the bar, holding his head. There was a man behind the bar, cleaning the bar, and polishing glasses. He walked past them and down a long hallway. At the end of the hall, there was a door. He walked in without knocking. The man behind the desk stood up quickly, as if startled. Before the man behind the desk could say anything, he spoke. "I'm Cain." Cain was about six feet tall. He had graying hair that was buzz cut so closely to his head he looked almost bald. While he was clearly middle-aged, it was tough to see how old he was. He had a very straight posture and quick walk that made him seem younger than he looked. He was incredibly confident and walked as if he could—and would—go anywhere he pleased.

The man's mouth opened slightly; he was unsure what to say. He finally said, "Yeah. Yeah, man, we were told to expect you."

Cain spoke again. "You will take my orders and give me what I need, without question."

The man nodded. He had an accent that was hard to place; Eastern European or Russian, maybe. "Of course; we were told you are in charge while you are here. Our home is your home." An awkward silence settled between them. Then the man said, "If you need anything—drugs, women, anything…"

Cain interrupted, "What I need is for you to do what I say, when I say, and that is all."

The man nodded nervously. "Sure, man. Sure."

Cain said, "Now get out! This is my office while I am here."

The man stared for a brief moment and then started grabbing his things. He reached into a drawer, pulled out some more things, and then, with his arms full, he hustled out the door.

Cain sat down, took his arm, and raked everything on the desk onto the floor beside it. He got out his phone and opened a message that read: "Begin your search in the industrial section. Proceed there immediately." He closed the message and then stared silently out the window.

CHAPTER 6

David felt himself coming awake. It was early. He sat up and rubbed his eyes. He swung his legs around and sat to the side of the bed. It was just after 6:00 A.M. He wasn't sure why he had awakened. He rubbed his eyes again and ran his fingers through his hair. He started to open his eyes and take in his surroundings. He looked around the sparse room, dimly lit in the morning light. As he looked toward the door, he saw a man standing there! He jumped to his feet, felt his heart race. He looked for something, anything to defend himself.

The man spoke. "Ruth asked me to come and wake you."

David looked at him with a shocked expression. He realized this was the man who had saved them the night before. He put his hand on his chest. He said, "You scared me to death!"

The man was expressionless. He seemed to ignore the statement. He said, "I don't think we have had the chance to meet." He stepped forward and extended a hand. "I'm Ezekiel, but most people call me Zeek."

David shook his hand and mumbled, "David."

Zeek replied, "I know." An awkward silence settled between them. David assumed he would turn and leave now that he was awake. Instead, he just stood there, staring at him. David felt he should say something, but he found himself at a loss for words. Zeek finally spoke. "Isaac said you were a non-believer." David nodded. Zeek continued to stare at him expressionless and then he said, "An atheist?"

David nodded a second time. He didn't know why, but he seemed to feel better each time he acknowledged it. He was proud that he could see the world as it was, not the fairy tale place these people made it out to be. Zeek continued to stare at him. With his face never really showing expression, he said, "Atheism fascinates me." Now David stared. Zeek continued, "I always felt I had to have something to believe in. How do you go through life with nothing?"

David replied, "Acknowledging that there is nothing else is what helps me embrace my life. By knowing what we have here is all there is, I know how to make each day count and enjoy what is here, in front of us."

Zeek was quiet for a moment, and he nodded his head thoughtfully. He said, "I've never been able to believe there is nothing. I've always believed there has to be something more." He stared away as if lost in thought. A few moments later he said, "A person can't sustain themselves without something to believe in. Even if they believe in the wrong thing, even if they can't get fulfillment from what they believe, even if they can't find the answers to their questions, it doesn't mean the answers aren't there; it just means they haven't looked in the right places."

David began to think now. His thoughts went to his mother again. David remembered how lonely she was, how she missed their father and hoped he would return before he died. David remembered how she constantly looked for answers in a book of made-up stories that she read before she went to sleep every night and never found them. He was lost in that thought for a moment, and then realized he hadn't responded to Zeek. David said, "I guess you're right. If you can't find the answers, then you must be looking in the wrong places."

Zeek nodded his head slowly again. Another awkward silence settled between them. Zeek stared off again, looked back at David, and then said, "I'll let Ruth know you will be out in a few minutes." With that he silently turned and left the room.

David stared out the window of the car. He could see the old smoke stacks coming into view. At one time, this must have been a major, industrial park, he thought.

As if reading his mind, she said, "All these jobs went overseas years ago. Now these empty buildings and properties house the homeless communities for the city. The police have come and cleared them out multiple times, but they always come back. These large structures give them natural protection from the weather."

What would Tim be doing here? David thought. The car came to a stop in a wide area near the side of the road.

"We'll walk in from here," she said. David got out, looking puzzled. She said, "We don't want to park too close to their area. We could lose the car." This gave David a shiver. They walked up a long road that wound into the park. An old, faded sign stated that they were entering restricted property. There was a fence that had multiple holes in it, and in places it was torn down completely. They walked into an internal road in the park. The road was full of pot holes. The buildings were in neat rows. They walked down what looked like a deserted street. They passed a couple of people. One was pushing a shopping cart, her long hair hanging down over her face. Presumably, the cart was full of her belongings. A man was also walking by with a slow gait and a walking stick. Both didn't speak when they walked by.

When they turned the corner, it looked like they walked into some type of city. The sidewalks were lined with shelters of every type. Some looked to be made of simple cardboard, while others were canvas-covered structures. Some looked like they had mountains of paper on them. "Wonder what they do when it rains?" David asked.

"Shh," she said. "We don't want to offend anyone. Do you have the picture?"

David nodded. Isaac had given him a picture of his brother this morning. It was a fairly recent picture. They walked up to a woman who had an infant. The scene was heart-breaking. The child was crying, probably from hunger. David held up the picture of his brother and asked, "Have you seen this person around? He is my brother, and we are trying to find him." She shook her head no and then disappeared into her cardboard home with her baby.

They moved up and down the streets of the industrial park. The residents were very cooperative, but no one had seen Tim. After several hours, they felt like this was a dead end and decided it was time to leave. Both of them were tired; they had been doing this for a long time. They began walking out. As they approached the entrance area, a group of SUVs came up the road. She placed her hand on David's arm. "Wait; something about this doesn't look right." She pulled him down a side street. It was the street they started on when they first arrived. As the SUVs approached, they turned down the same street and began to speed up. Homeless people began to scatter, and one running across the road in front of an SUV was run over. She began to run now, and David followed; the SUVs were coming down the street behind them. They caught up to them and pulled in a circle around them. She grabbed David. "Stay behind me!"

Imps began to pour out of the vehicles. It was clear that their intention was to surround them. Before they could get into position, she spoke to David, "We are going to have to move quickly. Stay close to me, and keep up!" She reached into her jacket and pulled out several smoke grenades. She quickly pulled the pins and began to scatter them on the ground. The imps attacked. The first one came at her, firing shots wildly in the smoke. She pulled her oversized knife with lightning speed and cut off his arm. She moved into the smoke and began swinging the knife wildly. David was so close to her he kept bumping into her back as they moved through the smoke. He could hear her grunts as she moved. David thought it felt like she was cutting their way through the jungle. He was amazed at how strong she was.

They finally seemed to get through the chaos and the smoke began to clear. They broke into a run. They darted down another street. A small child ran out in front of them; her mother, running close behind, scooped her up and ducked into a cardboard shelter. David could hear them coming, but he was afraid to look back. They darted down one street, then another. Finally, they stopped.

"Where now?" David asked.

"I don't know," she replied. They were lost. They were at an intersection of several different streets in the industrial park. They had to pick one. "This way!" she shouted, and they began to run again. When they turned the corner, they saw they had run into a small group of imps. David was tired of feeling helpless. When she went into action, so did he. She moved in one direction, he in another. He kicked one man, who quickly fell to the ground. He then started to wrestle another one down. The imp tried to pull a gun, and he and David began to wrestle for control of it. Meanwhile she was cutting down the other imps. One managed to get off a shot that got her in her left arm. She screamed out in pain, but a few seconds later, she had cut the man down.

All of them were dead now, except the one David was wrestling with. They rolled around on the ground, each temporarily gaining an advantage, but neither able to sustain it. The gun they were wrestling over came out of their hands and fell to the ground. They continued to struggle. Finally David delivered a knee to the man's groin, and he let out a groan. David rolled and came up with the gun. The man lunged at David just as he got it in his hand. David fired, and the man fell to the ground. David was out of breath. His chest heaved. She came over and put a hand on his shoulder. "Are you all right?"

David noticed her arm bleeding and said, "I think I should be asking you that."

She glanced down at her arm and then said, "It's just a flesh wound." She looked back up at David and said, "We've got to keep moving."

"Which way?" David asked.

Just then another man appeared at the end of the street. He stared at them with a blank, hard look, like he was looking through them. He started to slowly walk toward them. She spoke to David, while never letting her gaze leave the man slowly walking toward them. "This is not an imp. You need to go now."

David felt his stomach turn over. He didn't understand how, but he knew she was right. The woman pulled her long knife out again. To David's surprise, the man pulled one also. David felt like this looked like something out of the Middle Ages. As she postured herself in a fighting stance, David saw blood slowly drip from her injured arm. The man did not move into a fighting stance; he just slowly walked to her. As he got closer, he began to walk around her in a circle, totally ignoring David. David's mind began to race. Should he help her? Should he do something? For the moment, he just stood there, frozen. The two stared at each other for a long moment, and then the man moved in and swung his large knife. He was older, but had blinding speed. She easily deflected the first blow. He began to walk around her again; a few more quick swings, a few more deflections by her. He was testing her, looking

60

for weakness. She was clearly on the defensive. David wasn't sure why. The man moved in again. He began to violently swing. She began deflecting his blows and then offering swings of her own.

Their feet began to move now. He was strong; it became clear to David that he was stronger than her. She seemed to be a little more agile than him and, for now at least, she was keeping pace with him. They were moving with incredible speed. He began to back her toward a wall.

Just as it looked like she was going to back into it, she quickly turned, jumped up toward the wall, pushed off with her feet in an incredible motion, and came at him in a quick attack. Her knife just missed his head as he moved his head sideways, toward his right shoulder.

David began to notice why he wasn't getting tired and was able to keep up with the much younger opponent. He wasted no movements. David had been exposed to this in his own martial arts training. You must move with efficiency; wasted movements waste energy in a fight. This man seemed to be better at this than anyone David had ever seen. As she moved, in what seemed like a flurry of movement, he moved very little. But what he did do counted. It now began to occur to David that he may actually wear her down.

They were close to each other, their knives locked together. As he pressed in on her using his superior strength, she was pushed back and was able to use her leg to kick him away. They both stopped for a moment, just staring at each other. As her chest heaved, David began to see that he was correct. She was the one getting tired. David began to realize that he needed to do something to help. If he killed her, David was clearly not going to be a threat to him.

He moved in again. They both began to swing wildly. They were moving so fast it was hard to see who was doing what. Suddenly his knife came down on her right arm. It looked as if he sliced it to the bone. She let out a scream. She dropped her knife to the ground. He slowly walked over to her and then looked down at her. He spoke in a deep tone. "If you want to pray to your God, do it now, and do it quickly."

David understood what this meant, and he began to run at the man. He wasn't sure what he could do, but he knew he had to do something. As he approached the man, the man turned and looked toward David. As David was almost at him, he tried to jump into the air and kick the man away. He felt himself go flying backward. He was stunned; he didn't even feel the man touch him. He fell hard on the ground, several feet away, with the wind knocked out of him.

On the ground, the woman's eyes bulged. The man had not touched David, but somehow he had sent David flying through the air. The man raised his knife and turned it in a stabbing motion. He reached down and picked her up with his left arm; his strength was incredible. As he drew his knife back to stab her, she was able to swing a much smaller knife down and slice his face. He dropped her and staggered backward, blood getting into his eyes.

She found her knife, secured it, and then moved to retrieve a gun from the ground. Just as she got to it, she felt herself get thrown into a nearby wall. When she hit the ground, she realized he was too far away to have touched her. He moved in slowly. She was on the ground. He still had his knife in his right hand. He raised it over his head. David was just coming to his feet. He cried out, "No!"

As the knife went over the man's head, it flew from his hand. He turned and stared at David in surprise; the first emotion David had seen him show. He slowly pulled a gun from his jacket. As he began to swing it upward toward David, David felt fear rush through his body, and he screamed out again, "Stop!" David instinctively put his hands out in front of his body. The man flew into a nearby wall. He was dazed. He began to groan and roll around on the ground. David and the woman stared at each other, both shocked at what had happened. David then quickly came over to the woman and helped her up off the ground. He put one of her arms around his shoulder. She insisted on retrieving her knife from the ground. Neither really spoke, but they both understood they had to get out of here.

David began to help her limp away from the man as fast as they could go. They limped together down the first street that David saw. David could hear noises behind them; they had to do something. The woman was losing consciousness. David turned down an alley that led to the side of an old building. When they got about half way down the alley, David saw a window that had boards on it. David helped her gently to the ground and then kicked out a couple of the boards. He helped her to her feet and then pushed her through the opening he made. "This is going to hurt a little," David said as he pushed her through. She fell to the ground on the other side. David heard her groan as she hit the floor on the other side.

David climbed through. She was unconscious now. David picked her up in his arms and carried her through the factory. It was dark and dirty, he could barely see. He wanted to get deep into the place. After some time of moving through the building, he went inside a room that was bare. It was probably an office or storage room. He went in, closed the door, and locked it behind him. He realized that without her he was totally alone and virtually defenseless now.

Judas walked into the church. He had a meeting here today. He admired the architecture of the large building. He had always enjoyed looking at the art in churches. He had spent many hours in a church. In spite of all they had learned about one another, he didn't think the Christians ever understood how much time his people devoted to church. As part of their training, they were required to spend hours listening to different preachers and different faiths. Satanists were required to know the Bible like any Christian. They could probably quote scripture better than most Christians. Judas had been taught that the best way to manipulate your enemy was to understand their ways. Judas had never told anyone, but he actually enjoyed it. There was something about being on the doorstep of your enemy and walking among them that always gave him an adrenaline rush.

He nodded to a couple of people as he proceeded through the building. He was to meet his contact here. He assumed that it made them feel safe. He wondered if there was any specific reason for them wanting to meet at a Catholic church.

He saw the confession area and he looked around and then went inside. He knew the procedure. With a smile on his face he said, "Should I make a confession to you?"

"Is that supposed to be funny?" the voice on the other side said.

His smiled faded and he said, "What information do you have for me?"

There was a pause. Judas let the silence sit there; he had learned to be patient, especially when dealing with traitors. The act of betraying your loyalties was often a trying experience. It required them to wrestle a little with their convictions. He knew he would give him the information if he had come this far. Finally the voice said, "I won't be able to help you much longer. I just can't take this anymore. I need to make it official and switch sides soon."

Not much surprised Judas anymore, but this week he seemed to be getting surprised more and more. Switch sides? he thought. This person actually thought he would be serving with them? What in the world were they telling him? While they took great pride in working traitors, they would never let them into their inner circle. At best they could work like an imp, but then only temporarily. Their faith taught them that a traitor will always be a traitor and that they could never be fully trusted.

Judas knew this better than anyone. He chose the name of the greatest traitor in the Bible. He liked that he carried the name of the man who betrayed Jesus. He carried it with pride. He felt it showed his commitment to his master. He spoke softly to the voice on the other side. "In time we will discuss your options. I have just been assigned to you and this area. I need to know more about the…current situation."

There was another pause. Then the voice said, "We still don't know where he is."

"Where *who* is?" Judas asked patiently.

"Tim," the voice said.

"Tim? The missing soldier?" Judas asked.

"Yes," was the reply.

Judas took a long, patient breath. "We are looking for him now, and we'll find him before the Christians do. Our resources are vastly superior to theirs."

"He may be defecting," the voice said.

Judas considered this and then said, "Defecting. Do you really think that both of you are…considering serving my master?"

"I don't know," was his reply.

Judas was now silent. He considered the possibilities. The odds that more than one of them was turning traitor were pretty low. He thought of all the possibilities. It even occurred to him that this was some type of a trick. He then considered that it could be true. Either way he felt they should proceed cautiously and patiently. "Let me look into this, and we will contact you again soon. I appreciate your information. You are on the path to true freedom. We look forward to guiding you to the true path to eternity."

He stood up and started to leave the box when the voice spoke again. "There's more."

Judas paused, sat back down, took another long patient breath, and then said, "Go on."

After a brief pause, the voice said, "He has the Testimonial with him."

Judas felt his breath catch, and his mouth went slack. After all the surprises this week, he now felt something he hadn't felt in years: shock.

Judas exited the church. He was walking quickly. His pulse was racing, and he could feel the excitement pulsing through him. The Testimonial, he thought. He couldn't believe it. How could the Christians be so careless? If it was really in the open, it could spell the end. This was big, it was huge. Possibly the biggest mistake made by either side in two thousand years of warfare.

He dialed a number into his phone. The voice on the other side said simply, "Yes?"

Judas said, "It's real; all of it. The Christians have a traitor, and the man has the Testimonial. We need to devote all our resources to this. If the Testimonial is in the open, we could deliver a blow—maybe even *the* blow—to end this war, once and for all."

There was a long pause on the phone, and then the voice on the other side said, "We will send you additional resources."

Judas said, "I need to find out more about this Tim. Who is he? How long has he been serving? Where did they recruit him? I will need everything we have. I need to be more informed. I don't even know his full name or where he's from."

Another long pause and then, "We will send the information. Cain will take care of the brother and the soldier protecting him. You focus on finding the Testimonial. All other considerations are secondary. Understood?"

"Understood," Judas repeated. The line went dead.

David had her head in his lap. He had torn both of his shirt sleeves to wrap a make-shift bandage on both of her arms. She was right; her left arm was not serious, but her right arm would need serious attention and many stitches. She had hit her head, and he could tell she was in a lot of pain. David felt helpless without her. There was no way he could even begin to stand up to these people without her. The way he figured it, their best chance was to stay hidden until they could escape. She had been out for hours, and he had just sat there, frozen, with her head in his lap. He didn't know what else to do. His mind had raced with everything that had happened.

She began to awaken. David gently stroked her head. "It's all right. You're going to be okay," he said.

"Where are we?" she asked with her eyes still closed.

"I'm not sure; some abandoned factory," David said. She tried to get up, but the pain in her body was obvious. David pulled her back to his lap and said, "Listen, you are in no condition to be doing anything right now. I'm not sure, but I think they are looking for us. I really think we should wait this out and then try to leave in the morning."

She began to open her eyes. Her eyes caught his, and they stared at each other for a long moment. Then she said, "How did I get here?"

"What is the last thing you remember?" David asked.

"It's fuzzy; I remember you picking me up and us running. I remember falling through a window. I think that's it."

"That's most of it," David said. "Only you didn't fall; I pushed you through a window and then carried you here. You have a bad bump on your head. I'm not sure if they gave it to you or I did when I pushed you through the window. You have been unconscious. You will need to see a doctor for your arm, if we make it out of here." She rubbed her head with her left, good arm. David said, "You know, I have never gotten your name."

She smiled a little. David thought her smile was beautiful; he had never seen it before. She said, "I guess you should know it. It's Ruth."

David repeated, "Ruth." They were both silent for a moment and then David said, "Do you have a middle name?"

"We don't have middle names," she replied.

"So, Ruth is like your group name?"

She couldn't believe he was calling them a group. She said, "When we get anointed, we take a biblical name. We get to choose. I love the story of Ruth. It was the name I chose. It is my only name now."

"I would like to ask you some questions," David said.

"And I would like to ask you some questions," Ruth said as she rubbed her temples with her fingers, "but I don't know if I will be able to answer all your questions."

David considered this and then said, "Okay. Let's see if we can give each other some answers. Who was the man you fought with?" David asked.

"He was a soldier."

"You make it sound like you are at war," David said flatly.

"We are," she responded plainly.

David looked up, took a long breath, and then, as if searching for his next question, said, "What is that knife you guys carry?"

You guys? she thought to herself. She said, "We call it the *blade*; it's our weapon of choice."

David stared at her for a moment then said, "Why?"

Then she said, "It has been our primary weapon for centuries; since the beginning, really. The technology for weapons is great and keeps getting better. When we have to fight, we tend to be in close quarters. Guns and grenades have a place for us, but when we fight, we don't find them as useful as the blade. The Satanists have kept theirs, too, for presumably the same reason. Okay. It's my turn. What is that power you have?"

"Power?" David repeated.

"Yes, that man. I have heard of him. His name is Cain. We have heard of his power. No one else has it. That is, until now, we have never witnessed anyone else with it." She paused, waited for David to say something. He just stared at her blankly. She said, "How long have you had it?"

David said, "I'm not sure. I noticed it right after we first met. I have seen it a couple of times. It just seems to happen sometimes. I'm not sure how. Usually I have to be upset or angry."

"David, there is…" She started to say something and then thought better of it.

"What?" David asked.

"I think it would be better if Isaac explained. I don't think it's my place."

There was a silence that settled between them. Finally, David said, "What now?"

Ruth said, "I agree with you. I think we just wait until morning and then try to get out of here."

Suddenly they could hear noises coming from outside the room they were in. David froze. Ruth tried to rise up again, but the pain forced her back down. They were in the factory. David could see the bouncing beam of flashlights. The room they were in was bare. It had a window with wire in it. There was nowhere to hide. David scooted over to the corner and pulled Ruth with him. Their only hope now was that the darkness of the corner may help them. If they were discovered, there was no way they could resist. As they closed in, David could hear them talking. There were at least two of them. One of them was complaining about having to work into the night. The other one was agreeing with him.

"They're getting closer," Ruth whispered.

David could hear their voices plainly now. "Those two are long gone; I don't know why we have to keep looking for them."

Ruth grabbed David's hand and put it in her own. She closed her eyes and began to pray, "Oh, Lord, we are in your hands now." David rolled his eyes, but he let her hold his hand. She continued, "We are in your care; please protect us."

David could hear them moving outside. A light started to move around the room. They tried to open the door, but David had locked it. The light panned all around the room. David laid his head on Ruth's stomach. The light came over his back, just as he laid down on her. There was a pause, and then they moved on. "The Lord protected us," Ruth whispered.

"We got lucky. Those imps, as you call them, don't seem to be the most dedicated bunch." David never raised his head. Ruth never asked him to. In this awkward position, her head on his legs and his head on her stomach, the two of them, exhausted, eventually fell asleep.

David and Ruth got back to the church just before noon. They had slept till dawn in the factory. They got back to the car, but it was trashed. After a long walk, they finally found a cab. Ruth was exhausted from the effort, and she was very weak.

Zeek's trip to the church had turned up no clues to where Tim might be. His contact was tied up with confessions, and it took Zeek some time to speak with him. Once he did, the priest told him Tim had went underground, but he didn't know anything more. He promised to keep him informed if he heard anything.

Zeek took Ruth to the doctor. David found himself sitting in the small kitchen with Isaac again. It seemed he always ended up back here. Isaac poured him a cup of fresh coffee. He inhaled it; he needed a strong cup after the morning he had. Isaac sat quietly across from him. After a few sips, David spoke, "I feel like my world has totally changed."

Isaac spoke softly, almost in a whisper. "You have been exposed to a side of the world that you never knew existed. When we expose people to it, it is usually slow, gradual, and controlled. You have had to see all this in a very short time. We never intended this for you. Events have forced this on you...and us." David didn't respond. He just sipped his coffee and stared off in thought. Isaac said, "Ruth told me about your confrontation with the Satanist soldier."

"Cain," David said, as he stared off.

"Yes," Isaac said. He continued, "Ruth told me you saved her life."

"I hadn't thought of it that way. She has saved mine, and kept me alive since we met."

"She's doing her job," Isaac said simply. Then he said, "She told me how you saved her."

David stared into his eyes for a long time. Finally, he said, "I don't know how I did it. It just happened."

"We have only known of one other person having that kind of ability. Co-incidentally, he was the person you were using your ability on," Isaac said.

"What does the Bible say about this?" David asked.

"Nothing," Isaac said. He continued, "The Bible is our source of wisdom, guidance. It is the blueprint for our lives. It doesn't always answer all our questions. Sometimes its wisdom can provide us with more questions than answers, but it points us in the direction we need to go to find them."

David said, "What do we do now? I mean, how are we going to find Tim?"

Isaac said softly, "We will get back to that. Right now I think we need to continue to talk about your...power. David, there is a prophecy that I would like to tell you about."

"A prophecy?" David asked.

"Yes," Isaac nodded. He continued, "In the thirteenth century, a soldier prophesied that there would, one day, be two people who would have these powers manifested physically. They would be able to do things that seemed impossible. Many years ago, we were made aware of a Satanist that seemed to have these powers. He is one of their best. Many thought that he had no equal. We tried to take him out; several times, actually. We lost some of our best people in the effort. We came to the conclusion that we could not. He has been going around the world, un-checked. He has done a lot of damage to us over the years."

After a long silence, Isaac continued, "We never understood how or why he has the powers he has. We do know that he seems to grow stronger as he has aged. I think he has learned how to use them, control them more effec-tively over time. Now, that brings me to you."

David looked up, back into Isaac's eyes. He had a scared look as he stared at him. Isaac said, "You seem to have similar powers."

David turned his head back down and began to stare into his coffee. For the first time since all this had started, he began to feel fear. He had no idea what was going on. Isaac's speech continued to be soft, low, almost a whisper. "David, the prophecy that I am referring to is not accepted by all our people. Many have dismissed it. Many have chosen not to believe there is anything to it. Even after what we have seen in Cain, many still think it is a coincidence or that it was taken out of its intended context."

Isaac stared off for a moment and then continued, "That's the thing about us, David. Everything is built on faith; faith in God. And, at times, we have to have faith in each other. The problem is that people are imperfect by nature. We all make mistakes, all of us. It's much harder to believe in an individual than it is to believe in God." Isaac continued to pause periodically, giving David a chance to comment, but David continued staring into his coffee. Isaac spoke again. "The prophecy stated that two people would have this power: one a Satanist, and the other…a non-believer."

Again silence, and again no response from David, so Isaac continued, "The prophecy said that the unbeliever would arise and become the greatest soldier anyone had ever seen."

Finally David turned his gaze back to Isaac, but he still had nothing to say. "I'm sure you can see why I find recent events…interesting."

David spoke now. "Do you believe in the prophecy?"

Isaac was the silent one now. After a long pause, he finally replied, "I didn't when I was young. Once we became aware of Cain, I studied it in more detail. There are so many similarities in our two sides. When we become anointed, we leave our given names behind and choose a biblical name. They do the same. We use the blade. They have a similar weapon, but for different reasons. We use if for its efficiency and effectiveness in close quarters. They use it for its brutality; its ability to injure an opponent, to decapitate them, to make them suffer.

In spite of our war, there is somewhat of a mutual respect between us. When they take one of ours, they normally give them a minute for a final prayer. When we have to take one of theirs, we believe we should give them a final moment to repent."

David was not sure where all this was going, but he stayed silent and let Isaac take him wherever he wanted this conversation to go. "I came to believe that it was possible, that there was something to the prophecy, but I have never fully endorsed it. Now, after meeting you, I am beginning to believe that it was from God. This is not a popular belief with my people." David continued to stare at him. Isaac said, "The real issue now is that if the prophecy is true, then I am looking at the realization of it. And, quite frankly, I find that very scary."

For a man like Isaac to talk about being scared gave David pause. For a man of such faith, such confidence in himself and his beliefs to be scared seemed out of place. David asked, "It scares you that I could be the one?"

"No," Isaac replied, "it scares me that there could actually be one at all. The prophecy says that this person will have to choose a path. It says that they will have to choose one side or the other. It says that if they choose the Satanist side, they will wreak great damage to our people and the world. It's possible they could win the war for the Satanists. If they choose our side, they can help us win the war. Either way this person will win over many people for the side they choose and bring great harm to the side that they don't. I believe this person may be able to deliver a total victory for whichever side they choose" That hung in the air for a minute. Isaac looked at him for a long moment, and he said, "The fact that you don't believe at all tells me that you will have a very impartial point of view; at least initially. It also tells me that you have closed God out of your heart."

Isaac wanted David to say something, but he continued being silent. David finally said, "This is so much to take in."

Isaac reached across the table, patted one of David's hands gently, and said, "If I can be of a help, please let me know."

David looked at him for a moment and then said, "You don't want to begin pushing all your beliefs on me?"

"You have a lot to figure out. I have learned over the years that all my pushing will do nothing if the person doesn't want to hear what I have to say. I would like the opportunity to answer your questions and to discuss your doubts, but I think you will have to give me that opportunity. I can't force it on you."

David appreciated this. He was developing a respect for this man. Isaac, sensing that David needed a break, changed the subject. "Did you know that I knew your mother?" David looked at him in shock.

"She's going to be fine," a voice boomed from behind them. It was Zeek. "Where is she?" Isaac asked.

"Still at the hospital," Zeek said.

"You left her there?" Isaac asked.

"Yeah, I didn't think I could do her any good. They wanted to keep her for observation. I didn't think I could do anything for her, and I thought you would need me here."

Isaac said, "You should have called me first. This is a delicate situation. She could be in danger there." Zeek stared at him for a moment. Isaac understood; he was embarrassed to have this scolding in front of David. Isaac said, "We will speak of this later."

A noise came from down the hall. Isaac and Zeek exchanged a look. Isaac said, "David, please stay here for a moment." As Isaac and Zeek proceeded down the hallway, David ignored Isaac's request and followed distantly behind them.

The two proceeded down the hallway. As the hallway opened up to the sanctuary, Isaac and Zeek saw they had visitors. The two proceeded cautiously into the opening. David stopped at the end of the hallway. There was a large group of men and women fanning out around the sanctuary. There was a large man in the center of them. The tall man had a crew cut and graying hair. He stared past Isaac and Zeek to David. Isaac made eye contact with the man and shook his head in a defiant *no*. This made the man smile. Isaac and Zeek moved to parallel each other and immediately began to assume a defensive posture. David felt fear begin to grip him. The man stared at Isaac, then David, then Isaac again. He said, "We have come for him." He motioned with his head toward David.

Isaac responded in a calm voice, "You will not take him from here without a fight. What makes you think you can come into God's house like this?"

The man smiled again. He asked, "Do you know who I am?"

"Yes," Isaac responded.

The man gave him an intense look. Then he said, "I will be taking him; one way or the other. He will be leaving here with me."

Isaac looked back at David and spoke softly, but intently. "David, leave now!"

David wasn't sure why, but he froze. He couldn't move or think clearly. He kept staring at Cain. He couldn't understand why, but he felt like he was glued to the place he was standing. Every time he and Cain locked eyes, he felt something inside himself, something he could not explain, but something he could not ignore.

Isaac reached his hands behind his back in an awkward manner and, from under his loose shirt, he pulled a blade. Zeek quickly drew his in the same, practiced manner. From several different directions and without warning, the imps attacked. Zeek was powerful; he chopped and sliced. What amazed David was Isaac. They were hopelessly outnumbered, but Isaac fought with the speed of a young man. Like Cain, he had an efficiency about him. His moves were cat-like. Both he and Zeek were cutting through the imps quickly. David felt a surge of hope; maybe they just might even the odds and have a chance.

David noticed that Cain was not attacking. He was just watching. Watching like David was watching. The two made eye contact again. Cain didn't seem to want to get involved in this fight, and no one was attacking David.

Isaac and Zeek moved apart now. Isaac ran toward a pew and jumped into the air. His agility continued to amaze David. David would never have thought him capable of this. Zeek didn't have Isaac's agility, but he was incredibly strong. At one point, several imps were converging on him at once, and he spun with his blade and cut two of them down at once. His swing, going a full, 360 degrees, sent two other ones to the ground, though not mortally injured.

Isaac and Zeek were fighting all over the sanctuary now. They fought almost in a circle of Cain. He didn't look at them at all. As the fighting was going on, he kept staring at David. David exchanged looks with him. He wondered if Cain had the same sense he did. David could not explain it. It was like something in him was awakening; something that he never knew was there. Unlike Cain, David would stop, periodically, to watch Zeek and Isaac. Each time he brought his gaze back to Cain, he saw that Cain never stopped staring at him. David tried to think what emotion this was causing, but he had to admit that Cain's stare was intimidating. He felt like he should help, but all he could do was continue to watch. In a sense, he felt helpless, like he couldn't move or wasn't supposed to move.

Finally Isaac and Zeek moved close together. The fight had clearly worn on Isaac. His chest was heaving, he was sweating. Zeek didn't look much better. They moved together, as if they had practiced this. Their backs were touching, and their blades were raised defiantly, ready for the next round.

"That's enough," Cain said in an authoritative voice. Many imps lay dead or dying around the sanctuary, and many more still circled Isaac and Zeek. Cain said, "If you want to pray to your God, do it now." To David's surprise, Isaac did. He immediately closed his eyes and mumbled a short prayer to himself. David could not see Zeek; he faced away from David, but he thought Zeek probably did the same thing. Isaac opened his eyes and stared at Cain defiantly, his blade still raised. Cain moved through the imps. They parted for him, and he came within about six feet of Isaac. The two stared at each other for a moment. Cain said, "Get back. I will kill this one myself.

The imps immediately began to spread their circle. Cain didn't have a weapon; he seemed to want to talk with Isaac. "Before I kill you, I want you to know you will lose. Everything you have fought for will have been for nothing. We will wipe you out; all of you. Your dying faith will not outlive me."

To David's continued surprise, Isaac smiled now and said, "You will never kill us all. We serve the true God, the true Lord, and Master of this world. Your path will lead to only death and eternity in hell."

With lightning speed, Cain pulled a blade that was holstered on his back. He slowly approached Isaac. Suddenly Isaac's face showed shock. He looked down to see a blade protruding from his abdomen. He slowly looked back up as he fell to his knees. David opened his mouth to scream, but no words came out. To David's shock and horror, Zeek was standing behind Isaac. He bent over and, with one, quick motion, pulled the blade from Isaac's back. He looked up at Cain and said, "I can't do this anymore. I'm changing sides now. We can kill David and then all that's left is to find Tim. With my help, you can defeat them all!"

David felt like a small child who could do nothing but watch. He stared in horror. How could he have done this? He looked back toward Isaac, who was still on his knees. Isaac had been staring at David. Just as their eyes met, David understood that Isaac was hanging on, hanging on to tell him something. He mumbled a single word and then fell, face first, on the floor. Blood began to pool around his body. David still could not make a sound, but he felt a tear come down his face. He began to process what Isaac had said, what had been Isaac's final advice to him. The word was a simple, one syllable word, and David understood him clearly. "Run!"

CHAPTER 7

David wanted to run. He just didn't know how. He felt frozen to the spot he was standing. Both Zeek and Cain stared at him now. David didn't know what to do. All the imps in the room started to form a semi-circle around him in the doorway of the hall. They stood as if waiting for orders from Cain, but none came. Cain stared at him for another long moment and then said, "You and I seem to have something in common." He let that hang in the air for a moment and then said, "Some have said we are destined to be enemies, but I don't believe it has to be that way. I think we could be friends."

Everything in David told him this was wrong. This man didn't look as if he had any friends. David just continued to stare at him.

Zeek moved from behind Cain to his right side now. He said, "What are you doing? Just let me kill him. I can do it now, and we can be on our way." Without moving his feet, and with one, quick, fluid motion and without using any other part of his body, other than his right arm, Cain cut off Zeek's head. He didn't even look at him as he did it. His gaze never left David. Again David's mouth came open and, again, he could not say anything. He stared in disbelief as Zeek's head and body both fell to the floor.

Cain said, "I hope that shows my sincerity."

David finally found his voice. He said, "I may not be a Christian, but I will never be a Satanist."

David braced for the attack now. It never came. Cain stared at him for a long moment, as if debating what he would do next. Then he said, "I don't think you are thinking clearly. I want you to consider why you aren't a Christian. Maybe it's because deep down you know that something is wrong with the whole thing. We are not the people you think we are. We are followers of the true god, the true lord and master, the god that tells the truth and doesn't distort it with false prophecy, and the god that will rule this world. I have spoken to him, and I can tell you he is real. I would like to give you the chance to see that for yourself. There is more to the story than the Bible tells you. There is another side of the story. The Christians are the ones that try to manipulate, who try to convince everyone their way is the only way. I am going to give you a gift while you think about that: your life. I'm going to let you leave here freely. I want you to consider what I have said. We have a great opportunity to work together, to prove the prophecy wrong. We don't have to be enemies."

David absorbed this. He stared at Cain for a moment and then turned and ran down the hallway. Cain stared at him until he was out of sight. Cain pulled a small cell phone from his pocket. He punched in a number, waited for the voice on the other side to answer. He said, "I'll need a cleanup crew at the church." After he listened for a moment, he said, "No, the situation has changed. I want to talk to the Chairman."

Judas was going through the information on the screen. He was learning who Tim was. The reports were recent, before his disappearance. After some time, he began to get frustrated. He needed more detailed information. He pulled his cell and called a number. The voice on the other side answered, and he said, "I need to talk to records.

After a moment, the voice on the other side answered with a polite, "How can I be of assistance?"

Judas said, "I need information on this Tim. What you have sent me is reports our people have compiled on him. They are not organized to my satisfaction. I need a more organized report. I want it as far back as we can get. I need to know where this guy is from, where he went to school, everything."

"Just a moment," came the reply.

"Okay."

She said in a very pleasant voice, "Give me a minute, and I will see what we have on him" Judas continued reading as they were talking. She said, "We seem to have a lot of information on this one. I will not be able to send it all at once; it will have to come in several attachments."

As Judas was reading, something caught his eye. "Hang on a minute." He read intently. His eyes widened.

"Hello? Are you still there?" The voice came from the phone.

Judas stared at the screen. A look of utter horror came over his face. As the woman continued to ask if anyone was there, he slowly moved his hand down, away from his head, with the phone still in it. As it reached his side, he dropped it on the floor, lost in whatever he was thinking.

David rushed out the back door of the church. He was in a panic now. He didn't know what to do. Everything was spinning out of control. He tried to clear his head, to think clearly. Isaac was gone, and Zeek had betrayed him, had betrayed everyone. He ran until he felt like he would collapse. He didn't know how many blocks he had run, but he finally stopped.

Exhausted, he sat down on the side of the street. His mind was still racing. He thought about going back to his apartment and then felt silly for thinking that. Everything had changed now. He wasn't sure if he would ever really get to go home again. He put his head into his hands. He took long, deep breaths and tried to gather his thoughts.

Then it hit him. It hit him hard. "Ruth!" he said aloud. Then he ran off, looking for a taxi. David had to run several more blocks before he found one. He had no money, but he was desperate. He tried to think. They would come for her. She had no idea what had happened. She would not be ready. He had no way to call her. He didn't even know what room she was in. He was thankful that Zeek had said what hospital he was taking her to before he left with her. He just hoped he was being honest. That bit of information and Ruth were all he had left. He tried to think, tried to get a plan together in his head.

He had no way to pay the cab driver. He would start there. He would have to get out somewhere close to the hospital, but not to close. He would have to try to outrun this guy. The man driving the cab had tried to converse with David, but David's lack of response to his questions told him that this one wanted to be left alone. David looked in the front seat: college books. A picture of his family was taped to his dashboard, just above the meter. He had a wife and daughter. David hated that he could not pay him. He kept telling himself that it was life or death. They were getting close now. David said, "Stop here, please." The cab came to a slow stop. The man seemed kind of sleepy now. He seemed to have had a long day. He let out a yawn as he said, "That'll be $33.46." He then yawned again. This yawn was bigger than the first. He put his hands over his face and rubbed back and forth, trying to wake himself up.

David saw his chance and said, "I'm sorry!" He jumped out of the back of the cab and began sprinting. David expected to hear the man yell or scream, but he heard nothing. After some time, David began to slow his running; maybe he had just pulled away. He slowed to a jog. Then he heard something and looked back. The man was running at him, full force now. He had a tire iron and was charging at David. David felt the adrenaline rush and took back off now. He was running with everything inside of him. He turned down an alley, with the man close behind. Whatever fatigue the cab driver had before, he was not showing it now. He had clearly done this before. David felt his strength begin to drain. He could not keep this pace up much longer. He hoped he could get to an area that was populated. He thought if he could get to a public area, he could lose the man. This was the city after all.

David turned another corner and then realized he had turned to a dead end street. He stopped now. He looked for an escape, but he could find none. He turned to face the man. The man came to a stop about twenty feet in front of David, his chest heaving from the run. Out of breath, he said, "Now, you owe me $33.46. Pay me now!"

David said, "I have no money. I'm sorry, I really am."

The man said, "Then I'm going to take it out of you." He moved forward, and David froze again. He did not know why this was happening. He had never felt this way before. He just watched the man walk toward him, with his tire iron in hand. He had anger in his eyes, frustration. Everything began to feel like slow motion to David. In the moment he swung the iron, David saw his family, his picture in his cab, his books. This was not a bad man. He had a family; he was trying to better himself.

As the iron came toward David's face, David instinctively held out his hand to try to defend himself. The iron stopped about an inch in front of David's forehead. The driver looked shocked. David looked as shocked as the driver. In the past, when David had seen this power, he was angry or upset or even scared. This time he felt none of those emotions. He felt empathy for the man trying to injure him. He had no aggressive feelings toward this man. It felt different than before. He felt a certain peace about himself. The power felt different this time. He felt more connected to it somehow. He seemed to have total control of his surroundings. The man's expression changed from anger to fear. He let go of the iron. It hung there in midair for a moment, as if on a string. Then David felt himself let it go. It fell to the ground. The man was now the one frozen.

He started to walk backward, stumbled, and then fell. David reached down and picked up the iron. The man, still on his back, began to scoot himself backward with his feet in quick motions. David walked up to him with the iron, and the man's fear quickly turned to panic. David quickly walked to him, and the man, now feeling cornered, put his forearms in front of his face, preparing for the blow. He closed his eyes tightly and thought of his wife, his daughter, what would they do without him. He opened his eyes and there was a hand in front of him. An open hand, as if wanting him to put his hand in it. The man stared up at David, who looked back at him with soft eyes. Surprised, he slowly, carefully put his hand in David's, and David helped him back to his feet. The man stared at David in disbelief at what had just happened. David, who had the man's left hand in his left hand, now raised the tire iron in the right hand. The man flinched, but David turned the iron slowly and placed it in his other hand. The two men exchanged a look and then David said, "I'm really sorry to have done this to you. You are a good man. Someone's life depends on me getting here. If I had money, I would have paid you." The man simply nodded.

The look in David's eyes gave him a peace he could not explain. David said, "Don't leave this behind." David now released the iron into the man's hand and said, "You will need it if you get a flat tire." The man again nodded but seemed to be frozen. David said, "Go home to your family."

The man turned and started to walk away. David watched him leave. The man looked over his shoulder a couple of times as if to re-assure himself of David's intentions, but he never saw David coming for him.

As he turned the corner, out of sight, David, who was watching him, was actually thinking about this new power and how it felt different each time he used it. Today he felt something he had never felt before, but he had no idea why.

He suddenly remembered that he had to get to the hospital. Ruth could already be dead. He started sprinting and turned down the next street, trying to find his way to the hospital.

David walked into the hospital. He had run from the alley he was in. He was panting breathlessly. He put his hands on his thighs and bent over, trying to catch his breath. People in the waiting area stared at him. He straightened, walked over to the receptionist. She looked like the typical, over-worked employee with her hair pulled back, her glasses hanging on her nose, and her head buried in the computer. She said, as if very aggravated to be interrupted, "Yes?"

David said, "I'm looking for a patient. She was admitted this morning."

"Name?" she said simply.

"Ruth," David replied.

"Last name?" she said in a monotone.

David realized he did not know her last name. He said, "I don't know it."

She looked up from the computer at David. David knew what she was thinking, he was thinking it himself. He said, "We have just recently become friends. I heard she was admitted earlier today.

The woman looked back down, typed some key strokes into her computer, and then said, "There has been no one admitted today by the name of Ruth. Could she be under a different name?"

"Yes, but I have no idea what it could be." David thought of Isaac now and how he said they give up their given names when they are anointed. He thought they probably don't change them legally, which means she would be under her given name. David didn't know what to do now. Feeling desperate, he said, "Isn't there any way that you could check? She was brought in a little after noon today and was admitted. Isn't there a way that you could give me a list? I could go and see which is her."

"I'm sorry, I can't," she replied. She pushed her keyboard away and said, "I'm afraid you will have to get more information and come back."

David saw he was getting nowhere. He wordlessly walked away from the window. He didn't know what to do now. He walked over to the waiting area and sat down. He thought about her injuries. He was at the main entrance.

He thought that she might have come in through the emergency room. He sprung to his feet and asked a passing worker, "Which way to the E.R.?"

The woman pointed down the hall and said, "Two rights, then a left and straight down the hall, all the way to the double doors."

"Thanks!" David said as he walked briskly away. He got to the emergency room and saw a station for check-in. He felt he would not be able to get any more information there. He looked around and then decided to walk outside. He saw the ambulance entrance. He walked over where a couple of EMTs were loading a folding bed into their ambulance. They seemed to be having some trouble, and David instinctively went to help. He said, "Here, let me help you."

He assisted in getting the rolling bed loaded. The man and woman both said, "Thanks!"

David said, "No problem."

They got in the ambulance, closed the door, and left. Another EMT came out of a door behind David. David spun to see that behind the secured door was another person coming down the hallway, not far behind. David had an idea. He walked toward the door. It closed behind the EMT, who had just exited. David pretended to start to enter a code into the pad by the door. When the next person came out, he pretended to be startled and then smiled. The person returned the smile in a cordial way. As they exited, David entered.

He walked down another long hallway. There was a lot of activity. No one seemed to notice him at all. He quickly mixed in with the crowded E.R. patients. There were curtains pulled in all areas. David saw a man cradling an arm in a sling. Behind another curtain, a little boy was holding a compress on his head, his mother holding him on her lap, with her arms around him. David saw a desk in the corner.

He walked up to the woman and put on his best smile and said, "Hi!"

She looked up and enthusiastically said, "Hello!" She was much younger, probably not long out of school. She had a pretty smile, brown eyes, and hair to match. David could tell that she liked him by her smile. He was never good at flirting. He always preferred directness. He always guessed that was why he didn't date much. He never cared for the cat and mouse games some men and women liked to play. He was always direct and to the point. While these were admirable qualities, he had learned most women didn't appreciate them; at least not in the beginning stages of dating. They liked a little flirting, a little romance.

David smiled broadly, leaned in, and said, "I could really use some help."

She just smiled back and said, "Sure. I mean I'll try. What do you need?"

David said, "I am looking for someone. I only recently met them, and I don't know their name. I'm really worried about them. You see, they go by a nickname, and I don't know their real name. They were admitted a little after noon today."

She smiled and said, "Let me see what I can find. What were his injuries?"

David hesitated. He was making this up as he went, and he was worried if he said the wrong thing, he could lose this woman's support. He said, "It's not a he, it's a she."

The woman had a noticeable change in her expression. She didn't respond; she just looked at her computer and started looking. David began to worry. He said, "Her husband is a good friend, and he travels abroad. She was mugged, and he asked me if I would check on her. He's in Japan right now, and he is desperately trying to get home." He laughed and tried to act embarrassed. He said, "I have been to their house for dinner several times. She always goes by Ruth, and I have never asked her real name. I wanted to ask him on the phone, but I think they told me once and I forgot. I really didn't want him to know I didn't know his wife's name."

She looked back up, and her smile returned. "Yeah, that would be pretty embarrassing." She giggled.

David said, "I really appreciate your help. I was freaking out thinking I might have to call and ask."

"I'll see if I can keep you out of trouble," she said and winked at him. David continued to smile. He felt like this was going to work. Then she said, "It shouldn't be a big deal. Just give me her last name, and I can pull it up."

David continued to smile, but inside he was panicking. He had to say something fast, he was fumbling in his mind, and then he said, "You see, that's part of the problem. She is one of those women who wanted to keep her maiden name. When she married my friend, she kept her last name." She looked back at him with some suspicion now. David pretended not to notice, and he said, "I feel like this kind of stuff only happens to me."

She looked at him for a few more moments, and as she looked back down at her computer, she said, "I know what you mean. I have the same feeling sometimes."

David noticed she didn't have a ring on her finger. She was definitely flirting. He said, "Well, maybe we could exchange stories sometime."

She looked up, smiled, looked him over, and then said, "I would like that."

David lowered his head, tried to look embarrassed again, and said, "So, do you think there is any way I can find her?"

She said, "Yeah, tell me what was wrong with her."

David said, "Both her arms were injured. I think my friend said that she was cut badly on her right arm."

After a few more seconds, she said, "Okay, I think I have her. Her name is Mellissa…"

She stopped and looked at David. She smiled and said, "We're really not supposed to give this kind of information out. I'll leave it at that. She was brought in a few hours ago. She is on the third floor, Room 319."

She looked back down at her computer, made a few more key strokes to close out her system. She spoke as she looked back up and said, "Listen…" She was surprised to see that no one was standing in front of her desk. He was gone.

David was running full force down the hallway now. He bumped into an older nurse who said, "Slow down! No running in here!" David ignored her. He finally found the elevator. It was packed with people. He looked and saw a sign for the stairs down the hall. He sprinted to the door. As he entered, he took the stairs, two at a time, until he was on the third floor. He came out of the door and then started looking for the room. He noticed that all the odd numbers were on one side, and the even numbers were on the other. He ran by the nurses' station, and they all gave him a concerned look. He slowed down, smiled nervously, and then said, "Sorry, I know I'm not supposed to run. I was looking for Room 319."

By this point, he knew what direction to go, but he didn't want them to call security on him. They wordlessly pointed in the direction he was already going. He took a deep breath, smiled, and said, "Thank you very much" He tried to walk casually away, but he doubted he did a very good job.

He got to the room. His heart was racing, and he just knew he was too late. He came in, and she lay there, motionless, on the bed. He shouted, "Ruth!"

To his surprise, she immediately sat up and rubbed her eyes as she said, "David? What are you doing here? You shouldn't be out by yourself."

As she woke up, she looked him over. He looked awful. His hair was wet with sweat, and his clothes looked like he had slept in them. David said, "Thank goodness you're alive."

She looked at him with a puzzled look and said, "What are you talking about? Is Isaac with you?"

"No," David responded.

She asked, "Does he know you came here? It's not safe for you to travel without protection."

David stepped back out, looked down the hallway, and then said, "We have to go, now!"

Ruth said, "What's going on, David?"

"No time to explain; get your clothes on," David said.

She slowly got out of bed, her arms clearly aching. "Keep your voice down." For the first time, David noticed they were not alone. There was a curtain pulled around another bed. David looked at the curtain and then looked back at Ruth. She said, "Her name is Judith. We prayed together earlier. She just had surgery on her hip."

"Hello there," came a voice on the other side of the curtain.

David didn't respond. He moved back to the doorway. He could see the nurse's station. He noticed a group of people: two males and one female. They were asking the nurse for directions. David recognized one of them from the church earlier. He quickly closed the door. He said, "They're here!"

He quickly opened the curtain. The woman appeared to be in her eighties. She had long, solid white hair. She smiled at David. Before she could speak, he said, "I don't have time to explain, but we need your help." She stared at him, with a puzzled look. David said, "Our lives are now in your hands."

The three imps came down the hallway. The woman opened her purse and looked down; the syringe was there. This should be easy. As they strode casually down the hall, she spoke at a whisper to the two men. "Check your weapons." The men reached their right hands inside the left side of their jackets to ensure their guns were ready and to verify the safeties were off. They weren't taking any chances.

They entered the room. They hoped she might be sleeping. The syringe could be injected into her I.V. or into her directly. She would be dead in seconds. When they entered, they saw the first bed was empty. It looked like it was recently slept in. The second bed was behind the curtain. She exchanged a look with the other two men, who then moved to flank each side of the curtain. She quickly pulled the curtains open with a quick movement. In front of her was an old woman, probably in her eighties or nineties. She said, "Well, hello."

The young woman stared at her for a long moment. Her legs were suspended in the air. She said, "Could you please empty my bed pan?" She motioned to a bed pan, on the floor beside her bed. "It has been awful, having to inhale that for so long."

The woman didn't speak, she just looked around. There was a wardrobe. Other than that, the only other place she saw was the bathroom. She motioned with her head in each direction. The man to her right walked to the wardrobe and the one on her left walked to the bathroom. Neither found anything.

The young woman finally said, "The woman in the other bed, where did she go?"

The older woman smiled and said, "She left about an hour ago." The young woman stared at her for a long moment, without saying anything. The older woman said, "Won't you pull up a chair? Judge Judy is getting ready to come on. I would love some company."

After another moment, the young woman said, "Let's go."

After they left the room, the older woman said, "I think it's safe now." From under the bed, lying in the confined space beneath the bed, beside the bed pan, David began to scoot from under the bed. The space was so tight; he had to turn his head sideways to get out from under the bed. With a groan, he got up. He reached for the old woman's legs, which were suspended in the air a result of her surgery.

David said, "I'll try to be gentle." Judith closed her eyes as David gently lifted her legs. From under the sheet, beneath her suspended legs, Ruth slowly un-rolled from the tight ball she was in. She eased off the foot of the bed. David tried to gently lower her legs back into the braces in which they were suspended. Ruth moved to the side of the bed and squeezed Judith's hand. "God bless you," she said to Judith.

Judith smiled and said, "This is the most excitement I've had in a long time. My grandkids will never believe me."

Ruth went into the bathroom and changed out of her hospital gown. David moved to the doorway. He said, "It's clear."

Ruth looked back at Judith and said, "We will see each other again."

Judith smiled as they left the room.

David led the way. They had to go down the hall, around the opposite side from the nurses' station. The corridor made a circle around the floor, with the nurse's station in the middle. They had to go by the nurses' station to get to the elevator. David hoped by circling around and passing by the other side they would not be noticed. David instinctively grabbed Ruth's hand as they walked by. Fortunately it worked. The nurses were busy and didn't even look up to see who was passing by. David wanted to proceed with caution, so he explained that he didn't want to take the elevator.

After going down three flights of stairs, they emerged on the first floor. David said, "I think we should try to find a back exit."

"From the hospital?" Ruth asked.

David gave her a look that said, I know. They both understood that there could still be people looking for them, and Ruth was in no condition to fight. David pulled her into a crowded waiting area. They sat and began to think. David was so happy he had found her alive, but he knew they needed to get to somewhere safe. It was possible there could be people monitoring the main and emergency entrances. They sat there for several hours. They were afraid to leave, but they were also afraid to just sit there and be noticed.

As they sat there, David noticed a door that employees kept going in and out of. An idea came to him. He sprang up and said, "Come on, I think I may be on to something." David approached a hospital staff member and said, "Miss?" The young woman stopped and looked up from her cell phone. She was young, probably just out of nursing school. She had brown hair, pulled back tightly, with only a few bangs hanging down. Her green eyes looked at David through stylish glasses. David smiled nervously, looked around, and then said, "My wife and I just came from the maternity ward. We just had a little girl."

The young woman looked down at Ruth's stomach, looked the two over, and then gave David a skeptical look. David said, "We are adopting. The biological parents are both drug addicts. They signed the paperwork this morning, but they are harassing us."

The young woman said, "Okay, let me call security for you." As she began to raise her cell phone, David put his hand on her forearm. She looked surprised as David touched her, and she stepped back a step. David also stepped back, tried to give her an apologetic look, and said, "They have already been involved. They made them leave the hospital, but they told us that they could not make them leave the parking lot. We are afraid to leave through one of the main entrances. My wife is worried they might try to confront us."

She looked at Ruth, who tried to put on a concerned look. David asked, "Is there a side exit we might take?" The young woman looked them over carefully, as if trying to decide if they were being honest. She partially raised her cell and then looked at it for a moment as if pondering calling security.

She took another look at them and Ruth said, "Please."

The young woman sighed and said, "There is an employee entrance. No one is allowed to come in that way, but I don't think it would be a problem if you went out that way."

She took them across the hall and through a door. They went down a hallway and stopped at a door. She said, "This door leads to the parking garage on the east side of the hospital. I hope you get your daughter home safely."

David thanked her, and Ruth grabbed her arm as they exited and said, "You have no idea what this means to us."

David and Ruth left the parking garage from the back side and walked for a few blocks. Ruth wanted to call Isaac, but neither of them had a phone. They found a diner, and David asked, "Do you have any money?"

"A few bucks," Ruth replied.

David said, "Let's go in and get a booth." Ruth agreed and they proceeded in the diner. The diner was nearly empty at this hour. It was one of those twenty-four hour places. At this time of night, there were only two employees. David asked for a booth in the corner.

As they sat, Ruth could see something in David's eyes. She asked, "What is it?"

David proceeded to tell her about Isaac, about Zeek, and about Cain and the imps.

As he finished, her eyes were full of tears. They kept rolling down her face. David reached across the table and put his hand on hers. She quickly pulled it away and said, "No! I can't believe it. Zeek, Tim, and I have been through so much together. Now Tim is missing, and they are both dead!"

She sobbed. The waitress approached the booth, ready to take their order, but David waved her away. David said, "I know you are going through a lot now. I am, too. We have both lost everything." David paused, and he felt himself starting to feel emotional. His voice cracked as he said, "When I left the church, all I could think of was getting to you."

Ruth looked up into his eyes for a moment. David felt embarrassed. He didn't let his guard down around people. He had spent years putting up walls. Walls that he never let people knock down. Walls that made him feel safe. He never let anyone in. He rubbed his hands over his eyes and then said, "I don't know what to do anymore. I feel lost. I don't know what we are supposed to do now."

Ruth straightened, composed herself. She wiped her eyes and gave David's hand a reassuring squeeze. She said, "I do know what to do. We have to find a phone."

CHAPTER 8

C ain was sitting at the office, in the club. Two bodies lay on the floor in front of him; the two men who had been sent to kill the Christian soldier. The woman was sitting in the chair across from the desk, directly in front of him. Her hair was matted with blood. Her face looked disfigured. It was horribly swollen. Her left eye was swollen completely shut. Her right eye was swollen, but she could still see out of it. She was staring at Cain with her one, good eye. She had been cut in multiple places. Cain shot her in the left shoulder and then the right shoulder. She screamed in pain. Her body was limp, but somehow she was still sitting upright. She was sobbing uncontrollably. Two other imps stood by the door on either side. They both stared with frightened looks on their faces.

Cain said, "I gave you a simple task. You let her get away. She had to be right under your nose the entire time!" He hesitated and then said, "You couldn't even keep her from leaving the hospital! We don't tolerate failure here!" The woman continued to cry. Cain seemed to calm himself; he spoke in measured tones now. "Is there anything else you haven't told me?"

Tears rolled down her face. She said, "Only one thing: a nurse told us that a tall, dark-haired man was going to her room just a few minutes ahead of us." She sobbed more and then said, "I'm so sorry. Please give me another chance. I won't fail you again."

Cain's eyes filled with fire. She could see them turn red. His entire face turned red, like it was on fire. The two imps exchanged frightened glances at each other. She felt her limp body rise off the chair and into mid-air. The two imps by the door recoiled in fear. Cain's hands were still at his side, but it was as if his stare held her there, in mid-air. She slowly began to turn until her body faced the floor. Cain spoke in a deep, dark tone. "We do not give second chances!" With a motion of his hand, she shot forward and then down. Her head made contact with the corner of his desk as it came down, and it snapped back, breaking her neck instantly. She hit the floor hard with an incredible thud. Cain's face seemed to slowly return to normal. He said, "Get them out

85

of here! Take them far away and then bury the bodies deep." The two imps scrambled to start dragging the bodies out. Cain said, "Tell the others what you have seen here. Make sure they understand the price for failure."

He sat back in his chair. He had been waiting for a call for hours. Finally his phone chirped, and he answered it. "Yes?"

"Cain, I got a message that I needed to call you." The female voice on the phone was the unmistakable voice of the chairman. This was the leader of the worldwide Satanist movement. Cain was the only soldier who could summon her this way. She never talked to soldiers. She always delegated through subordinates. She had lots of them. In fact, Cain was the only solider who truly knew who she was, where she was. But Cain was special. She understood this. He had a power that they didn't understand, but they believed came from their god. No Christian, or anyone else for that matter, had that kind of power. She believed Cain was destined to deal the Christians a blow or wipe them out altogether. The decline in Christianity, since the mid-twentieth century, was a sign that their time was over. She had come to believe that Cain could be the one to help them deliver the final blow.

Cain said, "I have been waiting for hours."

She said, "I know. You have to remember the time difference. I'm on the other side of the world right now."

Cain said, "I know where you are."

There was a silence. Then she said, "What is it that has made you contact me?"

Cain said, "The prophecy."

She was silent again. Cain imagined she was stunned, but she would never show emotion. Finally she said, "Go on."

"The other one has been discovered. I have seen his powers. They are real, but he doesn't know how to use them."

"Is he a Christian?" she asked.

"No."

This simple word sent chills down her spine. She was a ruthless woman. A woman who wasn't afraid to kill, steal, or destroy anything or anyone in her way; she had done this her entire life. You didn't get to be in her position without being ruthless. She was a confident woman. She rarely felt herself uncertain. She rarely found herself afraid. But to hear the one word Cain said to her gave her all these sensations at once. She knew this meant the prophecy was true. The prophecy was clear that one would be a Satanist and the other would be a non-believer. She composed herself mentally and said, "How did he escape you?"

"I let him go," Cain said simply.

Again, she felt herself stunned. She felt her anger boiling up inside. "You let him go?" she said. "I want him dead. I order you—"

"Order me?" Cain interrupted. "You don't order me. I serve our master, not you. I follow your instructions only because I believe he is guiding you." There was silence. Cain continued, "I do what I do and allow you to do what you do, only because I don't want your job. Don't forget that. If I feel you have begun to think that you really command me...I'll erase you."

She took all that in. She was furious, but she knew not to speak. She knew she had to choose her words carefully. As much as he had angered her, she also knew he was right. No one could kill this man. He was too powerful. He was a weapon that her god had given her, given their cause. She had to wield that weapon, and it was not easy. He had been loyal; he had done everything they had asked of him. She had always wondered why he didn't try to be more of a leader, but she knew he liked being a soldier. He liked the killing, liked using his powers to hurt Christians. She knew he believed it was what he was meant to do.

If she was nothing else, she was political. She again composed herself and asked, "Why did you choose to let him go?"

Cain said, "I thought there may have been a chance we could convert him."

She considered this. She wasn't sure how to respond. She carefully went over several possibilities in her head. She finally said, "Do you believe that is what our master wants?"

Cain said, "It's what I want. I haven't had a chance to pray, but I will speak to our master soon. He works through me."

She asked, "What do you want to do?"

Cain said, "This matter needs our full attention. All our resources need to be brought to America."

She said, "You know our people are all over the world. You want us to bring them all to the least important theater in the world? We are winning in America; we have been for decades now. Our influence keeps growing there."

This was all common knowledge. Cain said, "What happens here will make everything else unimportant."

A long silence settled between them. She finally said, "I will put as many resources as possible at your disposal. You know I will have to meet with the Grand Council before I can make a move like that."

"Then do it quickly," Cain said.

"What do you want to do?" she asked.

"Find him. Convert him or kill him. Our entire existence could depend on this."

No one talked to her like this. No one talked to her this directly. She was still fuming, but she also knew he was the only person in the world who could kill her." She said, "What about the defector?"

Cain said, "I could care less about him."

She wondered if Cain knew he had the Testimonial. She briefly considered withholding that from him for now, but she decided that if he found out from anyone else, it would not benefit her. She asked, "Are you aware that he has the Testimonial?"

Cain smiled. Smiling was something he almost never did. Without answering her directly, he said, "I think our master has signaled us: the Testimonial, the prophecy. I think it's clear that we are at the end."

The end? she thought. She wanted to ask, but sensed he would elaborate.

After a pause, he continued, "We are at the end of this war. Our master has put it all before us. We find the defector, take the Testimonial, and either convert or kill the non-believer. We wipe them out."

She felt she was supposed to say something, but she was at a loss for words. She finally asked, "What do you intend to do now?"

Cain said, "I intend to find the non-believer. I intend to show the Christians that this generation is correct when they say we are living in the last days. It's over for them."

David sat in the car. He had enjoyed a meal with a wonderful family. They had fed him exceptionally well. They had used the payphone at the diner to call them. They had come right away to pick them up. Ruth hugged the necks of the kids and the man's wife. The man had provided them with an old car, but he assured them it would get them where they needed to go. David just wished he knew where that was. They had wanted to pray. David thanked them and told them he would wait in the car while they prayed.

Now the man walked to the car with Ruth. Ruth opened the driver's side door, and David could hear them talking now. "It's a long drive. You will need to be careful." Then he reached into his pocket and gave Ruth a wad of money.

Ruth said, "No, I can't ask anything more from you."

She tried to give it back to him, but he would not take it. He said, "You will need this for the long trip."

David wondered again where they were going. Ruth grudgingly accepted the money and got into the car. The man leaned in and looked at David. He said, "God bless you."

David smiled and nodded his head, trying to be polite. He said, "Thank you."

They drove away. They drove for some time with neither saying anything. They found their way onto the interstate when David broke the silence. "Nice people. What church are they with?"

Ruth smiled a little and said, "Does it matter?"

David said, "I was just curious."

"They are Jehovah's Witnesses," she replied.

"You guys really get help from them all," David said.

Ruth replied, "We don't represent a faith. We are here to protect them all. We don't judge."

"I know," David said, "Isaac went over all that with me."

Ruth was silent for a few miles and then said, "David, I have been going over what you told me happened at the church. One thing you never explained to me is how you were able to escape."

David had dreaded talking about this. He had been going over it, as well. He didn't understand what had happened. He said, "He let me go."

Ruth looked over at him and then back at the road. "He let you go? I don't understand."

David said, "Me, either."

Ruth said, "Why would he let you leave? I mean, he killed both Isaac and Zeek."

"Zeek had betrayed you," David interrupted.

This was particularly hard for Ruth. They had fought and bled together. She could not believe he had just turned on Isaac, especially after all Isaac had done for him. She believed Zeek had somehow been corrupted, used by them. She said, "Would you mind telling me how it happened?"

David cleared his throat and then said, "There really wasn't much to it. He told me that I should consider joining him. He told me that we could be friends."

Ruth looked at David again, this time a little longer before turning her attention to the road. She said, "What did you say?"

David said, "I told him that I may not be a Christian, but that I would not be a Satanist."

Ruth felt chills go all the way up her back. She physically felt herself shiver. She knew the prophecy. Everyone did. She wondered if he did. She said, "Well, I'm glad you made it out of there in one piece. They are ruthless, relentless, merciless people."

"I'm not so sure," David said. He continued, "I mean, if they were as bad as everyone thinks, why would they just let me go? I wonder if there could be more to them."

Ruth said, "David, they tried to have you killed!" Ruth couldn't believe he was saying this.

"Yes, but you are at war. He thought I was on your side."

Ruth felt herself getting angry, but she sensed that this needed to be a debate, not an argument. They would be in the car together for roughly two days. She said, "Aren't you? On our side, I mean?"

David said, "I'm very grateful for all you have done for me and for all Isaac did for me, but I'm an atheist. I...don't have a side. I got into this to try to find my brother. I still want to."

A silence settled between them. Ruth said, "For an atheist, God certainly has his hand on you." David gave her a puzzled look. Ruth continued, "David, have you considered all the things that have happened in the last few days? From me getting to your apartment, just in time to save you, to what we went through at the industrial park, to you getting to the hospital just in time to save me?"

David said, "We have been lucky."

"Lucky?" Ruth said incredulously. "Luck had nothing to do with it."

"What about my power?" David asked. "Do you believe it comes from God, too? If you do, then how do you explain that Cain has similar powers?"

Ruth said, "David, there is a prophecy that I think you should know about."

David said, "Yes, Isaac told me about the Christian that prophesied all this would happen a long time ago."

Ruth was silent for a moment and then she said, "David, could it be possible that you are afraid to acknowledge that there is something going on here, something bigger than you or this world?"

David answered this with a question of his own. "Do you think you could be afraid that this is all there is? That you will live what years you have here, and that is it? Do you think that you need to believe that there is some kind of power over us that will let us live forever? Have you considered that it takes strength to see the truth?"

Ruth said, "No, I know that there is a God in heaven, and I plan to see him one day."

David replied, "Okay, give me one piece of hard evidence that there is some great power over us—anything."

Ruth said, "It doesn't work like that. You have to have…"

"Faith," David interrupted. "I know all about faith. My mother preached that stuff to me for years. I never saw anything but a bunch of people praying for someone. It's a win-win for you so-called Christians. If the person recovers, it's because of God. If they die, some preacher will preach that it was the will of God, and we just don't understand it."

Ruth saw this getting out of control, so she decided to change the subject. "You need to get some sleep; we have a lot of driving ahead of us. We will have to take turns driving."

David said, "Don't you think it's time to tell me where we are going?"

"Command; we are going to Command."

David asked, "What is Command?"

Ruth said, "Command is the center of all our operations in the U.S."

"They told you we needed to come there?" David asked.

"No, they're not expecting us," Ruth replied.

"Okay, that brings me back to my original question: Where are we going?"

Ruth smiled and said, "Salt Lake City."

David thought for a moment, looked puzzled, and said, "Utah?"

Judas had been in a panic. He had called everyone and anyone he knew. Now, more than ever, Timothy had to be found, and he wanted to be the one to find him. He seemed to have vanished without a trace. Judas needed to know what had happened to the brother. No one seemed to know. He had made several calls to find out about the status of Cain and the defector, but no one was telling him anything. He had no leads, and the defector was his only contact. He felt his next move was to make contact with him again and make him give him something, anything that could help him find Timothy. They had met once, but it had not yielded any clues to where Timothy may be.

He decided it was time to call his superiors. He hated this. He would rather call anyone else, but he had tried everyone else. He punched in the numbers on his phone and waited for an answer. The voice on the other side said, "Judas, we were just going to call you."

Judas said, "I need to make contact with the defector again. He has been in communication with you, and I need to know how to get a message to him."

There was a pause on the other side, and then the voice said simply, "He is dead."

This hit Judas hard. His mind began to race. His only lead was gone. He didn't understand how. He asked, "How did he die?"

"Cain killed him," came the reply.

Judas began to get angry. He said, "I know that Cain is powerful, and I know we are all supposed to look up to him, but why would he kill our only lead to the Testimonial?"

"He had his reasons," the voice on the phone said.

"You support those reasons?" Judas asked.

"We do," was the simple reply. They continued, "Cain will be pursuing the brother and the only soldier left protecting him. You will stay focused on finding your mark."

Judas said, "What do you want me to do now? My only lead was killed, and the soldier has vanished. There are no leads to follow."

After a pause, the voice on the phone said, "You figure out how to find him. That's why we brought you here. That's what you need to do."

"Fine," Judas said simply and ended the call. He put the phone away in his pocket and then said aloud to himself, "Well, Cain, it looks like my only lead is the brother. You and I will get to work together after all."

CHAPTER 9

After two days of near-continuous driving, David awoke to see the twin peaks coming into view in the distance.

"We'll be there within the hour," Ruth said.

"Salt Lake City," David said aloud. "Can you tell me why Salt Lake City?"

"I don't understand," Ruth replied.

"I mean, why is the headquarters for the U.S. in Salt Lake City?"

Ruth said, "It's actually been here for many years. Our headquarters has moved a few times in the history of the U.S."

David took an impatient breath and said, "I understand all that, but why Salt Lake City now?"

Ruth smiled. She was intentionally stretching out the answer. She thought he was so handsome, and she loved the way his eyebrows furrowed when he got aggravated. She asked, "Have you ever heard of the way that the U.S. government came to put the gold depository in Fort Knox?"

"No," David replied.

"Well, the government was concerned about the threat of foreign invasion. They knew that if the U.S. was ever invaded by a foreign army on the east coast, it would have to move through the Appalachian Mountains of Virginia, West Virginia, and eastern Kentucky to get to it. For that reason, they decided to place it in Kentucky."

David let out another breath and said, "Your point?"

Ruth smiled in spite of herself. She didn't want to, but his *eyes*— she thought it was the eyes that she found so attractive. She loved to watch the expressions he would go through. She didn't know what the future held for each of them. She knew it was possible she may never see him again after they got to Command. She was worried what would be said to her. She was worried she was wrong to bring him here. She had practically worried herself sick over the last two days. Now that they were getting close to their destination, she was enjoying just talking with him. She would miss him. She wanted to remember him just like this. She looked at him for a moment, making notes of his features. He was so handsome. She answered him, "Salt Lake City is known for many things. One of the lesser known facts is that it has the largest Christian population of any city in America. So, if the Satanists ever moved on us, we would be in the friendliest place possible, where they would have the hardest time penetrating the local population."

David didn't respond. This felt almost military, he thought to himself. He had worried over Tim. So much had happened since all this had started. He had to admit his time with her had been the best part. He found himself smiling at her often. She was so beautiful. He wondered if she could see through him. While he didn't agree with her on a lot of things, he had to admit he was surprisingly attracted to her; surprisingly because he had always controlled this aspect of his life so well. He thought she was one of the most perfectly beautiful women he had ever seen. He sighed to himself. After all these years, he finally found a woman he really liked, and she was unavailable.

They moved through downtown and then across the city. Ruth seemed to know exactly where they were going. She clearly had been here before. They seemed to be driving back out of the city now. She stopped at a large building that seemed to go up several stories. David got out of the car. He looked up. There were large letters on the brick building that read, "Church of Jesus Christ of Latter Day Saints." David decided to stop asking questions after the Jehovah's Witnesses, but he couldn't believe how many different faiths supported these people.

They went inside. David didn't know what to expect. The grounds were simple. No decoration and very little lawn, but it was well-maintained, and there were no other decorations. They entered the building. The inside matched the outside, as it had very little decoration of any kind. Everything seemed to be very plain. There appeared to be a lot of people coming and going. Each spoke a polite greeting as they passed.

They found their way to a desk. The receptionist said, "How may I serve you?"

"We're here to see Moses," Ruth said.

"Oh...um...let me get someone for you," the receptionist said.

In a few minutes, a woman came out. As she walked down the hall, she had a very business-like manner, until she got within a few feet. Then her expression changed. She beamed and said, "Ruth! Oh my, it is you!" She rushed to give her a hug. She said, "I didn't recognize you dressed...like that."

David wasn't sure what that meant. Ruth was wearing simple jeans and a tee shirt. Her long hair was pulled back tightly.

"Sara, this is David."

Sara extended both hands and shook David's hand. "Welcome," Sara said. Sara was a middle-aged woman. She appeared to be in her fifties. She was very plain. Her hair was halfway between brown and gray. She didn't seem to care. She had hazel eyes and pale skin. David recognized right away that her best quality was her warm, welcoming smile, with perfect teeth or dentures, David decided.

David said, "Thank you." He didn't know what else to say.

Ruth said, "We need to see Moses."

Sara glanced toward David then looked back at Ruth and said, "It's very unusual that you are here. Is everything okay?"

"No," Ruth said.

Sara waited for some explanation, but Ruth simply waited patiently to be taken to Moses. Realizing no explanation would be offered, Sara said, "Wait here, please. I'll be back in a few minutes."

A few minutes turned into an hour. Finally, Sara came back. She had the same smile, but she was now flanked by two, large men. They reminded David of Secret Service agents. Except these men had shaved heads and wore polo shirts. They looked like body builders or ex-football players. As Sara approached, both men wore expressionless faces. Sara had the same welcoming smile. She said, "Moses will see you now."

Ruth walked by the desk, David followed. As he attempted to walk past the men, one put a hand on his shoulder. The hand was gentle but firm. David immediately got the message. He stopped and said, "Ruth!"

She turned and saw David was alarmed that they were going to be separated. She knew this would happen, but she didn't realize it would happen so soon. She tried to force a smile and said, "It's all right, I promise."

David just stared at her. Sara walked back to David, put a reassuring hand on his arm, and said, "You are safe here. Everything is okay. Just give us a few minutes." David, still staring at Ruth, just nodded. As Sara turned to follow Ruth, David sat down in a nearby chair. The two men stayed with him and stood close by. David understood now. They didn't trust him.

Ruth entered Moses's office. She was nervous. She had only met with him a few times, then briefly and formally. As she entered his office, the room had not changed. It was a small, simple office. The only extravagance was the large, padded chair he sat in and several computer monitors around the wall, behind his desk. This was, after all, the way they tracked information now. Moses was on the phone. As Ruth and Sara entered, he said into the receiver, "I'll call you back." He hung up the phone and stood up.

As Ruth approached him, she extended a nervous hand. He reached across the desk and gently shook it. He said, "Ruth. I must say, you have surprised us by coming here this way." Ruth just stared at him, and then, as if continuing the same thought, he said, "Unannounced."

She swallowed, took a deep breath, and said, "Yes, I know this is not… appropriate." Moses had always seemed like such a large figure to her. He was

African American, about five feet, eleven inches tall. He kept his head shaved but, occasionally, it would grow just enough to see that he had lost it all on top of his head but had a little on the sides. It was common for men in their fifties, she had thought. He had deep, dark, penetrating eyes. He always kept his face clean shaven and always dressed well. Today, in a collared shirt and sweater, she felt he looked a little more informal than she was used to seeing him. He was a man who commanded respect just by his presence, and he possessed an unusual intelligence. He was well-known for sizing people and situations up quickly. He was a man of action and had a reputation for being a very hard working, results-oriented man. Ruth had always been intimidated by him. With everything she had heard, combined with his position, she always found him to be a mountain of a man. His ramrod-straight posture always made him look taller than he was. She tried to take steady breaths and dreaded everything she would have to tell him.

He sat back in his chair as if letting her begin to tell him what she needed to. Ruth cleared her throat and began, "There is a lot I have to tell you. I don't know where to start."

Moses sat there calmly and said, "Start at the beginning."

Ruth considered this. She said, "I'm not sure where that is…for you. What was the last thing Isaac told you?"

He stared at her calmly, with a level gaze. He said, "About what?"

Ruth swallowed again and said, "About Timothy and about David."

Moses stared for a moment and then said, "Does Isaac know you are here? Did he order you to come here with him for some reason?"

Ruth looked down now. Moses patiently waited for her to answer him. When she looked back up, her eyes were full of tears now. She said, "Isaac is dead."

To her surprise, this didn't elicit a response from Moses. He stared at her thoughtfully and repeated, "Dead. How did he die?"

Ruth wiped tears from her eyes. She said, "He was killed by Zeek, but I think Cain somehow made him do it." Again Moses didn't show any emotion. He continued to stare. She could tell he was thinking now, processing what he had been told.

After a few moments he asked, "Where is Ezekiel?"

Ruth began to cry again and said, "Dead."

A silence settled between them. Moses kept staring at her, but to her it felt like he was looking through her, thinking of something else. Then he asked, "Did Cain kill him also?"

"Yes," Ruth replied.

Moses continued asking patient questions. "How did you escape?"

Ruth answered, "I was in the hospital. David came there and saved me just minutes before they came for me."

Moses' facial expression changed somewhat, but Ruth could not read him. He asked, "Why did you come here?"

Ruth said, "I didn't know what else to do. With both of them gone and Tim..." She didn't know what to say about Tim, so she moved forward in her chair and repeated, "I didn't know what else I could do. I felt we needed to come here."

Moses asked, "You didn't think you should call first?"

Ruth felt like a little girl who was being interrogated by her father. "I was afraid to call."

"Why?" was the simple question from Moses.

She said, "Zeek betrayed us. He was working with them."

"You have proof of this?" Moses asked.

"David told me how it happened," she replied.

Moses sat forward in his chair and asked, "So you are basing everything on what this person has told you? You brought him here, not knowing his intentions?"

She looked down, knew she was being scolded, and looked back up at him again. Her face looked like that of a girl who had just been scolded by her parents. She said, "I believe him."

At this Moses sat back into his large chair again. He said, "We will need to do a complete de-briefing with both you and him. I want the rest of the Apostles in on this. Go clean up and get something to eat. You will come back in two hours, and we will go through everything."

Ruth got up. Moses didn't rise or say anything else. As she got to the door, he said, "Ruth." She turned, and he said, "I am glad you are still alive."

She wasn't sure what to say. She simply nodded, forced a smile, and walked out the door.

Ruth returned as he had directed. She had a quick lunch with David. She reassured him that everything was okay. He was visibly worried, but he seemed to trust her. When Ruth came back, she was directed to a large room. When she entered, she was facing the entire Apostolate. There were three men and three women. The Apostolate always had been made up of six people. When they were in their infancy, this had been one of the questions: How many people should be on The Apostolate, the lead committee? It was deemed six to honor the six days that the Lord used to create the world. Each country had their own. These six reported directly to the worldwide headquarters and made all the key decisions for the U.S.

Ruth sat. There were no introductions. Moses asked her to begin and to brief them on everything. Moses had not told her what his last conversation with Isaac was like. She had no idea what he knew and didn't know. She felt he didn't want to tell her. She started with her assignment to watch David.

She took him through everything that happened, including David's special abilities. This part gave her looks of both surprise and concern. When she finished, she was expecting to be dismissed, but they seemed to want her to stay.

"Does he know of the prophecy?" This question came from Ester. Ester was the youngest member of The Apostolate. She had long, blond hair that flowed down her back, but today it was pulled up in a tight bun. She had creamy white skin and blue eyes. She was one of the youngest to ever be put on the staff. She had moved up quickly. A formidable soldier, she once fought three Satanist soldiers at once, killing two. The other fought her to a draw. The battle had left her permanently disabled. Her right leg was injured, and she now walked with a limp. She was small, barely five feet tall, but she was fast and stronger than she looked. Many thought she had been advanced because of her injury, but anyone who knew her knew this wasn't true. Her exceptional intelligence matched her physical abilities.

Ruth said, "Yes. Isaac had told him of it, and I discussed it with him briefly on the way here."

Ester said, "What are his thoughts on his powers?"

Ruth considered this then replied, "He hasn't shared them. He seems to only be able to tap into his powers when his emotions are high. He doesn't understand them."

"What if he is lying?" This question came from Solomon. Solomon was in his thirties. He had prematurely graying hair and hazel eyes. He had a keen intellect and had the reputation of always being the one to ask the tough questions.

His question caught Ruth off guard. "Lying?" She paused, and they all stared at her. She finally said, "To what end?"

"Well, you brought him here."

Ruth stared for a moment, leaned forward, and then said, "While they don't know the location of all our bases, they know the location of our headquarters, just like we know their headquarters are in New York City. What advantage would they have by coming here? He is under guard, we will be watching him."

Ruth felt her voice raising a little. She instinctively pulled back into her chair and grew silent. They all looked at her for a long moment. Then discussions broke out all over the room. First one and then another. The noise of if all became deafening. As the conversations progressed, they got louder. There were suggestions to try to convert him to Christianity and calls to imprison or kill him.

Moses, who had been quiet so far, finally spoke in a voice so low Ruth wondered how they all could have heard him. "I want to speak with him."

Everyone else in the room immediately grew silent upon hearing this. Ruth said, "I'll go and get him."

She rose, but Moses spoke again, his low voice still commanding. "No, not now; I need to pray first. I need time to reflect on what we have heard. I will meet with him this evening, after dinner"

Ruth nodded and then turned and left. As the door closed behind her, Ester asked, "Do you believe her?"

Moses said, "I don't know."

"I am questioning this entire situation," Solomon said.

The rest of them were still silent. Moses knew what they were thinking. It was totally against their protocols for Ruth to come here like this. Was she really that desperate, or did she have another agenda? Could they be working together? If not, what if David was using her? What if he killed Isaac and Ezekiel? As all this raced through his mind, he knew he needed to pray, to meditate. The possibility that the prophecy was coming true was very concerning, especially since there was no way to predict what David would do or what path he would choose. Moses knew he could be seeing the beginning of the end.

Judas approached the entrance to the club. It was evening, and it was just beginning to get busy. A line was beginning to form. Judas walked by the line and approached the bouncers who were standing guard at the entrance. He attempted to walk past them. One put a hand on him and said, "Back of the line."

Judas looked up into the large man's eyes. He said, "I will be going in. If you do not remove your hand, I will, but if that happens, you won't be able to use it anymore."

The man looked into his eyes and saw something that gave him pause. He could see something dark, something he was not used to seeing. He removed his hand but did not stand aside. He said, "We have orders that no one gets in."

Judas opened his mouth to say something when the man heard something in his ear piece. He instinctively put his hand to his ear to listen. When he was done, he moved aside and said, "Cain says he is waiting for you."

Judas walked by and into the club. Judas entered the office, Cain's office. He sat down wordlessly. Neither man spoke for a moment. They knew of each other but had never met face to face before. They were two of the best; possibly the two best the Satanists had. Finally Cain spoke, "What are you doing here?"

"I'm trying the find the soldier," Judas said simply.

"Then find him. Why are you here?" Cain asked impatiently.

"You killed my lead, my only lead," Judas responded.

"You know we do not allow these people to live. I felt he had exceeded his usefulness," Cain replied.

"Did you? Did you happen to think that he may have had clues; clues to where we could find the soldier?"

Cain stared at him for a moment. No one talked to *him* like this. He considered killing him, but he knew that would serve no real purpose. He decided that he would let him live; at least until he was sure he would not need him anymore. Cain decided this conversation needed to come to a close. Cain said, "What is it you want?"

Judas did admire his directness; it reminded him of himself. He said, "I want to go with you."

Cain stared at him for a moment and then said, "Why?"

Judas said, "Because I have no other leads. You are going after the brother and, right now, he is my only hope of finding the soldier."

Cain stared for a long moment. He said, "Very well, you will be under my command."

This surprised Judas. He said, "Your command? I report to the same people you do."

Cain said, "And they report to me."

His stare was cold. Judas felt it. He knew this man was dangerous. He knew his powers made him feared and respected. He decided he could push him no further. He said, "All right, while I am with you, you are in charge. If we find the brother, I'll need to interrogate him. I'll use him to find the soldier and the Testimonial."

"No," Cain said in a strong voice. "The brother is mine and mine alone."

Judas didn't understand. How was he supposed to get anywhere like this? The truth was he had no other options.

Cain spoke again. "I will convert him, or I will kill him."

Judas felt his mouth come open. He didn't understand this at all. He wasn't sure what to say. He finally asked, "Why would you want to convert him"

Cain said, "It's the prophecy. He is the other half of me."

Judas was stunned. He asked, "He has the same powers you have?"

Cain nodded and then said, "He is so weak. In addition to his lack of experience, his lack of training, and his lack of faith, I have already discovered he has another weakness I can use." Judas stared at him. Cain said, "He seems to have a special affection for the female soldier protecting him. He went to the hospital and prevented us from eliminating her. She could be useful. I may be able to use her to convert him or, if necessary, to kill him."

Judas sat back in the chair, stunned. Cain began talking about his plans. He was bringing additional resources to America. He was planning a major strike on the Christians. He was becoming upset, talking about the wrath he would bring to the Christians, but Judas didn't look at him, not directly. He stared off, lost in thought, after what he had learned about Timothy. He didn't think anything else could shock him. Now he was learning something about the brother that shocked him that much or more. He could feel Cain's anger, his hatred toward the Christians. He knew if Cain knew what he did, he would be beyond angry. He would be absolutely furious.

David entered Moses's office. He didn't know what to expect. Moses greeted him with a smile. Moses didn't rise, but he motioned to the chair in front of his desk and said, "Come in, David, sit." David sat down. Moses said, "Ruth has briefed us on everything you have been through." David nodded. Moses said, "You were with Isaac at the end?" David nodded again. Moses stared at him for a moment and then said, "He was my friend." David continued nodding. Moses said, "Can you tell me how he died?"

David said, "I thought Ruth explained— "

"Ruth told me what you told her," Moses interrupted. "I would like to hear it from you."

David stared at him for a moment and then took a deep breath. He said, "He was protecting me." David stared off as if re-living that moment as he spoke. "He fought so hard. I didn't know he could fight like that. In the end, Cain was too strong. He was going to kill him, but Zeek did it first."

Moses didn't respond. He didn't want to show emotion to David, but he was fighting back tears. He knew if he spoke, his voice would be broken. Both of them sat in silence for a moment, David clearly waiting on him to speak next. After a few more breaths, Moses said, "Did he say anything to you before he died?"

David looked at the floor. He then looked back up and said, "He told me to run." David looked at him for a moment and then looked down at the floor again. While looking at the floor, he continued, "He fought all those people, gave his life. In the end, he died protecting someone he barely knew; someone who didn't share his beliefs. He gave up his life to protect me, and now he is gone. It's such a waste."

Moses replied, "He is not gone. He just moved on, crossed over to a better place."

David didn't respond to this. He had heard things like this his entire life. People like Moses needed to believe this because they were not strong. They could not fathom that a good man was gone and that was it. They had to believe he was going to live on in some imaginary place with pearly gates. The fantasy let them go on and gave them peace. He wasn't going to dispute that. He tried to remind himself he was doing this for his brother. For his mother, he corrected himself.

Moses asked, "Why do you think he let you leave? He could have killed you."

David didn't respond for a moment. That moment had been on his mind, almost continuously since it had happened. David gathered his thoughts and said, "He said that he wanted me to consider being his ally. He said we didn't have to be enemies. He let me go to prove his sincerity."

Moses absorbed this. It was definitely unexpected. It was a smart play, he had to admit. "What are your thoughts on that?"

David didn't hesitate this time. He said, "Look, I don't believe in this fantasy world you guys have going on. I am an atheist." It felt good to say that. He had struggled with it for so long; even felt guilty. Now, in spite of everything, he felt he was finding himself and something about stating it publicly—being proud of it—felt good to him. David continued, "I don't want any part of your holy war—either side. I want to find my brother and then go home."

David expected Moses to argue this, but he didn't. He leaned forward and looked deep into David's eyes. He said, "Do you really think you will ever be able to go home again?"

David wasn't sure what he meant by this, and he stiffened. Moses, as if understanding, continued, "Don't misunderstand me, David, you are not a captive here. You came here of your own free will. You are temporarily under our protection. If you choose to leave, we will not stop you. What I mean is, after all you have seen and after what you have discovered about yourself, do you really think you can just forget it all and go back to a normal life?"

His words hit David like a sledge hammer. David wanted to debate this with him, but as soon as Moses said the words, David knew he was right. He slumped in his chair, looked down toward the floor. He suddenly felt deflated. There had been so much to think about, he hadn't considered this was a one-way trip. In the back of his mind, he always thought he would go back and pick up his life at some point. Even if he could somehow make peace with it, he knew there would always be people who would see him as a threat. Moses could read him like a book; somehow David knew this.

As if understanding he would need to reflect on this and try to come to terms with it, Moses changed the subject. "Do you know why your brother would have disappeared?"

This was the first time anyone had asked him about Tim since he got here. David was still looking at the floor. He looked back up at Moses and said, "I don't know Tim; not really." Moses stared, and David continued, "He is my brother. I am all he has. I feel obligated. Since he became a member of your... since he joined you, we have not kept in touch."

Now Moses nodded and then said, "David, we are not in the habit of losing our people. Tim had been a very solid soldier for us. We had no indication he would suddenly go missing."

David felt he was supposed to respond to this, but he wasn't sure what he was supposed to say, so he just waited on Moses to say something else or to let him go.

Moses, as if understanding this, asked, "David, have you ever heard of the Testimonial?" David stared at him blankly. Moses clearly wasn't going to move forward until he answered.

David finally said, "No, what is it?"

Moses said, "When we began, not long after Jesus died on the cross, it was determined that we would have a book. The book was called the Testimonial. The Testimonial was just that. It was a testament to our people. Over time, it became one of our most sacred traditions. We have an archive of them in our world headquarters. We start a new one, once every hundred years on a specified date." He paused, giving David a chance to absorb this and then continued, "The Testimonial is a book that details all our members—*all* our members. It also chronicles their recruitment and who they were before they joined us. When we anoint someone, they have to leave that life behind. We are not allowed to have attachments, they compromise us. Like priests or nuns, we are forbidden to marry or have relationships. As part of the anointing, a soldier will chronicle their life in the Testimonial for posterity. It lists who they were before and who their family was. For us the decision to become a soldier is final. There is no going back to these lives. We all understand that, before we accept the anointing. The ceremony of documenting this in the Testimonial is our way of saying goodbye to that life and hello to a new life, protecting Christians for our Lord. Once they go through the anointing, we go to great lengths to ensure they can never be traced back to those families from which they have come. The safety of our families, our loved ones, is essential. Our people have no fingerprints, for example. We have them removed. We do other things to totally erase any path back to their original lives."

Moses paused again. David just stared at him. Why in the world was he telling him this? David wasn't sure what the relevance of this was.

Moses continued again, "Could you imagine the harm that would come to us if this book was to fall into the hands of the Satanists? Could you imagine what would happen if they could know the identity of our every member and could know how to go after their families?"

The wheels were turning in David's head now. He still didn't know why Moses was telling him this, but he was beginning to understand why Tim had not been there for his mother. He was beginning to understand why his mother understood and didn't hold it against him. He thought about his mother's burial again, about the look on Tim's face that day. This thought made David change the subject. He asked, "My brother came to my mother's burial in defiance of you, didn't he?"

Moses nodded and then said, "He showed a moment of weakness, and he put you in danger. We should have moved him right away. Isaac wanted him to stay with him for a while longer, after he accepted the anointing and before we sent him somewhere else. Such things have happened before. Thankfully, no harm came to you. We had to put you under surveillance for several months to make sure. We considered disciplining Tim, but Isaac spoke out for him. He convinced us that saying goodbye to his mother was the last thing he needed to do. We were going to move him somewhere far away...when Isaac felt he was ready." Moses trailed off, as if thinking about that decision.

David felt an anxiety he had never felt before. He was beginning to understand his brother. It must have been incredibly hard for him: to lose his mother and his brother. In a lot of ways, David was seeing the situation for the first time. Tim risked everything important to him just to say goodbye.

As David was thinking about this, Moses patiently watched him. David felt like Moses could read his mind. Moses was gazing directly at David and, after David looked away and considered what he had heard, he eventually brought his gaze back to Moses again. When he did, Moses brought the subject back to the Testimonial again.

"David, we move the Testimonial all over the world. In the ninth century, the Satanists found out where it was and tried to take it. They almost succeeded. After that we decided that it was best to keep it moving. We randomly ship it all over the world. That way it makes it nearly impossible to pinpoint. Only I and the rest of the Apostolate know where it is at any time while it is in the U.S. That is, besides the soldiers who currently have it in their care."

David wasn't sure what the point of all this was. Moses' next words brought it all into perspective. He said, "David, when your brother disappeared, he took the Testimonial."

David absorbed this. He could see why they were so concerned now. Why would Tim do that? He didn't know. He still didn't know what he was supposed to say. Finally he said, "So what now?"

Moses said, "I need to meet with the rest of the Apostolate. I need to pray again. We will let you know."

David rose to leave. As he was approaching the door, Moses spoke again. "David, one final thing." David turned, and Moses said, "Your power. How does an atheist explain such a thing?"

David had also thought a lot about this. He said, "I don't know. Maybe it's a physical gift or the next stage in human evolution. Whatever it is, I still don't think it has to do with your Christian prophecy."

Moses stared at him for a long moment. David thought he was going to say something, but he didn't. Now Moses looked down, nodded his understanding, and David left the room.

After David left, Sara entered from a side door in the office. She had heard the conversation. Moses leaned on her. He had come to trust and confide in her. She could tell how troubled he was. She put a hand on his shoulder. She said in a soft, low voice, "He doesn't know."

Moses nodded slowly, agreeing with her. He said, "He will eventually find out, but I don't know when the right time to tell him will be."

David was given a room. He was truly exhausted. It was simple, plain, but it had everything he needed: a hot shower, a shave, and a comfortable bed. David had just showered. He had been given clean clothes. He got out of the shower, dried off, and pulled on the pants they had given him, a simple pair of jeans, and lay on his bed. He wondered what he was supposed to do. He was truly lost. He was no closer to finding Tim now than when he started. Every question he had asked seemed to lead to more questions.

He heard a knock on his door. He threw on the tee shirt he was given and went to the door. He opened it slowly. A woman was standing in his doorway. Her head was lowered, and David assumed she wanted to come in. He said, "Um, would you like to come in?"

She wordlessly entered. As she raised her head, David realized it was Ruth. She looked so different. She had on an ankle-length skirt and plain blouse, and her hair was long and flowing, down to the small of her back. David was stunned to see her this way. She smiled. David said, "Wow, I've never seen you like this."

Ruth said, "This is me. This is who I really am."

David felt sincerity as he said, "Well, you are truly beautiful."

She blushed upon hearing this. She moved over to the bed and sat. David could tell something was wrong. She said, "I came here to tell you something." David didn't ask, he just waited and stared at her intently. She said, "Moses met with the Apostolate." She paused and then continued, "They came to some decisions." Another pause. David could tell whatever she was going to say was difficult. She took a deep breath and said, "There is some good news. They decided that you will stay under our protection...for as long as you want. They are going to continue to search for your brother."

David didn't blink. He just stared. He knew there was more. She looked down and ran her hands across the front of her skirt to straighten it. David could tell this was some type of nervous habit. She looked back up at him and said, "I'm leaving."

David didn't know what to say. He was shocked. He said, "Why?"

Ruth smiled again. She was fighting her emotions; it was obvious. She said, "They have decided that I need to take on a new assignment."

David stared at her incredulously. "What could be more important than this?"

Ruth forced another smile and said, "David, they feel that I am too close to you."

David walked to the bed and sat down beside her. He said, "But we have not done anything wrong."

Ruth said, "I am going to be moving to another country. I can't say where, but I am needed there."

David stared for a moment. He asked, "So when do you leave?"

"Tomorrow," she said flatly.

David asked, "So after today, I won't ever see you again?"

She looked down, toward the floor, and nodded.

David asked, "So this is it?"

She continued to nod. David's mind began to race. They had shared so much in so little time. He didn't know what to do. He thought they had more time together. He hadn't even considered she would be out of his life so quickly. David began to feel the sum of his experiences over the last few days. So much was uncertain, so much was unknown. He could be dead by the end of the week. He wanted to say something, but he didn't know what. He couldn't let it end like this. She was going to leave, and he would never know where she was, how she was, or if she was safe. There had been so much going on that he had not faced his feelings for her. He felt his emotions welling up. His mind raced, and he began to think about how he may never get this chance again.

She began to rise, but David put his hand on her shoulder and pulled her back down. She sat but didn't look at him. She looked straight ahead. He wasn't sure what to say. He didn't know if she felt anything for him. He knew he didn't have much time. Whatever he was going to say, he had to say it now, but he didn't know where to start. He had never been close to a woman before. He felt nervous. As he thought of everything he had been through, he was learning how fragile life was. He couldn't let her leave without telling her. He grabbed her face and turned it toward him. He started to speak, but her eyes stopped him. They were full of tears. They hadn't started to come down her face yet, but he could see them welling up. For a moment, he held her face there, in his hands. He wanted to tell her so much, but he couldn't figure out what he was supposed to say. He looked into her eyes. She returned his gaze. At that moment, a tear started down her cheek. Without letting go of her face, he wiped it away with his thumb. In that moment, all doubt left him. In that moment, he knew beyond the shadow of a doubt.

He gently pulled her to him and began to kiss her. Part of him was scared; scared she would reject him. He knew how wrong this was, but he couldn't help it. She was consenting to the kiss, but she was not kissing him back. He could feel it, but he didn't care.

He stopped. She pulled her head back a little, but he still held her face in his hands. He wanted to say it in a confident voice, a manly voice, but when he said it, his voice cracked with emotion. "I love you, Ruth. I just had to tell you that before you leave me forever. I think I always will."

She just stared at him. He suddenly began to feel foolish. She clearly cared for him, but maybe that was all. Maybe her caring had given him a false impression. He was still holding her by her cheeks, but his grip started to loosen.

As his hands began to come off her face, she stopped them with her hands. She kissed his hands and put them back on her face and closed her eyes. David wasn't sure what to do now. He wasn't sure what this meant. Then she opened her eyes and said, "I love you, too, David."

She leaned in and began to kiss him now. This kiss was different. They were kissing each other now. David had kissed women before; he had made out, but he never felt like this. The kissing became more passionate. They began to hold each other as they kissed. David began to caress her long hair. Ruth began to rub her hands across his broad back. As the passion grew, David found her neck. He began to kiss it passionately. She looked up and let him move his head across her neck to the other side. She could feel his breath now. They were letting go; letting go of the world, and the problems, and for tonight, just this one night, they would just have each other.

David laid her back on the bed. He began to rub her calf. It was so incredibly smooth, like silk to his touch. He felt her shiver with excitement. His hand began to move up the skirt to her thigh. His head was kissing her neck and began to move down, toward her chest. David felt her hand on his chest, but it wasn't to touch his chest, it was to stop him. She didn't speak, and he didn't need her to. They both knew they couldn't do this. He loved her too much, and she knew this wasn't right. He knew it would disrespect her, and he couldn't do it to her. He stopped. He laid his head on her chest, and she put her arms around him. They just lay there together.

They both realized they may never see each other again. They may never feel this way again. All they could do was savor this moment, for the last time in their lives. After a long time, Ruth got up and brushed her hands through her hair and ran her hands over her skirt. For the second time in his life, he had to let go of a woman he loved. This was different than with his mother. Ruth wasn't dying. She was leaving. He wanted her to stay. He wanted her to want to be with him, but deep down, he understood.

As she proceeded to the door, David followed her. As she approached the doorway, she looked back at him. Ruth could see it in his eyes. She grabbed his hands and pulled them to her mouth and kissed them. She said softly, "My feelings for you will not change. No matter where I am or what I am doing." They both began to cry. She forced another smile and said, "I will get to see you tomorrow before I go." David leaned in to kiss her again, but she turned, left the room, and shut the door behind her.

CHAPTER 10

The next morning the Apostolate met early. There was still much to discuss. The debate over David had created a level of tension to which they were not accustomed. They had to work out the details. They had decided Ruth would go to South America. It was a good next step in her career. David would need to be relocated to another location, but they hadn't decided where. Moses sat with the five other members. They had agreed that David should be part of the conversation. They had also agreed Ruth should be there. There was plenty of time before her flight. They felt she could help persuade David. They felt he might listen to her if he didn't agree with their decision. He was not a prisoner, and they would need his consent for any decisions involving him.

David entered the room. He noticed Ruth. She had on street clothes now: a simple blouse and jeans. Moses said, "David, we are here to decide the next logical steps to take regarding your care."

David looked around at the different members. He said, "My care? What about Tim?"

Moses said, "Your protection and finding Tim are two separate issues. We need to secure your safety. We will have people looking for Timothy. We will find him."

David said, "I didn't come here for your protection. I came here to find my brother. I'm not going to be protected while you look for him."

"We have already lost two people to your whims. We will not lose a third." This came from a man to David's right. He was large. Because he was sitting, David could not tell how tall he was, but he had a barrel chest, a shaved head, and arms so large they looked like they were going to burst out of his shirt. He was African American; he had a round face and dark eyes. David felt his temper start to flare up. He looked at him and said, "And you are?"

Instead of speaking, Moses spoke for him, in a soft voice. "David, this is Jeremiah. Our vote to protect you was not...unanimous."

David stared at him for a long moment. He said, "I didn't come here to ask for your protection. I came here for my brother. Either you can help me find him, or I will do it on my own."

Moses started to speak, but Jeremiah, leaning forward, spoke in a loud voice and said, "You would have died long ago if it were not for us. You are only here today because we have kept you alive. You will not survive twenty-four hours without our protection. The Satanists—"

"Let me go..." David replied in a loud voice. Everyone stared at him now. He sat back in his chair and continued in a softer tone. "...of my own free will!"

A silence settled over the room. After a few moments, Moses said, "David, what is it you want? We cannot effectively search for Tim and protect you at the same time. We need to get you out of this country, where we are certain you are beyond their reach, at least temporarily."

David started to speak, but as he did a siren began to sound. The Apostolate members quickly stood up. Moses asked everyone to wait, and he moved to the door to look down the hall. The sound of glass breaking could be heard. Shouts and screams were coming from both directions down the hallway. Moses shut the door, and he said in a surprisingly calm voice, "We are under attack."

The other members began to move toward the door. David said, "What weapons do you have?" Everyone ignored him.

Ruth, still next to him, said, "We don't carry weapons here."

Moses spoke in a commanding voice now. "Let's move; we need to get to the lower levels. Moses opened the door and then looked back at David and said, "We need to keep him out of the line of fire and get him to a safe room!"

David and Ruth exchanged a look. As if understanding his question, Ruth said, "We have safe rooms on the lower levels. Once inside you won't be in danger."

Jeremiah put a beefy hand on the back of David's neck. He said, "Go! I will watch over him!" He leaned into David's ear and said, "Go where I say and how I say. I won't let you cause any more of our people to die." David didn't respond to this.

They moved into the hallway. They were running in a line. They still couldn't see anything, but as they advanced, they began to run into smoke. Moses, who was leading the way, yelled back, "We need to get to the armory! From there we can make our way down!"

The hallway led into a large room. As they entered, there was an explosion. They couldn't tell where it came from, but the building shook. The sprinkler system came on above them. Water began pouring all over them. A few of the large soldiers David who saw when he first came here came at them from the opposite direction. This time they were armed with guns. They both had some type of rifle and both were wearing side arms. As they approached, Moses said, "What's going on?"

They said, "Sir, we are under attack! They are coming from every direction! We were trying to get to you!"

Moses said, "We need to get to the armory!"

At that the men wordlessly turned and led them down another corridor. David was running in the middle of the group with his head lowered, to try to get under the smoke. The corridor ended in another large room. Shots started coming from the direction they were trying to go. One of the big men was hit, and he fell back. The other grabbed Moses and pulled him down. The rest of the group began to scramble for cover. Moses managed to get the gun from the large man who was shot. He moved with the other man to the doorway. Through the open door, Moses could see a large number of imps coming toward them. He scooted on the floor to the doorway they were trying to escape through, he used his foot, and kicked the door shut. He said, "We have seconds, take cover!"

Solomon kicked over a large table, and he and a couple of the Apostolate got behind it. David was lying on the floor, under the thick smoke, with Jeremiah's hand on his back. He wasn't sure what to do. After a few seconds, the door exploded open. Imps poured through the door. The thick smoke was the only thing that kept them all from being executed. It gave them some protection. Jeremiah rose, and as he took his hand off David's back, he said, "Stay down!"

David rolled to try to see what was going on. He saw Jeremiah grab one of the imps and slam him down hard. David was amazed at the large man's strength. The imp hit the floor so hard that David felt he must have broken a number of bones, if he even lived. Jeremiah took the man's gun and his knife. Fights began to break out all over the room. David saw one imp shoot one of the Apostles in the head, at point blank range. She was lying on the floor and didn't see him behind her. David didn't even have time to cry out to warn her.

The fighting continued. David crawled through the room, trying to see where Ruth was. The large room quickly became a war zone. David could hear people crying out and continuous gun fire. David wanted to help, but he wasn't sure what to do. He felt a hand on his back; it strongly lifted him up. It was Jeremiah again. He said, "Move!" He pushed David through the door and down the hall from where the imps had come.

It was just David and Jeremiah now. The smoke was clearing in the direction they were going, but the sprinklers were still going strong. The corridor was long. As they moved down the corridor, David saw a figure on the other side, and the figure held a gun. The figure stared at them for a moment;

David thought it might be an ally. Then a shot rang out. It went past David, but hit Jeremiah in the arm. He fell back. The figure with the gun stared at David for a moment. David felt a chill; he didn't know why, but he could sense something. The figure lowered the gun and slowly walked in the other direction. The gun shot was deep in the left arm of Jeremiah. The bullet must have been a high caliber. The hole in Jeremiah's arm was huge. He was clearly in pain. David grabbed him and began to drag him toward the nearest room that branched off from the long corridor. Jeremiah protested, told David to leave him, but he was losing blood fast and David was worried he was going into shock. He was heavy. It was taking everything David had to drag him.

As David was getting him through the door, he heard someone running toward them from the room where the fighting was coming from. It was Ruth. She helped David get him into the room, and she shut the door. David looked up at her and said, "I'm glad you're okay."

She didn't respond to this. She said, "Moses was shot several times. I think he is dead. Several of them have gotten killed. We don't have much time!"

"What do we do now?" David asked.

Ruth pulled Jeremiah's long sleeve and tore it from his injured arm. She then tied it tightly over the bullet wound as he groaned. She then looked out the window. She couldn't understand how their defenses were breached. Where was the police? She looked down. There were shrubs and bushes a couple of stories down from where they were. She said, "David, we have to jump. Hopefully the bushes will break your fall."

David looked but didn't see how they could make the jump and not break some bones. His fear of heights didn't help matters any. Jeremiah was holding his arm and was beginning to get up. He slowly moved to the door and looked down the hall. He said, "They will be on us any minute!" Jeremiah looked at Ruth and said, "They did this to get him!" He motioned toward David.

Ruth said, "Our only hope is to jump, kick out a window, and get David to a safe room in the lower level.

Jeremiah said, "You and him go; I will hold them off! They'll be here any second!"

"No!" Ruth screamed. "You have to take him!" Jeremiah started to protest, but Ruth said, "It will only take your hand scan to access the door." In that instant, he knew she was right. Only one of the six could access the door. As the realization of her sacrifice hit him, he put his hand on her shoulder and said, "God go with you."

"And with you!" she replied.

David said, "No!" as he moved toward Ruth. Jeremiah grabbed him with his good arm and ran toward the window with him over his shoulder. He sat David in the window and positioned him for the long fall. David was wiggling,

trying to break his hold. Ruth moved to the door and then, with water streaming down her face from the sprinklers, she looked back. Her eyes made contact
with David's. For an instant, they just stared at each other. She moved her
lips, but no words came out. What she said was unmistakable to David: "I
love you." As she said it, she turned and began firing her gun and running
down the hall.

Jeremiah pushed David out the window as he screamed, "Ruth!"

As they fell, Jeremiah pulled David around and on top of him. It all happened
so fast, but David could tell he planned it this way. He had positioned David so
that, as they fell, he was able to turn David to be on top of him. They hit the
bushes hard, with Jeremiah and the bushes breaking the fall. They lay there for a
moment. David was the first to speak. He said, "Are you all right?" Jeremiah nodded and groaned. His arm was aching. David was amazed at this man's tenacity.
As they began to move again, David started to raise his head, but Jeremiah pulled
it down quickly. There were imps all over the grounds. Jeremiah kept David's
head pulled down until it was clear. They moved a few yards along the side of the
building. Alarms were sounding, and screams and gunfire could be heard. In the
chaos, they were able to move along the side of the building unseen.

Finally they came to a window, close to the ground. Jeremiah kicked it
out. He said, "Normally that would have set off every alarm in the building,
but the alarm is already triggered." The window was small; they were just
barely able to slip through. As they moved through the window, they fell again
into a room inside the building. It was pouring water again. The sprinklers
were still going strong. Alarms were going off all over the building. As David
and Jeremiah got to their feet, they were looking into the barrels of guns.
Two guns, to be exact, held by two imps. One of the imps said, "That's him.
This will score us big points with the boss."

Jeremiah grabbed David by his arm and pulled him behind him. Even
now, in all the pain he was in, he was still protecting him. David couldn't help
but be touched by his dedication for a man he didn't trust. The two began to
debate killing Jeremiah. Just as it looked like they would shoot him, David
said, "Wait! Cain said he would give me a chance to consider joining you."
The two men looked at each other with puzzled expressions. David continued,
"I can see now I don't need to be on the side of these losers." As he said it,
he pushed Jeremiah to the floor hard and then kicked him in the back. One
of the imps smiled and pointed his gun at Jeremiah. David said, "Let me do
it. This guy is a real jerk. I shot him in the arm, but he still managed to force
me here. He was trying to get me to a safe room, so I could not let Cain know
I wanted to go with you guys."

The two looked at each other and exchanged glances. It had been said that
Cain was hoping to make this man an ally. They were given strict instructions

that nothing was to happen to him until Cain made a decision. It was also said that if he would not be with them, they would kill him. The water from the sprinklers was coming down so hard it was like being in a rain storm. David walked over and, with an open hand, motioned for a gun. Inside he swallowed hard. He knew what he was going to do was hard, but he knew he had to do it. He kept telling himself that sacrifices had to be made to stay alive, and he hoped he could do this right. One of the imps reached behind his back and pulled out a hand gun and gave it to David.

David walked back to Jeremiah, who was leaning up and looking through the wall of water coming down on them. David kicked him in the head hard, leaned over him, and fired two shots into his head. Jeremiah lay motionless. David looked back at the men and said, "Let's go!"

The two men turned. As they did, David shot them both in the back numerous times. Both men went down, and blood began to flow with the inches of water on the ground. David rushed back over to Jeremiah. What had looked like two shots in the head were actually two shots above the head, but the hard kick was real. David reached down and helped the big man up. David said, "Sorry." Jeremiah didn't speak; he just gave David a look that showed he understood. David helped him to his feet as he groaned in pain.

They moved out the door into a large area. David and Jeremiah began to run, with Jeremiah in the lead. They found a stairwell that took them deep into the building. Finally, after several flights of stairs, they found the bottom floor. As they entered, there were no alarms, no sprinklers. Everything seemed calm. They moved until they found a large opening. The chamber they moved into was huge. It was about half the length of a football field. It had a very high ceiling. The room was round and had several doors that went in a semicircle at the end of the room. Beside the doors were large, square pads. David assumed these must be the hand scanners Ruth was talking about.

Jeremiah said, "We've never actually used these before. We thought this building was impregnable, but in case of a catastrophe, these safe rooms were designed to protect our leaders." They began to run toward one. As they approached the door, both men suddenly flew off their feet and hit the floor, hard. David sprang up and saw Cain on the other side of the room behind him.

The two men stared at each other for a moment and then Cain spoke. "It's time for your decision." David tried to take in the situation. Cain was flanked by another man. David wasn't sure if he was an imp or a soldier, but his instincts told him he was a soldier. He had blondish-brown hair, combed straight back on his head. He stared at David in a way that David could not understand. It wasn't hate or even skepticism. He had an emotion that David could not make out. There were several imps in the background. As they stared at each other, neither of them spoke.

David didn't know what to do, so he stalled for time. "What happens if I join you?"

Cain said, "I will train you, I will show you how to use your powers. Together no one can stop us. I have heard the prophecy my entire life. It was clear to me many years ago that I was one of the chosen two. I had a long time to think about what would happen when I found the other one. I give you my word that you will not be harmed if you join us now. If you don't, I will kill you here and now. Your time has run out."

David still held a gun in his hand. He raised it at Cain and said, "What if we kill each other?"

Cain made a motion with his hand and said, "Bring her. I was going to offer her to you as a reward, but I can see you have chosen death."

David felt his heart drop. Cain had Ruth by the hair now. He had taken her long hair and wrapped it in his hand and was holding her in front of him. He was gripping her so hard that both her hands were reaching up, trying to take the tension off the hold he had on her hair.

Ruth screamed, "David, no!"

David's mind raced. He said, "What makes you think I care about her?"

Cain let out a chuckle. "I know you have at least a mild affection for her. I saw the way you fought for her before at the industrial park. I know you went to the hospital to keep her alive." David and Cain exchanged another stare. Cain said, "You will die now. There is nothing that can be done to prevent it, but I am willing to let her live."

David thought for a moment and then he said, "Why should I believe you?"

Cain said, "Because I have no reason to lie. Look at the fire power, look at the weapons we have. You have a pistol and a broken down soldier, bleeding on the ground behind you." Cain let that hang in the air for a moment and then said, "If you lay down your gun and accept your fate willingly, I will let her live. Do you think one female Christian soldier really makes a difference to me?"

David thought about it. Cain could see the wheels turning in David's head. He loosened his grip on Ruth's long hair, and he continued to speak. "You have my word, sworn in front of my god, that no harm will come to her."

David stared for another moment and then slowly began to squat to the ground and lay down the gun. While David was doing this, Ruth made eye contact with Jeremiah. She motioned with her eyes toward the safe room. Jeremiah understood, but didn't know what she planned to do. While Cain was fixed on David, Ruth slowly reached toward the buckle of the pants she was wearing. With a soft turn, a small knife fell into the palm of her hand. She pushed the blade between two fingers and made a fist. With one, quick motion, she twisted and jammed the knife into Cain's shoulder and screamed, "Now, Jeremiah!"

Jeremiah turned and lunged at the door. His open hand touched the pad, the light over the door turned green, and the door opened. Cain staggered back, and Ruth kicked the other soldier beside her. She was then swarmed by a large number of imps. They threw her to the ground and began to kick her. She screamed in pain. David put his hands up in front of him and screamed, "Ruth!" A wave of energy left his body, like a tidal wave going across the room. It hit the group of imps and threw them across the room. More imps from behind began to fire their weapons now. David screamed, but he felt a strong hand on him. He felt his body quickly twist around. Jeremiah had grabbed him and spun him. With two, quick steps, Jeremiah shoved him into the safe room and dove in behind him. David was still screaming Ruth's name when Jeremiah shut the door.

Cain came to his feet. He was furious. He screamed, "Who was the one who captured her?" Two imps came forward, very scared and nervous, and stood before him. He pulled out a gun and shot them both between the eyes. He looked at the rest and said, "Remember, while our rewards are great, our punishments are equally severe."

Judas moved to the woman and pulled his gun to execute her. Cain said, "Not yet! The police will be here soon. We have used all our time. We keep her alive for now."

Judas looked at her and then at Cain and said, "Why?"

Cain stared at the door to the safe room as he said, "Because he will try to find her. He's already dead; he just hasn't accepted it."

David was on his stomach. He was out of breath. As he lay there, next to Jeremiah, who lay next to him, also on his stomach, he noticed blood beginning to pool under Jeremiah's body. David said, "You're hit!"

Jeremiah groaned and said, "Yes, I know. I got hit as we were going through the door."

David rolled him over. The bullet had hit him, just above the hip, and passed all the way through the front of his body. Jeremiah said, "How bad is it?"

David said, "I'm no expert, but I think you got lucky."

Jeremiah said, "God must still have some work for me."

David made no comment, but his expression showed Jeremiah he didn't agree. Jeremiah sat up with another groan. David removed his shirt, clogged the bullet hole from the back, and ripped what was left of Jeremiah's shirt to plug the hole in front. David said, "Keep pressure on it." David helped him lie back down, and Jeremiah pressed in from the front on the hole, above the hip. David said, "How do I get the door open?"

"You don't," Jeremiah replied. He continued, "Once you enter, it only opens from the outside, and only by one of the six, either with their hand or remotely with a command code."

David lay down on the floor, next to Jeremiah. David and Jeremiah just stared at each other for a long moment as both of them lay there, exhausted. Jeremiah said, "You saved my life."

David said, "I'm pretty sure you saved mine a few times in the last hour."

In the silence between them, they both recognized the bond that had formed in the short time. They both had found a new respect for each other. They both lay there, exhausted and breathing hard for several minutes. As their breath slowed, David asked, "How long will we be in here?"

Jeremiah said, "I don't know. It could be minutes, hours, or even days."

They both pondered the situation. Jeremiah looked at David for a long moment and then asked, "Why don't you believe?"

David considered this and then asked a question of his own: "Why do you believe?"

Jeremiah said, "Because when he touches you, when you feel the spirit, you don't have to question it anymore."

David said, "Well, I have never been touched." With that he turned over on his back, his face looking up toward the ceiling. As they lay there, side by side, David said, "This isn't over."

CHAPTER 11

They had been lying there for over four hours when the door suddenly opened. David was expecting Moses or one of the Apostolate. Instead it was a member of the staff; one of the large men who protected the members. He opened the door, snapped to attention when he saw Jeremiah, and said, "Sir! I have orders from Ester to bring you to the Command Center!"

Jeremiah got up and was assisted by David. They were taken to an elevator. With their injuries, David was glad they didn't have to climb any stairs. The Command Center was just that. It was a vast room of monitors and maps. It had been trashed in the attack. Monitors were hissing, and sparks were flying. Wires hung in disarray from the ceiling and were strewn across the floor. The room was buzzing with activity. It had a large briefing table at the center, but the activity seemed to be coming from the far end of the room where there was a group of people. Water was still in the floor and everyone sloshed as they walked. There were many people coming and going.

As David and Jeremiah entered the room, Ester was giving direction to several people. She was visibly upset. As David and Jeremiah got closer, they could hear her, in a loud voice, say, "I want to know what happened to our security! I want to know how this happened! I want an update in one hour! Now Move!"

People began to scatter. David and Jeremiah got close to her as she was handed a pad. She read it and then gave it back and said, "It's one piece of a big puzzle; keep at it!" The aid with the pad ran off quickly in the ankle-high water. Ester stopped for a moment and ran her hands through her long hair. She had dried blood in her blond hair and across her forehead. David couldn't tell where the injury was, but it looked as if the blood had been smeared. Her clothes were tattered. She shut her eyes for a moment, looked up, and then brought her head back down as she noticed David and Jeremiah. As she stepped toward Jeremiah, her limp seemed more pronounced. David assumed the fight had taken its toll on her. She moved toward Jeremiah and gave him a brief, hard hug and said, "I'm glad you're okay."

Jeremiah didn't respond; he just glanced around the room and said, "What's our status?"

She said, "I am still getting the information together. It's coming in pieces. What I know is that they breached our defenses. They couldn't get around them, so they tripped all our alarms at once. By the time the police arrived, it was all over. They had strategically staged car accidents in a ten square block radius around the church to seal it off and prevent anyone from getting here. They seemed to know exactly how long they would have to attack and leave the building." She leaned back on a nearby table and rubbed the thigh of her bad leg.

Jeremiah said, "How many have we lost?"

"Too many," came her reply. She took in a long breath and looked at Jeremiah as she spoke. "We are still counting the bodies and the injured." She seemed to just notice Jeremiah's wound, which had clotted. "Speaking of which, you need to see a medic." She pulled a phone from her pocket, punched a button, and then said, "Get someone to the Command Center; Jeremiah is here, and he is injured." She looked back up at Jeremiah and then said, "They got three of us."

Jeremiah took this in. A tear rolled down his cheek. David was surprised to see such emotion from such a big man. Jeremiah said, "Who else is left?"

Ester said, "I'm temporarily acting as the Overseer. Moses has been hit… several times. He is on the way to the hospital. In the chaos, he put me in charge. He didn't know if you made it, but he told me to check the safe rooms. I disabled the doors remotely from here when the power came back on and sent someone to get you. I've called a briefing in two hours."

Someone arrived and began to dress Jeremiah's wounds. Ester said, "We are gathering our intelligence now. What people we have are cleaning the building and getting all the evidence we can from the attack. We will meet back here. As of now, we are on alert. I'm ordering everyone to arm themselves."

Jeremiah nodded and then went to change clothes and arm himself.

David walked the corridors and saw bodies everywhere. People lay in contorted positions. Not just Christians, but imps, as well. He thought of these people and how they had passed into nothingness now. They all believed a lie…both sides. They gave their lives for some ridiculous holy war and now all their potential, all they would ever be, was erased; erased from existence. He shook his head and wondered if he could be responsible, if he and Ruth coming here put these people's lives in danger. He wondered about her. Where was she? Was she being tortured? The thought of her being hurt was more than he could tolerate. He felt something inside him now begin to boil.

He couldn't describe it, but he knew he had to go after her. He didn't know where she was. The frustration drove him crazy.

When the two hours were up, he went back to the Command Center. He saw a lot of people surrounding Ester as she began to get reports. While there were a few people gathered around the large table, it wasn't nearly as many as he had imagined. Ester sat at the head of the table. She had Jeremiah to her right, still nursing his wounds, and about half a dozen people, including Sara, near her. The meeting was getting started as David entered. He noticed everyone was armed now. Everybody seemed to be carrying side arms, and both Ester and Jeremiah had blades on their backs. Ester was beginning to get everything started when she saw David taking a seat.

A person who David did not know said, "This is a private meeting." David stopped and stared.

Jeremiah said, "I agree, but this man saved my life. Without him I would not be in this meeting. I think he should be allowed to stay." David gave him a small smile.

Ester said, "David, I'm going to let you sit in on this briefing...as an observer." The message was clear: David's thoughts and opinions would not be considered. David nodded and sat down.

Ester said, "I know that we have been through a lot. I appreciate what you are all doing. It's going to be a long night. I spoke with our world headquarters. They want us temporarily focused on containment right now. They agree that I am temporarily in charge. Moses is in critical condition; it doesn't look good, and they don't know if he will make it." David saw concerned looks all around. "Our first priority is to secure and clean up the building. We are still counting the casualties." She looked to Sara and said, "What's our status up top?"

Sara cleared her throat and said, "By the time the police finally got here, it was all over. I told them we had been attacked by some terrorist group." This seemed to get a lot of concerned looks all around. "I told them that, fortunately, while we had injuries, no one had died. They wanted to know if we were pressing charges, but I told them we hadn't decided."

"No one had died! What do you call all these bodies around the corridors?" David said, incredulously. Ester looked at David the way that a teacher looks at a student for talking out of turn.

Sara continued, "That will hold them for now, but they will be back. We will need to clean this up fast."

Ester looked at another woman David didn't know. She said, "What's the status of the injured?"

The woman tapped a pad on her desk and said, "Of the live ones, we have eleven who didn't appear to have fatal injuries, but who were serious enough to need to go to the hospital. We have spread them out with fake IDs and taken them to the various hospitals in the area. We had two others that bled out before we could save them." She lowered her voice in a somber tone and said, "There are three others that are beyond help." She paused, composed herself, and said, "I have people with them now. They are in rooms, praying and waiting to cross over."

The amount of thought they were putting into things blew David away. The way they went to great lengths to protect the privacy of their conflict amazed him. Ester said, "I want around-the-clock patrols of the outer grounds. All our efforts need to start with the upper levels, and we can work our way down here." She looked to another man David didn't know and said, "Set it up. Some of them will need to get some sleep now; others will need to get to work. I want six-hour shifts, four rotations." The man nodded. Ester said, "One final thing: with regard to David..." Everyone looked in his direction. Ester said, "I feel the original decision still stands. We need to keep him protected." She looked at David now. "We have people in route. They will be here in forty-eight hours or less. They will take you to a secure, undisclosed location. Until then you need to stay down here and stay close to myself or Jeremiah."

With this the meeting seemed to be breaking up. David watched some of them rise. He looked incredulously and said, "What about Ruth?" The people rising stopped, and they all looked toward Ester. She was rising herself, but she sat back down.

She said, "Our intelligence thinks they are in route to Las Vegas. They have a base there. It is one of their most secure locations. We will not be attacking them now; it's not the time." She stared at David for a long moment and then said, "Ruth is a casualty of war. We will avenge her death."

David said sarcastically, "I thought you believed that vengeance was your God's."

Ester said calmly, "David, we are at war. It's different than in life. We will retaliate, but now is not the time."

David looked around the room, and he said, "So, you are all willing to let her die!"

No one responded. Finally Jeremiah said, "A lot of people have died already. We won't risk more to save one soldier."

David stood. Feeling his blood boiling, he said, "What kind of people are you? What kind of people would let their own die like this and do nothing about it?" No one responded. David stared at them all, incredulously. He said, "If none of you are going to help her, then I will!" David turned and started to the door.

Ester stood and said, "I've had just about enough! Enough of our people have died for your ungrateful protection! You will respect our decisions, or you will leave!"

David heard this and became furious. He turned and said, "I'm going to get Ruth!"

As he said this, something came off his body, like a white wave of energy, directed at Ester. The pulse knocked her back into her chair hard and sent the chair scooting across the floor until it hit the wall and Ester fell out of it. A couple of people went to help. The rest just stared at David in amazement. He wanted to say something. He wanted to apologize. He stared at them all now, feeling his anger reside a little. He couldn't decide what to say. Finally he mumbled, "Sorry." He then spun and left the room.

David went to the armory. It was a large room, and it had a variety of guns and knives in wall cases all over the room. The cases had been in glass, but most of them were broken open now. Broken glass was all over the room. Several were missing, taken in the attack, he presumed. He wasn't sure what he should take. He grabbed a large, black, cloth bag. He picked up a hand gun. He grabbed a rifle. He stopped for a moment and looked at the hand gun. He had no idea how to use it. He knew he had to go after her. He knew he loved her. He would rather die trying to save her than to not do anything and stand by while they killed her. He went to another rack that had ammunition. He started filling his bag. A voice from behind said, "That's not the right one. You want the boxes in the bottom of the case."

The voice was Jeremiah's. David didn't look back at him. He just stopped, threw the ammunition back out of the bag, onto the floor, and then pulled the correct ammunition out of the bottom of the case and began to put it in the bag. David spoke without looking. "Are you here to stop me?"

"No," Jeremiah said, flatly. "I'm here to reason with you." David ignored him. He continued packing his bag with various items. Jeremiah said, "David, there is a reason they went to Las Vegas. There is also a reason they call it Sin City; it is one of the most secure locations they have. They have a huge following there; vast amounts of the local population support them...both willingly and un-willingly."

That hung in the air for a moment. David was breathing hard. He stopped for a moment, and ran his hands through his hair. It was wet with sweat. He sighed and then knelt on one knee and started tying the bag. He said, "What would you have me do? Forget about her; ignore what they are going to do to her? I'm not made that way."

Jeremiah said, "You should respect her sacrifice. We are guardians. That is what we do; it's who we are. Do you think she expected anything from you? We never expect anyone to come for us. We never expect anyone to do anything for us. She would want you to leave her there, to respect the sacrifice she made for you. If you want to honor her, you let us protect you."

David sat now. He slowly spun his body around to face Jeremiah. To his surprise, Ester was with him. She hadn't spoken, but she was intently listening to their conversation. David looked at both of them for a moment and then said, "I can't leave her. I have to try to help her."

Ester spoke now. "Have you considered why they have such an interest in you? David, your powers make you special. We don't know why you have them. We don't know what purpose they serve in the grand scheme of things. They want you with them, or they want you dead. Think about it. It's the only reason she is still alive."

This statement got David's attention. He looked at her now with interest. She said, "There is no logic in taking a soldier alive. Both sides train their people to resist torture. We would do anything to protect our people. Even if they could extract information, they would only find out things they already knew. Our soldiers are kept out of sensitive matters for just this reason."

David absorbed her words. He knew they made sense, but he couldn't shake his feeling that he had to help her. He said, "I can't explain it, but I think I am meant to help her. I feel I have to do this."

"Meant to help her?" Ester asked. I thought you didn't believe."

"I don't," David said. Then he continued, "I don't believe in your God… or theirs. I only know I have these powers. I also believe I am the only person in the world who wants to help her."

Sensing they were not going to change his mind, Ester said, "David, your powers are special, but you don't know how to use them. The prophecy said you would join them or us. If it is true, you are destined to make a difference in this conflict; maybe *the* difference. Contrary to your beliefs, you seem destined to help one side or the other."

David stood now. He put the strap of the bag of munitions on his back. He said, "I don't care what your Christian prophecy says, I'm not destined to do anything." He walked past them, toward the door.

As he approached the door, Ester spoke in a low tone, without looking at him. She said, "It's not a Christian prophecy."

David froze. He heard the words, but he didn't fully understand what she was saying. He said, "Isaac told me a soldier—"

"It was a soldier," Ester interrupted, "but it wasn't one of ours." Ester turned to face him. David stared at her. Ester continued, "It was a dark time for both sides. Back then each side kept trying to wipe the other out. Each side thought they could win a total victory. There was killing on both sides. A Satanist soldier was taken captive in Eastern Europe. In the battle, her entire unit was wiped out. She was the only one taken alive. It was decided that she would be executed."

"She?" David asked.

Ester nodded. "Some of their most powerful soldiers have been women. Before she was executed, she was given a minute to repent. Instead she quoted the prophecy. Back then the executions were carried out by a member of the Apostolate. She recited the prophecy clearly. It was said her eyes turned blood red, and her face turned as red as fire. After she completed reciting it, she said it just came to her that she had not heard it before. Afterward she seemed to return to normal and then said she didn't remember saying any of it. They recorded her words, and we have all heard them since."

David processed all this. As he did, his stare never left Ester. She seemed to let him think it through. Finally David asked, "So the prophecy came from Satan?"

Jeremiah spoke next. "We never knew where it came from. She was executed within minutes of completing it. There has been much debate about this over the centuries, but it is possible. Satan knows a lot. He may have known this was coming. He may have had her recite the prophecy to keep us off balance. Some schools of thought say that because he had her recite the prophecy before the Apostolate, his intention was to guarantee that we would not believe it and not react when the time came."

David thought about it for another moment. He shook his head and said, "I can't think about this now. I have to go." Ester started to speak again, but David spoke first, shaking his head. "There is no time. I have to go."

He turned to leave again. As he did, Jeremiah said, "Stop." David stiffened. He knew they would resort to force. He braced for someone to try to restrain him. Jeremiah moved toward David. David stepped back and braced for an attack. Instead Jeremiah un-harnessed his blade from his back and gave it to David. He said, "You may need this."

David held it in his hands and looked at it. He knew he didn't know how to wield it. He nodded and then pulled the harness over his back. Ester was in front of him now. She gave him a cell phone. She said, "We will call you. We will provide you with what information we have. David nodded again and smiled. Ester didn't return his smile. She said, "Don't thank us. I still think you are going to your death. There is a small car outside. It has fuel and some supplies inside."

David stared at them for a moment. He said, "I'll bring her back." Neither of them said anything, they just continued to stare. He turned and started through the door.

As he left the room, Jeremiah said, "God go with you."

David didn't stop, he didn't respond. He knew there was no such thing as God. It was just a good idea, something to give them comfort. He knew if there was any chance Ruth could be saved, it was by him and now him alone.

Jeremiah and Ester stood looking out the door that David had just went through. Jeremiah spoke first. "Do you think we have done the right thing?"

Ester responded, still staring at the door, stone faced, "I think we have done the only thing we could. He has learned much, but he still doesn't know everything."

Jeremiah asked, "You didn't think we should have told him?"

Ester shook her head. "No, he isn't ready. There is no way of knowing how it would affect him."

Jeremiah said, "Do you think there is any chance he will return?"

Ester took a deep breath, looked at Jeremiah, and said, "If he lives now, it will only be because he joins them or because God keeps him alive."

David was driving; he had been driving for several hours now. When Ester said a small car, she wasn't kidding. The car was compact. David had seen these, but had never actually been in one before. It looked like one of those small European cars. David was driving on Interstate 15. Whatever plan he came up with, he knew it couldn't involve a fast getaway. The car wasn't built for speed. He thought he might actually see some kid pass him on a bicycle. He still had a couple of hours before he got to Vegas, but he wasn't even sure where to go.

His phone rang. It startled him. He had never heard it ring before. He answered it, "Yes."

It was Jeremiah. He said, "We have done everything we can to find out where she is. Unfortunately, we only have one lead. There is a construction site outside of town. It is one of theirs, and they have used it a lot lately. I'm going to text you the address."

"Thanks," David said.

"David, remember: they are expecting you." The line went dead.

David received the text and continued driving. He wouldn't admit it to anyone else, but he was scared. He didn't know how he was going to do this. He definitely could not take her by force. His only hope was to find her and somehow sneak in and get her out.

He drove into Las Vegas. He saw the sights of the strip. He drove by the hotels and saw billboards for the shows. He drove through the city and then into the outskirts. When he got within a mile of the site, he stopped and parked the car. He put on his blade and pulled a loose jacket that was left for him in the car over it. He grabbed his bag and started walking. The sun was hot, and the bag was heavy. He walked through a small housing development. He felt sweat forming on his forehead. He stopped to wipe it off. He crossed through a small field, the sand hot beneath his feet. He climbed a small rise. What he saw amazed him. He expected a building or a structure of some kind. The site was massive in size. It looked as if they were building an entire sub-division of houses. They were in the early stages. The houses were all just frames with foundations. It looked like they had started to put walls on a few of them. He could see where the roads and sidewalks would be, but no concrete had been poured yet. It was an impressive structure. He could see where the kids would be riding on bikes, and he could see adults watering their yards or washing vehicles in their driveways.

On the back side of the construction, against the desert, was a row of trailers that seemed haphazardly placed. They were in a scattered formation. The plain, white, construction trailers were a common site, David knew. He wondered if Ruth could be in one of them. He decided to wait until dark and move in under the cover of darkness to find out. David looked around and could see no activity anywhere. He decided to move into the housing area and find a place to wait. He moved in slowly. He heard a noise, looked around, but didn't see anyone. He spotted a large ravine on a rise, overlooking the development from the far side. He assumed this was dug for a water or sewer line. He decided he would move to there and wait. He was hoping he might hear or see something that would help. He crouched low, slowly walked down the slope, and then slid down the steep bank and into the ravine. He laid his bag down, as it was getting very heavy. He took a knee, glad for the break from the heavy bag.

After he caught his breath, he decided to climb up the opposite side and look into the housing area to see if he could see anything. He again heard a noise. But after looking around, he could find nothing. He started up the slope. Just as he was reaching the top, he felt someone jump on him from the back side of the ravine. He felt his adrenaline pump. He had to admit it was a perfect move. Whoever it was had perfectly landed on him and was holding him to the ground. David tried to twist, but he was pinned. He started to say something, but he felt a blade push gently into his neck. A man's voice whispered in his ear, "Do not move. Do not speak."

David nodded slowly. He tried to process what was happening. If this person wanted him dead, he would already be dead. Was he being taken prisoner? The weight began to come off him. He felt the blade come off his neck. After he was sure the person was completely off of him, he slowly turned around. When David looked into the eyes of his attacker, he was speechless. He slowly opened his mouth. Before he could speak, the man put his finger to his lips and said, "Shh."

David wanted to say so much to this person. He wanted to punch him. He wanted to kick him. He wanted to grab him, throw him to the ground, and beat the crap out of him. He had fantasized about what he would do, what he would say, if he was able to see this person face to face. With all the emotions running through him, when he opened his mouth, only a single word could come out. The word was a question, a statement, and for David, it was a revelation. David said in his lowest whisper, "Tim?"

CHAPTER 12

Tim slowly harnessed his blade and sat down in the red, clay-like mud in the ravine. David looked stunned, and the two brothers just stared at each other for a long moment. David thought he would be the first to speak, but Tim broke the silence. "What do you think you're doing?"

David stared back, incredulously, and said, "I am trying to save Ruth."

Tim said, "And you think you will do it all by yourself?"

David whispered loudly, "I got involved with her and these people trying to find you! Where have you been?"

Tim again said, "Shh." He scooted closer to David now. He put a hand on him and said, "I'm sorry, I never wanted to get you involved in this." After another silence, Tim said, "I was trailing you, but it looked like you were under our protection. I thought you were safe."

David said, "Tim, I think I'm entitled to some answers."

Tim looked at him patiently. He said, "Answers? What makes you think you are entitled to answers?"

David said, "I have given up a lot for you. I promised Mom that I would take care of you."

Tim smiled now. He said, "It looks to me like you are the one that needs to be taken care of, little brother."

David felt an argument coming on. He knew that was the last thing they needed. He sat back, his back leaning into the side of the red, clay mud. He said, "How did you find me?"

Tim said, "I spotted you when you came across the field. I have been trailing these Satanists for a long time. I trailed them here. I could tell they were setting up a base here, digging in for something. They left a few days ago. I lost them, but they were back within forty-eight hours."

David said, "Tim, they attacked the sanctuary in Salt Lake City."

Tim seemed surprised. He said, "How did you know about that place?"

David said, "I think there is a lot that we need to discuss."

125

As the day fell into afternoon and then into evening, David told Tim everything he had been through. He explained what happened with Isaac and Zeek. He told him about Ruth. When David told him how Isaac died, he saw Tim wipe away a tear. Then David told him about Salt Lake City and about the attack there. David did not tell him about his powers. He wasn't sure why; he just didn't feel that it was the right time.

As David finished, Tim looked down at the ground. He shook his head and said, "David, I'm so sorry; so sorry for getting you involved in this."

The afternoon had felt like old times for David, with him and his brother outside in the mud. His mind briefly flashed to a time when they were children, and they would play for hours until their mom made them come inside. He hadn't realized how much he missed it. It occurred to David that he had been the one talking and giving information all afternoon. Tim was listening but not offering anything.

David said, "Tim, I think I deserve to know what's going on. Why did you leave?"

Tim looked back up. He smiled again. He said, "Mom didn't want you to end up like me. When I decided to be anointed, she told me that we were two very different men. I wanted you to do this, too. I planned to try to recruit you, but Mom said no. She said you had to walk your own path, do what you felt was right. I know I look like Dad, but I've got Mom's heart. Mom always said you looked like her, but inside, you were our father."

David listened to him. He gave him a small smile. He knew he was telling the truth, but he also knew he was dodging his question. David said, "Tim, I need to know. I need you to make me understand. Why did you run away from these people who you claim to love so much?"

The smile on Tim's face vanished. He said, "I didn't run away. I discovered a terrible truth."

David said, "What truth?"

Tim stared at him for a moment. David thought he saw his mouth start to open, then close again. Finally Tim said, "David there are some things I have learned that have changed me, that has made me question everything. I had to find out for myself. I had to verify if what I found out really is the truth."

David could see him stalling again, not telling him what he wanted to know. David said, "What about the Testimonial?"

David saw shock on his brother's face. Tim said, "How do you know about that?"

David said, "When you pulled your little disappearing act I had to find out a lot of things that I didn't know about you."

Tim said, "David, I really am sorry you got dragged into all this. I want to repay you for the sacrifices you've had to make. Let's start with Ruth. I'm going to help you get her out. She's my sister, and I owe it to her."

"I want answers; I'm tired of your games," David demanded.

Tim said, "Okay, fine. Let's get Ruth out, and then I promise I will answer all your questions." David stared at him suspiciously. Tim said, "We don't have any more time to wait. It's getting dark. You know we have to move now."

David knew he was right. He said, "I'm holding you to this, Tim. I want answers when we get her out."

Tim nodded and said, "You have my word."

David said, "Now, we need a plan."

Tim had been casing the area for some time. He didn't know the situation, but he had been tracking the Satanist soldiers. He knew they were in one of the trailers. Tim said, "They are expecting you. You will never get close to her without them seeing you coming. Surprisingly, they have very few imps here."

David thought about it and then said, "Why do you think they don't have more of their people here?"

Tim said, "Imps are tools. They don't think they will need them to defeat you. There are two soldiers in there. They are very powerful. They know that you will be alone."

"How do they know that?" David asked.

"Because we would never come after her like this. We do have one advantage, though. They don't know I am with you."

Tim came up with an idea. It was bold, but David thought it was their best chance. Tim would slip in at dark and cover the housing frames with gasoline. David would circle around behind the housing area to the construction trailers. Tim will ignite the houses and show himself to draw them away. David would slip in to get Ruth. David wished there were alternatives but, he had to admit, this was the best plan.

The late evening was spent in preparation. Tim got fuel, and David prepared himself with his weapons. He had his hand gun and the blade Jeremiah had given him. He gave his rifle to Tim, and Tim gave him a knife.

At 8:00 P.M., they decided it was time. Tim said, "David, I would like us to pray together."

David said, "You go ahead, I'll wait for you." David was finding his patience to praying to someone who wasn't there, some imaginary God up in the sky, to be getting shorter and shorter. David turned his back to Tim.

Tim stared at the back of his head for a long moment. As he knelt, he said, "We do have a lot to talk about when this is over." Tim knelt and prayed for several minutes. When he rose up, he said, "It's time. You know what to do?" David nodded. Tim said, "Be ready for my signal; you won't be able to miss it." David nodded again. He started to walk away. Tim said, "David!" David turned wordlessly back toward him. Tim reached out and gave him a hard hug. David closed his eyes and hugged him back. They were two, very different men—almost polar opposites—but they were brothers. Tim was the only family David had, and he loved him. It was hard to admit sometimes but here, in this embrace, memories flooded back: them playing together as children; Tim looking out for him as a child; Tim teaching him how to ride a bike. Whatever else happened, they had a history together. They were family. Both brothers had a hard time letting go.

Finally David broke the embrace. They wordlessly left the ravine they had been in all afternoon and went different directions; much like their lives, David thought to himself.

David walked around the housing development. It was a lot longer of a walk than he thought. The housing area was large, and he had to stay out of sight and move all the way around on foot. The long jog around left him breathing hard. He emerged on the back side of the trailers. The lights were on in all of them. David saw movement in several of them. He had not seen a single guard of any kind. The fire hadn't started yet. The plan was for David to stay out of sight until the fires began. There were many trailers. David was worried it would take too much time to search them all. Even though he knew it was against their plan he decided to begin searching them. He wanted to find out where she was, as the worry was driving him crazy. He crouched low and began moving through the vehicles that were parked there. He slowly crept up to one of the containers and looked in the window. He saw a man inside. He was sitting with his legs propped up on a small stack of boxes, watching a small T.V. David knew she could be in one of the other two, small rooms, but he decided to move to another trailer.

He moved to the next one. This one had higher windows. This container had a natural gas tank located at the rear, near one of the windows. He climbed up on it to see inside. He looked in the window and saw men playing cards and drinking. He began to think these men didn't look like any of the other men he had seen. He noticed that some of them had guns strapped to their sides and, as he looked around the small trailer, he saw rifles stacked in the corner. He realized these men were ready to quickly go into action. He climbed down. As he made a small jump off the tank, he heard an unmistakable metallic click of a gun.

A man behind him said, "Freeze!" David stopped and started to turn when he felt the butt of the gun in his back. He fell to the ground. The voice said, "I said, freeze. You move again, and they'll be scraping your brain off the side of this trailer!" David froze. The voice said, "Keep your hands where I can see them, and turn around slowly!"

David complied. As he turned to face the man, there was a great light that suddenly came up, directly behind the man. Tim had lit the frames of the houses. The man could not help but reflexively turn and see the blinding light that lit the area like a sunrise. David knew he had to act quickly. He knocked the man's gun to the ground with his left hand and threw a right cross. The punch caught the man squarely on the jaw. David heard a pop, and the man fell backward. David dove on top of him. They wrestled on the ground. The man was strong, stronger than David. It became obvious to David he had to get away, get to the gun. The man was trying to position himself on top of David, but David kept twisting, trying to keep him from getting on top of him. The man's strength began to win, and David was slowly wrestled on his back. The man pinned David's arms to the ground with his knees and placed his large, beefy hands around David's neck. The choke hold was perfect. No air could come through to David's lungs. David began to panic. He tried to calm himself, but he knew he had seconds. He tried to twist, but it was in vain. The man was too big, too strong. David's left arm was pinned perfectly, but his right arm was pinned at the upper arm. David could still move his right arm from the elbow down. He felt his head pound, his eyes were watering. The man clearly wasn't going to let go. David twisted his right hand and tried to get the knife that was on his side. He could only touch it with the tips of his middle and forefingers. He had to gently tug at it with those fingers, for what seemed to be an eternity. He was finally able to retrieve the knife he had on his side. He had little leverage to work with. He could feel himself trying to black out. He pulled his hand back. With all the strength he could muster with his right forearm, he pushed the knife forward. He felt it go into the man's rib cage. The man groaned but would not let go. David pushed the knife upward. He could feel it hit something hard yet, amazingly, the man still wouldn't let go. David's eyes were beginning to roll back in his head. With his last bit of strength, he twisted the knife to the right and then to the left. Finally, just as he thought he would black out, he felt the man's hands loosening. He started to twist the knife back and forth in faster motions. He felt the large knee loosen on his right arm. He freed it and began stabbing over and over with his right arm. The man's grip finally let go, and he collapsed on top of David. David turned his head to the right as the large man fell on top of him. He wheezed as he sucked air in his lungs. He wanted to take the large man off of him, but he had no strength. He just lay there, trying to breathe.

In a construction trailer, far on the other side, Cain stared out the window at the fire. He spoke to Judas, stone-faced, still looking at it, "He's here."

Judas came to his side. Ruth was tied to a chair in the next room. She had been severely beaten. Blood dripped from her face. Her hair was soaked with blood and sweat. She was only half-conscious. She didn't raise her head, but she could hear their conversation.

Judas said, "I didn't think he would come; not by himself."

Cain said, "Send the imps to get him."

Judas said, "No." Cain turned to look at him with a look of anger. Judas said, "Let me go. I'll use them to distract him. I'll bring him to you."

Cain stared for a long moment and then turned back to look at the huge fire. He said, "Fine. Take them and go."

Judas started for the door. He picked up his blade and slung it across his back. As he opened the door, Cain said, "If you can't bring him back, don't come back." Judas stared at him; he didn't say anything and then left.

As he came out of the trailer, he picked up a walkie that was on his belt. He said, "I need everyone here at the main office." Within minutes the imps had all gathered. There were about a dozen of them. Judas said, "I want everyone to spread across the field. He is not a soldier. He will be easy to catch. Remember, I want him alive. If you catch him, radio me. I will deliver him to Cain personally."

They all nodded. On the other side of the housing development, opposite from the trailers, Tim was waiting. He had the rifle David had brought. He was an excellent shot. The scope of the fire he had started was amazing. He hadn't expected it to be so bright. He had the rifle scope to his eye. He was watching the trailers on the other side, looking for any sign of activity. He saw men start to fan out and move into the housing area. He took the first one he saw out with a head shot, then a second. He started to pick them off, one by one. By the time they moved down into the area where the flames were, he thought he had gotten half of them. He felt a little bit of hope. This might just work. He could pick the imps off, and David would just have to find Ruth. Once he got them all, he could help him. Judas was watching from the other side. He could see the flashes of the gun as it fired. He took off in a jog.

David pushed the large man off him. He rolled over. He was still gasping for air. He looked up and saw a group of men gathered at a trailer. Someone was giving them instructions, and then they all took off and went in the direction of the fire. David scrambled up to his feet and staggered off in the direction the men were in, coughing and wheezing as he went. Tim believed there were five or six of them left. He was moving his scope back and forth, trying to find one. He saw one, fired, but missed. The man scrambled off, out of sight. He saw one emerge from the fire and start moving up the hill toward his position. He fired. The shot caught the woman in the chest, and she fell back. They knew where he was. His position was compromised. He jumped to his feet and took off to find a new spot to survey the ground. He had been lying on a small hill that overlooked the housing development. He moved back toward the ravine in which he and David had spent the afternoon. Out of the darkness, he heard a shot. He immediately fell to the ground. The rifle fell off into the dark. He was stunned for a moment, and then he felt the wound on his left thigh. He had been shot. Tim grabbed his leg and moaned in pain. It had missed the bone, but he was bleeding. He didn't know if it had hit a vein or an artery, but there was a lot of blood. A man appeared. He had been jogging but, as he approached, he slowed to a walk. Tim couldn't make out his features, but he could see the figure against the flames behind him in the distance. He sat up. The man had a gun in his hand. He was aiming it at him. The man walked up slowly, out of breath now. He said, "Don't move!" He looked him over and said, "Take off your blade and throw it away!" Tim did as he was told.

The man squatted in front of Tim. Tim could see the surprise in his eyes. He said, "You're not him!"

Tim said, "No, but I know who you are!" The man stared at him for a long moment. Tim knew he had to do something. Imps appeared behind him.

The man looked back and said, "There are two of them! Go back! The other one is back on the other side. Tell everyone! Remember, I want him alive!"

Tim grabbed his thigh. He exaggerated his pain. He laid back and rolled. Tim only had one card to play, but before he played it, he reminded himself that he had to have faith—faith in God. He believed God had his hand on him. Even now, with a bullet wound in his leg and a Satanist soldier in front of him, he still believed it. He believed it because the leg that was shot, the leg that was pouring blood, was the same leg he carried his back-up weapon on.

The man walked circles around him now. He kicked Tim in the head. He said, "Tell me where he is! What is your plan?"

Tim continued to exaggerate his pain. He grabbed his leg. The man put his foot on the wound and said, "Tell me!"

Tim screamed out in pain. The man finally let his foot off and stepped back. Tim rolled over on his side, his left side. As he moaned in pain, he pulled up the leg of his pants, just a bit. The man started to walk in circles around him again. He said, "His only chance to live is for you to tell me where he is!"

Tim said nothing. The small gun attached to his left ankle was exposed. He prayed that God continued to watch over him and that the man didn't see it in the dark. The man kicked him in the back. Tim felt a sharp pain in his lower back. He groaned.

The man said, "We are running out of time!" The man came back into view. He started to pace back and forth in front of Tim. Tim's hand was on his thigh. He slid it slowly down his calf. As the man started to walk toward him again, Tim took a deep breath, tried to block out the pain he knew he would feel, and then, with all his strength, he pulled his leg up just enough to get to the gun. With it still in the holster, he fired a single shot that hit the man in his left shoulder. The man fell back and rolled out of Tim's sight.

David moved toward the trailer and looked inside. He only saw an empty room. He moved to another window and looked in. He could see Ruth tied up in a chair, her head hung down. He felt his heart race. He had found her! He looked across the room and saw Cain staring out across the fire-filled housing area. David didn't know what to do. He pulled his hand gun, crouched, and checked the clip. He moved to the back door of the trailer. He squeezed his eyes shut hard. Gathered all his courage, he opened the door as fast as he could.

Cain spun in surprise. David let out a yell and started firing his gun. As he fired, the bullets went all around Cain, and Cain ran across the room. David clipped his left arm with a shot, and he dove out of the window. David kept shooting until his gun was empty. He ran inside the trailer, pulled another clip, and slammed it into his gun. The crash course Tim had given him earlier in the afternoon on the gun seemed to have paid off. He looked out the window, but he saw no one.

He ran back to Ruth; she was half-conscious. She spoke in a whisper, "David, you shouldn't have come."

"You're welcome," David said. He moved behind her and started to free her. He wanted to cut her hands free, but he had left his only knife in the man who had almost choked him to death. She was bound with duct tape. He began to take it off her. He said, "I think I shot him, but I don't know where he went. Can you walk?"

"I think so," she said.

Tim rolled several times after he fired the shot. He hoped the change in his position would be enough so that if the man fired, he would not be in the area of the shots. He removed his belt, pulled it above the bullet wound on his thigh, and pulled it as tightly as he could. He looked for his rifle but could not find it. He saw his blade on the ground. He picked it up and walked in the direction of the man. The man was holding his shoulder on the ground. Tim approached cautiously. He had lost his gun when he fell, and he could not find it in the dark. He saw Tim coming at him and pulled his blade. He got to his feet. The two men moved toward each other cautiously. Both were injured and were not 100 percent. Tim limped on his leg. It was starting to get numb now, and the pain was subsiding. Judas felt the pain in his left shoulder, but he was right handed, so he could still wield his weapon with his right hand.

They began to circle each other. Tim made the first swing. Judas deflected it. It appeared to Tim that Judas was on the defensive. Tim moved closer, swung, and then he backed away. Tim swung again. This time his blade locked with Judas' blade. The two men pushed against each other. Tim pulled his blade down with a quick motion and cut Judas across his torso. Tim saw a change in Judas' expression. Judas came at him now, swinging wildly. Now Tim was on the defensive, deflecting his swings as he backpedaled and tried to get a solid footing.

David helped Ruth out of the trailer. He tucked his gun in the back of his pants and put his arm around her. He heard a shot fired at them. They ran together, as best they could, in front of the trailer and down the hill, toward the burning housing development.

As they approached the bottom of the hill, a woman stepped in front of them and said, "That's far enough." The two looked helpless enough. David had Ruth's arm around him and she looked like she was going to pass out any second. The woman pulled out her walkie and said, "I've got him and the woman. They are at the bottom of the hill, below the office."

As she was saying this, Ruth's hand was sliding down David's back. She removed his gun, and as the woman was talking on her walkie, Ruth shot her between the eyes. The woman fell back; she was dead before she hit the ground. Ruth held the gun tightly and looked around. David ran over, grabbed the gun from the dead woman, and said, "We've got to hurry. They're coming; I don't know how many are left. We are going to have to run through the middle of these houses." Ruth gave him a look. David said, "I know, but we don't have a choice now."

Tim was deflecting one swing after another from Judas. He had clearly made him angry. Tim could tell that Judas' skills were superior to his, but the injured left shoulder had prevented him from using his left arm. It had acted as an equalizer. While Tim's leg was injured, and he was limping, he had full use of both of his arms. He thought he sensed Judas tiring. Tim stepped forward to attack again. Judas began to give ground. Tim could feel it now with every swing: God had his hand on him, and he was going to help him to win this fight.

With every thrust or swing Tim made, Judas gave more ground. Tim was pushing him along the rise, in front of the houses. As they approached the edge of the hill, Tim thought he was close to finishing him. He pushed forward with everything he had. He used every combination, every move he knew now. He almost had him. Judas staggered back, right on the edge of the hill. As he stumbled backward, this was it! Tim lunged at him.

Suddenly Judas balanced himself, lowered, and swung his leg at Tim with a sweeping motion. The move was perfect. Tim was caught off guard, and he rolled down the hill, his blade tumbling away in the darkness. Judas stood, looked around and then at his shoulder, which was bleeding. His plan had worked; he had compensated for a younger, faster opponent by making him tire himself unnecessarily and then by tripping him. Judas knew the fall down the hill would either serve to further reduce him or may take him out altogether.

Then he slowly started walking down the hill, toward the flames; but more importantly, toward Tim. David was moving through the burning houses. He thought that it might be the adrenaline. He didn't know, but Ruth seemed to be getting more of her strength back. She was walking now without assistance, but still unsteadily. A shot rang out. Both he and Ruth went to the ground. They couldn't see where the shot had come from. David rolled again and then moved up into a low crouch. He looked around and saw someone in the distance. He looked over at Ruth, still on the ground. He said, "Stay here, and try to draw his fire. I'm going to move around and see if I can get behind him."

Ruth nodded weakly. She belly crawled behind a mass of dirt nearby and shot off a couple of wild shots in the direction of the imp. David moved around a burning frame. It was incredibly hot. Boards started falling from the roof of the structure. He ran through what would have eventually been a back yard. He came around behind where the person was supposed to be, but they were gone. He looked back in Ruth's direction and saw they were moving toward her, closing in on her. David took off running. The house they had been fighting around totally collapsed to the ground, and the wave of flames and the pulse of the fire knocked David off his feet. He fell to the ground, dazed. He lost his gun. He tried to get up, but he needed a minute to compose himself.

He finally was able to get to his feet. His gun was gone. He couldn't find it. He looked and saw the imp was down. He ran toward him. Ruth came limping out from the other side. She said, "I got him." David looked down and saw he was dead. Ruth walked up to him and put a hand on his shoulder. She was struggling to stay on her feet. She had been shot on her right side. David saw the blood. She looked up at him and, before he could speak, said, "It's not bad. He saw you go down, and I had to expose myself to him. He got off a shot after I did."

David was scared now. He was no expert, but she had been through so much. She had taken yet another chance for him. He just looked at her gravely and nodded. She seemed to sense his concern. She said, "I'm gonna make it." They started off again.

Tim's head pounded. He had fallen hard down the hill and was only a few feet from the fires now. He felt around; his blade was gone. His ribs ached. He thought at least one or two were broken now. He felt around for a weapon: a rock, anything. He couldn't find anything. In the distance, he could see Judas coming at him. He thought for a moment and then, with calm, he closed his eyes. He said an intense prayer to himself and then said aloud, as he opened his eyes, "Amen." With a renewed determination, he took his good leg and his arms and began to back himself toward the fires.

Judas walked slowly toward him. The fight had taken its toll on him. He was trying to rest himself, get his strength back, and he was walking slowly. He had him now; there was no reason to hurry. He had no weapon, his leg was injured and now, and he probably had a few broken bones. Judas thought about how he would handle him. He could see him feebly scooting away. He wasn't going anywhere now, Judas knew. Tim knew he was finished. He scooted away with as much speed as he could. Judas was closing fast. Tim was only a few feet from a burning house frame now. He could feel the intense heat and could hear the crackling noise of burning boards now. As Judas closed in on him, Tim sucked in a breath of air. It was painful because of the ribs he now knew were broken for sure.

He came to his feet. He knew what he had to do now. Judas stared in amazement. He could not believe he was able to get up after the fall he had taken. He approached him with confidence. Tim swung wildly with his right fist. Judas easily dodged the punch, kicked Tim in his injured leg, and watched him fall to the ground. Judas pulled his blade back out. Judas walked around behind Tim. He grabbed him by the hair, pulled his head back, and put his blade to his throat.

David and Ruth were trying to get across the burning area. David just wanted to get her back to the car. He wanted to get her away from here. They were so close now. They had almost made it. He imagined Tim was already in the vehicle with the motor running, just waiting on them to dive in the car so they could go.

Cain was walking through the fire slowly, taking his time. He felt like this was home for him. He saw this as a sign. He knew he would, one day, walk through the fires with his master. The heat had never bothered him. He always felt like it was a small taste of what waited for him in eternity. He slowly looked around. He savored this. He knew it was meant to confuse him, to throw him off balance, but he was right at home here. His master had again provided for him. He felt the hand of Satan was always on him, guiding him. Now he had provided him with the ultimate battlefield so he could complete his most important task. He would walk away from this field of fire at dawn, with David dead, and he would be the ultimate tool on earth in the battle for the souls of man. It was all clear to him now. He had never felt more alive, more powerful.

He saw a figure running toward him in the distance. As he ran up, he nervously said, "There are only three of us left! The other two have gone back to the office. We have to get out of here!"

Cain looked around and then calmly leveled his gaze at him. He said, "Leave."

The man stared at him incredulously. He said, "He is in here somewhere, but the heat, the smoke, and the flames are too much!"

Cain said, "Not for me! He is mine now."

The man stared and then said, "What are your orders?"

Cain looked around, then back at him, and said, "He will die a slow, painful death now and only by my hand."

The man didn't know what to say. After a moment he ran off into the flames and darkness.

Tim was at the end now; he had only seconds or maybe minutes left. He knew it in his soul. He had asked for strength, and he could only hope that God had granted his request. He sucked in another breath of air.

Judas was in his ear. He said, "Where is the Testimonial? I don't have to kill you. You don't have to die here. I just need to know where it is. Tell me, and I will let you escape. You have to give me something. If you do, I will give you your life."

Tim reached up and grabbed the blade by the tip. He pulled it away from his neck, blood now dripping off his right hand. Judas strained against him, but Tim had a strength now that had surprised Judas. Tim also placed his left hand on the blade. He ran both his hands up the blade. Both his hands poured blood now. He had his hands at the top of the blade, next to Judas' hands. Judas was directly behind him, leaning over top of him. His stomach and chest was directly on top of Tim's back now. He pulled upward as Tim pulled downward. Tim lowered his head to his chest. With all his might, he snapped it back and hit Judas in the nose with the back of his head. He pulled the blade downward with all his might, through his body. The blade came through his left side, just below his rib cage, out his back, and into Judas. Tim pushed as hard as he could and then pulled it back out. He felt blood come out of his mouth. He turned with the final strength he had asked for and shoved Judas into the burning house frame. Judas let out a shrill scream as he fell into the burning boards and flames. In spite of all the pain he was in and the fact that he was going to die any second, Tim smiled. He knew the Lord had granted his request. He rolled on his back now, and he knew he would not move again. Ever.

David heard a scream. He motioned to Ruth to keep following him. He looked and saw a figure in a burning house frame, screaming. He hoped it wasn't Tim. He ran in the direction of the burning man. He could see a figure lying on the ground. He ran up closer.

Ruth heard David scream. She saw David run to the figure on the ground. David looked down and saw it was his brother. Blood was everywhere. He knelt, picked Tim's head up, and cradled it in his arms. Tim tried to talk, but

David could not hear him. Tim tried to lift his left arm, but he couldn't. David thought he understood, and he lowered his ear down to Tim's mouth. Tim spoke in a light whisper. It was hard for David to hear him with all the noise around them. Tim said, "I don't have much time left. I have two things I need to tell you."

It was very hard for him to talk. He whispered something to David. David nodded, raised his head up, and then said, "Save your strength." When he looked into Tim's eyes, he knew he was going. He had seen this before. He had had to be there for his mother's end, and now he was going to have to see it again with his brother. David felt tears in his eyes. He smiled at Tim, stroked his hair, and said, "I love you, big brother."

Tim managed a smile back. David lowered his ear back to Tim to hear the second thing. Tim wanted to tell him, but he heard nothing. He raised his head up, looked at Tim, and saw he was gone. David let out a scream that pierced the night. He howled like a mad animal. He laid his head on Tim's chest and began to sob. As he lay there, with his head on his brother's chest, he saw a figure emerging from the flames. It was Cain. David began to feel a hatred he had never felt before; a fury he had never experienced. He thought about all the agony he had felt over his mother and the resentment toward his brother. He thought about how senseless his brother's death had been, believing in a God that didn't exist, a God that was only in his mind. A crutch for weak mindedness because he could not accept the world as it was. Instead of making him stronger, the Christians had made him weaker. They made him believe in something that wasn't there. They used his fears, his lack of perception, and his fear of the world and made him a tool in their bogus war. Now he was a senseless casualty.

David felt his blood boil. He had never been this angry in his life. He shook with fury. He stood on his feet. Ruth was sobbing. She said, "I'm sorry, David. I'm so sorry."

David looked at her, stone-faced. Even her apology angered him. Everyone kept telling them how sorry they were. Now it was his turn. It was his turn to make someone really be sorry. He said, "Get back to the car and leave!"

Ruth didn't understand. She saw David staring past her and then she turned around and saw Cain. She looked back at him and said, "David, no!"

David ignored her. He reached up, pulled his blade, and walked into the inferno to face Cain.

CHAPTER 13

David felt the heat coming at him from all directions. He felt like he was walking through an oven. The frames of the houses were engulfed now in flames. It had spread to the houses that Tim didn't light, and they were all burning now. It looked like something from a movie. The houses were all burning high into the sky. David was walking down a street that should be paved and houses that should have yards and driveways. Instead he was walking down a dirt road with housing frames on both sides that were aflame. At the other end was Cain, just standing there. For some reason he could not explain, he was not afraid. He walked toward Cain with no fear, no thought of his own safety. David was angry—angrier than he had ever felt. That fear was giving him purpose, giving him strength. He didn't believe in Satan any more than he believed in God. He began to think maybe he was destined to do something. Maybe he was destined to end this conflict. He was the only one who seemed to have clarity; clarity to see the truth and to see that there were no fairytale places or lakes of fire. There was only the here and now. Maybe that gave him an advantage. He would never look up or down for help. He would only look to himself and his inner strength. Perhaps that gave him an advantage neither side possessed.

As he closed in on Cain, he could see Cain's face now. He was smiling. David was holding his blade in his right hand at his side. Cain was doing the same. Cain said, "It's all clear now. I see it all perfectly. My master has delivered you unto me. You will die here tonight, here in the flames that honor my master."

A house frame collapsed to David's left. He flinched a little. Cain didn't budge, but he turned to look over at it. As the house frame collapsed upon itself, the heat from that direction became even more intense. Cain looked back at David and smiled broadly. He said, "Do you feel it? Can you feel it now, atheist?" David didn't respond. Cain said, "My master is all around us. He has been in the shadows long enough! He has chosen me to lead our people out and take back what was stolen from us two thousand years ago!"

He raised his blade at David. It was larger than any other David had seen. It had a serrated edge. Cain's shirt was soaked with perspiration. He reached up with his left hand and tore it off. As it fell to the ground, David took in his body. It had a reddish tint from the heat, David guessed. He had tattoos all over his body. Writing covered his chest, but David could not understand the language. He had arms that looked like tree trunks and biceps with veins bulging. Still David did not feel fear. He wanted to kill this man, and this man would have to kill him to stop him.

David walked closer. Cain didn't notice he was not scared of him. In truth he didn't care. The fire was a sign to him, a sign this was his moment. His time had come. He was not going to waste it. He was going to enjoy every second of it. David moved closer. Both men raised their blades up. David swung. Cain easily deflected it. Cain swung, David blocked the blow, but it threw him off balance, and he staggered back a few steps. David balanced himself then moved in again. They exchanged a few blows, each successfully blocking the other. Cain smiled again. Both men were beginning to breathe heavily.

Cain said, "Everyone you have cared about will die now. I will see to it. That soldier you care for. When this is done, I will kill her and lay her next to you and your brother, and I will celebrate over all three of your corpses. Your death will usher in a new era. The prophecy has been fulfilled, and I will be recognized as my master's chosen one."

David thought of Ruth, thought of him hunting her down and killing her. As his anger boiled, Cain raised his left hand and motioned with his hand for David to come over. David screamed out as he lunged forward. He swung wildly. The speed with which he was swinging the blade amazed even him. Cain was moving with equal speed. He was deflecting every blow. Cain was slowly giving ground as David swung violently.

Cain saw the fight clearly now. David was no match for him. His skill with his blade was laughable. He could cut him down at any moment. He was wearing himself out now. Cain was normally more aggressive, but he was seeing things with such clarity now. He wanted to savor this. He wanted to take his time, make him suffer. His master had provided him with this opportunity, and he did not want to waste it. David was predictable; his attack had a pattern that Cain had deduced in seconds and was easily deflecting. Cain could see David was wearing down. He waited a few more minutes until he was sure David was exhausted.

When the time came, he swung back hard, knocking David's blade back. He then punched him in the face hard, with the right hand that still held the handle of his blade. The punch caught David squarely on the face now. His nose poured with blood as he fell to the ground. Cain calmly walked over to him. He would cut his leg, possibly to the bone. He didn't want him to get back up. Then he would begin to work on him. This would be the defining night of his life. David was on the ground. His chest was heaving. Cain raised his large blade over his head and begun to swing down. He felt his feet come out from under him, and he fell hard on his back. In spite of the pain, he smiled again.

David had some training. This would make it even better. He came to his feet. As he did, David rolled and came to his feet with his blade at the ready. Cain began to attack now. David was moving back quickly with the barrage of blows Cain was giving him. Cain was superior to David in every way. David was beginning to see it. Cain swung over his head with a violent scream. David blocked the blow, and their blades were locked together. Cain then delivered a knee to David's abdomen. David staggered back. Cain swung. David tried to twist away, but the blade caught him on his right side and sliced straight down into his thigh. David staggered back as Cain delivered another swing, which he blocked, but the force of it knocked him off his feet. David rolled again, but he lost his blade a second time. Cain walked calmly toward him. David rolled, came up on his butt, and began to scoot himself backward as Cain walked toward him. David was scooting, trying to find something that could help.

Cain walked over David's blade and continued slowly gaining on him. David, realizing it was pointless, stopped and allowed Cain stand over top of him. He was finished, Cain was right. Cain kicked David hard in his leg. David let out a groan. Cain kicked him a second time, even harder, in the same leg. David knew he would have trouble walking on it now. Cain raised his blade again, and David braced for the blow he knew was coming.

Cain let out a scream and dropped his blade. David was confused. Cain fell to his left side on one knee. When he did, David could see Ruth standing behind him, holding his blade. She had cut him across his back. She said, "David, we have to go now!"

David now knew she was right. He acted quickly. He kicked Cain hard in the head, while he was distracted with the pain. He picked up Cain's blade and swung it into the fiery inferno of a nearby fire. He grabbed Ruth, and the two of them limped off together. David's leg throbbed. He was trying to help Ruth, but it was hard to help her and walk himself.

Suddenly Ruth fell off her feet. David stopped, looked behind, and saw Cain coming at them with a quick stride. David said, "Run, go!" He turned and limped back toward Cain. Cain pushed his arms forward, and a wave of energy came out of him that knocked David off his feet. David felt dizzy, the wave hit him hard. Ruth recovered and ran at Cain with her blade. She got closer to him than David did. A surge of energy came from his body, and he channeled it through his left hand at her. It knocked her off her feet. She fell to the ground, losing the blade. Cain calmly picked it up. Ruth was hurting; she had already been through so much. She rolled to her stomach and tried to get up. She moved very slowly, as she was clearly exhausted. As she came to her knees, Cain took the blade and sliced down her back. She let out a shrill scream. When she turned over, he looked at her wound on her shoulder. He stuck the blade in it and twisted. She screamed again. Then he sliced her across the front of her body. She screamed again.

David felt his anger again. He got to his feet and moved toward Cain. He tried to make something come from him, tried to use his power, but nothing came. Cain was still standing over Ruth as David approached him. He took a step over her body as she lay bleeding. David was exhausted now. He knew he had to do something, but he had no weapons left. He still had his fists. He balled his right fist. As he approached Cain, he swung. Cain easily dodged the swing and then returned with a punch of his own. It hit David just below his left rib cage. It knocked the wind out of him. David fell to the ground.

Cain was tiring of this. This had not been as fun as he had originally imagined. He wanted David down on the ground and wanted him to stay there. He raised his foot. He would crush his knee and then decide how much longer he would let him live. Cain raised his foot over his knee. David was helpless below the large boot.

At the last second, Cain felt a blow to the back of his head. Ruth had gotten to her feet and punched the back of his head with all the strength she had left. Cain fell forward, staggered several steps, but then recovered.

Ruth fell to her knees as she hit him, her strength gone. She looked at David and said, "David, please run!"

Cain came back at her now. He wasted no time. He took his blade and drove it into her abdomen. The blade went in her awkwardly above her left hip. Ruth fell to the ground, for the last time. David felt his blood boil, but he had no strength left. David sat up, but Cain kicked him in the head, hard. David saw stars. Cain stopped, took in his surroundings. He looked at the fires around him, his fallen foes on the ground before him. He was doing all of this in the presence of his master and lord. He felt like this would be the greatest night of his life. He smiled again. He said aloud, "Now is the time, master! Work through me!"

He turned and shot a wave of energy into David. The pain was indescribable. David felt pain in every inch of his body. Another wave of energy came out of Cain's body. This one was slow; it surrounded David, picked him up, and then slammed him to the ground. David was seeing stars again. Cain began speaking aloud: "Master, I call to thee! I serve thee! My power honors thee!" A burning frame behind him collapsed and fell to the ground in a ball of fire.

David, helpless now on the ground, thought he actually looked like a demon, with his arms spread and the fire all around him. Cain took a slow turn, taking it all in; it was blissful for him. As he turned slowly and watched all the fires around him, he said in a loud voice, "I serve thee, master! My name has long been removed from the book of life! Tonight I will have you write it in the book of death! I want to spend eternity with you! I pledge all I am to you! Work through me!"

He hit David with another wave of energy. Then he did it again. David was in agony now. Cain raised his arms and looked up, fire all around him. He said, "I will sacrifice him to honor you, lord! For the gift you have given me! To prove myself worthy!"

David knew he was going to die now. He had nothing left. He was lying on his stomach. He looked at Ruth. She was still alive, but very weak now. David made eye contact with her. As they both lie, helpless on the ground, all they could do was stare at each other. They would at least die together. As he stared at her, she mouthed silently, "I love you, David." David felt something inside himself. He wasn't sure what it was, but something was happening inside his body. In that moment, everything changed.

Something inside David awoke. Something he never knew was there. It was like a door was opened before him. In a matter of seconds, everything he thought he knew began to change. He thought back to his mother: his agony over her death; his resentment of her for making him promise to look after his brother; his anger over his brother, over his ridiculous beliefs; his anger for the way his brother left his mother; and for the anger for the father he never knew. In those few seconds, all that anger he had carried for so long was replaced by love. He could hear his mother's words now: "There may come a time you will have to face your hatred of him. There may come a time you will have to let it go...to be strong."

He could see it now: the hatred he had kept him from using this power. It wasn't hate or anger that unleashed it, not really. To truly use it, he had to feel love, he had to forgive. That gave him focus. He suddenly remembered the love he had for his mother and the love she had for him. He had no bad memories of her; he just felt her love for him. It was that love that gave him strength and that gave him courage as a child. He knew his mother loved him unconditionally. He remembered how he loved his brother. It wasn't his hatred of his brother that motivated him; it was his love for him, for his only brother and for the only family he had left in the world. In that instant, he forgave, and he loved like never before. In that peace and serenity, he found a vast strength. Then he came back into focus now.

As he lay there, on his stomach, he looked into Ruth's eyes, and he realized how much he loved her. He knew in that moment he would do anything for her. He had never loved a woman before, not really. He couldn't imagine life without her now. As he let go of the hatred he had carried for so long, he felt the power grow inside of him; a vast power. He could feel it in every inch of his body.

Cain reached his hands into the air. A wave of energy seemed to come out of the sky and into him. It seemed to flow through his body. He shot it out of him at David. When it hit David, his body seemed to absorb it. David didn't feel it at all. A shock washed over Cain. This had never happened before.

David felt no pain. He felt something surge through him, something give him strength. He felt something in him begin to awaken; he began to feel his power flowing through him. It was so simple now; how could he not have seen it?

Cain sent another wave into David, and again David's body seemed to absorb it. David began to realize now that his hatred had suppressed it. While it was totally new now, he somehow knew it was there; he knew how to use it.

David felt his pain going away. He slowly came to his feet now. Cain looked at him, incredulously. Cain sent another wave at David. This time David didn't absorb it. He held out his hands and seemed to send it back at Cain. The wave knocked Cain off his feet. Cain was shocked. He couldn't believe it.

Cain quickly got up. He said, "Give me the strength, lord!" He shot another wave at David. This wave was the largest of all. It looked like a tidal wave. It moved toward David like it would wash over him, consume him.

As it reached him, David again absorbed it; all of it. He closed his eyes for a minute and then looked up toward the sky and felt his new power flowing through him. When he brought his head down, he was looking Cain in the eyes. The look he gave Cain sent fear through him. For the first time in his life, Cain saw something that scared him. David looked at him with a glare. David had his hands at his side. He slowly raised them. He opened his palms, facing Cain.

As he closed them, Cain could feel hands closing on him. David raised him up into the air. Cain was powerless to stop him. David moved him around until he was in a horizontal position, high in the air. David then threw him high into the air. Cain fell to the ground with a sickening thud. He picked him up again. Cain looked at him with a bewildered look.

David pulled his palms back toward his body. This pulled Cain close to him. He brought him within just a couple of feet from his face. David didn't speak, but Cain understood the unspoken message between them. He had been beaten. Then he thrust his hands forward in a violent motion, and Cain shot through the air, over the houses and out of sight.

David slowly lowered his hands. He could feel his power subsiding now. He saw Ruth lying in a heap on the ground. He ran to her. Blood was everywhere.

He quickly grabbed her and held her head in his arms. In the distance, he could hear sirens. He said, "Hold on, help is coming."

She slowly raised her hand to his face and put it across his cheek. She was too weak to talk. She smiled. Then her hand fell, and she went limp in his arms. David screamed, "No!" He continued to hold her tight. Within minutes, fire trucks, ambulances, and police cars were arriving on the scene.

They found David still holding her. A young medic jabbed his fingers into her neck. After a few seconds, he screamed, "I've got a pulse! Get me a stretcher!" He put a hand on David and said, "Sir, she is still alive. I don't know if she will make it, but you have to let us take her."

David nodded and slowly let the young medic begin working on her. Someone else threw a blanket over David's back. Two firefighters began leading the paramedics with Ruth on a bed through the flames and to a waiting ambulance. David walked behind her. As they approached the ambulance, the medics shut the door. David started to protest, but another medic said, "Let them take her. They need to work on her."

David looked at him and said, "I want to go to the hospital she is going to." The paramedics nodded, and David was ushered into another ambulance.

CHAPTER 14

David arrived at the hospital and was treated for his injuries. For all he had been through, all he had physically were bumps, scrapes, a bad cut on his torso, and some badly bruised ribs. David was preparing to leave the emergency area when he was approached by a detective. The man was young. He looked like he was barely thirty, if that old. He was average weight and height. He had brown hair and a bushy mustache.

He introduced himself to David. "I'm Detective Rigdon."

David nodded and said, "What can I do for you?"

He gave David a sympathetic look and asked, "Are you all right?" David nodded again but didn't say anything. Detective Rigdon said, "What can you tell me about what happened out there tonight?"

David thought for a moment. He had no idea what he was supposed to say. Finally he said, "Detective, I have lost my brother. The only other person I care about in the world is in this hospital somewhere, and I don't know if she is alive or dead. Can't this wait?"

The detective looked at him thoughtfully. He said, "Yes...I guess it can." David started to walk away. The detective said, "Did you know any of the other people?"

"No," David said plainly. Without turning to look back, he walked out the double doors of the emergency room and into the main floor of the hospital. The detective studied him thoughtfully. His phone rang. He reached down and pulled it off the clip on his belt and answered it. He said, "Rigdon." He listened for a moment and then said, "Yes, sir. I'm at the hospital now. I just spoke with one of the survivors, but he didn't tell me anything." He listened and then said, "Yes, sir, there was a woman. I don't know her status." He listened for a few more seconds and then said, "There is one thing I learned that we didn't know. There is another survivor." After a few moments of listening again, he said, "I didn't understand it either, sir. Apparently he was in one of the homes; he was burned to a crisp. They don't think he will make it. He has third-degree burns on his body from head to toe and a stab

145

wound in his abdomen. The doctors say he should be dead, but somehow he is alive. He was able to speak, but we didn't get much information from him. The doctor said it was the worst burns he had ever seen. They airlifted him to the burn unit of a hospital in Los Angeles. They asked him his name. He said it was Osborne; we don't have a first name yet. If he survives, we'll get more.

David quickly went to find Ruth. He got off the elevator and discovered she was still in surgery. He sat in a waiting room for a couple of hours. Around 1:00 A.M., a doctor came in. David jumped to his feet. The doctor was an older woman. She appeared to be in her fifties. Some of her graying hair came out from under the surgical cap she was still wearing. She looked tired. Her paper mask was still hanging around her neck. He had asked the nurses her status several times, so he was sure she was told about him. He expected her to ask some questions about his relationship to Ruth. Instead, she asked, "Are you her next of kin?" David nodded. He felt like she was the closest thing he had to family right now. The doctor cleared her throat. She looked at him through her hazel eyes gravely. She said, "She is in very bad shape. She has lost a lot of blood. The stab wound was horrible. It severed several organs, as well as an artery. She has been beaten severely. She has multiple areas of internal bleeding. We can't stop it all. We did what we could and then we had to close her."

David just stared. He didn't know what to say. He felt like he had been hit with a sledgehammer. He felt tears coming up in his eyes. He said, "How long does she have?"

"Minutes," came her reply. "Maybe an hour or two, if she's lucky." She continued. She put her hand on David's shoulder and said, "We gave her something for the pain. She's sleeping. She won't wake up...she won't feel anything."

David wiped another tear from his cheek. He said, "Can I be with her for the end?"

The doctor said, "Yes, certainly. We'll fight to keep her alive as long as possible, but she won't last very much longer."

David was shown to a room. Ruth lay there, motionless. She was unconscious. David pulled up a chair beside her bed. He took her hand in his and held it tightly. More tears came now. He couldn't believe it was going to end like this for her. He couldn't believe she would go this way. He tried to think. Maybe there was more he could do. Maybe he could have her taken to another hospital. Maybe another doctor could do more. But as quickly as these ideas came to him, they vanished. He knew it was hopeless. He sat with her for an hour. He could see her slipping away. Her breath was becoming shallow. He watched her chest rise and fall. Each time it fell, he thought it might be the last time and then it would rise again. He felt so helpless. He wanted to do something. He had to do something. He just didn't know what.

He got up and began to pace by the foot of the bed. He had to face the truth in that moment. He had to face there was nothing he could do, nothing anyone could do. At that moment, he was so desperate he would try anything. He would do anything. For all the science in the world and all David's powers, there was nothing that could be done to save her. He loved her so much. He was going to do the one thing he had sworn to himself he would never do. He swallowed his pride. Pride he had carried for years, through all the ridiculous signs people thought they saw and all the hypocrites he had met to all the empty promises he heard made in the name of God. He kept his eyes open. He didn't bow on his knees. Then David, the atheist, did the only thing left he could do. Standing at the foot of her bed, he began to pray.

David said aloud, in a low voice, "I've never believed you were there. I never believed you existed. I'm not going to apologize. I'm not going to make excuses. I don't think I'm worthy of a favor from you. I'm not asking for one, but this woman has pledged her life to you. I don't understand how you could let someone who has been so faithful just die like this." David clenched his fists and began to cry again. He said, "If you are there, if you really exist, I'm asking you to save this woman, to make her whole again." David shook his head slowly and then said, "Amen."

At that moment, the machines she was attached to begin to make noises. Fast beeps and whines. A nurse came rushing in. She checked Ruth, hit the button by the bed, and said, "She's crashing!"

A crowd of people came flooding in the room. They began to work on her. One of them said, "Get me a crash cart, stat!" He felt hands on him now. A couple of people began to push him out of the room. The door to her room closed in front of David.

He stood there, in the hallway. He knew she was going to die now. He spoke to God again; this time he looked up as he spoke. He said, "Thanks a lot." David felt silly now. He couldn't believe he would even have tried something so ridiculous. He shook his head, rolled his eyes, and slowly walked to the empty waiting area. He sat down, put his head in his hands, and sobbed like a small child.

David sat in the waiting area for several hours. The time seemed like an eternity to him. He wondered if anyone was ever going to come to talk with him. He wondered how long she would survive. When he could bring himself to face it, he wondered how he would go on. His family was wiped out. His mother was gone, his brother was gone, and now Ruth. He was truly all alone now.

Just before 5:00 A.M., another doctor came to see David. This was a young man. He looked like he couldn't have been out of medical school long. He had a small build. He had brown eyes and brown hair that he combed to the side of a high forehead. He came into the waiting area. David was still the only one there. David wanted to get up, but he didn't have the strength. The doctor walked over and sat down beside him. He said, "I'm Dr. Owens." David nodded his head and then looked down at the floor and waited to hear the news he already knew. The doctor didn't speak. David raised his head and looked up at him through blood shot eyes and waited to hear it.

The young doctor finally said, "I'm very sorry." Upon hearing this, David bent over and put his head in his hands. He wanted to cry again, but he couldn't. He had no tears left; he was totally drained. The doctor continued, "I'm very sorry for everything you have been through tonight." David slowly raised his head back up to look at him. What more could he possibly have to say? The doctor stared at David and then said, "We still want to run more tests on her."

David lowered his head into his hands again. In a hoarse voice he said, "No, no more tests. Just let her rest in peace now."

There was a long pause. "Rest in peace," the doctor repeated. He said it as a statement, but he meant it as a question. Dr. Owens said, "She is not dead."

David heard the words, but he could not process their meaning. David slowly raised his head again to look at the doctor. David said, "What?"

The young doctor cleared his throat, looked around, and then back at David. He asked, "Has no one been out here to talk with you?" David slowly shook his head. Dr. Owens seemed to get more animated now. As if reciting a medical text, he read, he said, "At 2:43 A.M., the patient's heart began to race. The first nurse in the room thought she was entering cardiac arrest, but she never did. She then began to break out in a cold sweat. She soaked her sheets." He hesitated and then continued, "This is very unusual because there was no reason for her to do this. At 3:21 A.M., her heart rate stabilized. Her blood pressure began to climb, and all her vital signs seemed to return to normal. We ran some tests on her at 3:30 A.M."

He hesitated a second time. He started again a little more excitedly now. "We received the results of those tests at four o'clock. We believed the tests were flawed."

David asked, "Flawed?"

The doctor said, "Yes. We requested the machines we were using to scan her run a diagnostic. Then we ran the same tests with a different set of equipment. We received the results of these tests at 4:42 A.M. The second set of tests confirmed the validity of the first set of tests. And those results are... every trace of the internal bleeding is gone from her body."

David heard it, but he was so tired he still wasn't sure what he was saying. David again said, "What?"

Dr. Owens continued, "They're gone. It's almost like they were never there. The organs that were damaged are healing at an amazing rate. What looked like life-threatening injuries a few hours ago now looks like superficial wounds."

David continued to stare at him. David again said, "What?"

The doctor seemed to calm himself a little now. His voice lowered. He said, "We can't explain what happened."

The doctor started to say something else, but as he did, David got up and without another word and started to walk toward Ruth's room. When he entered, Ruth looked like she did when David left her. She was sleeping quietly on the bed. David pulled a chair over to her again. He put her hand in his. He kissed it again and again. He needed to be close to her. He wanted to climb into the bed and just hold her, but he couldn't. He took her hand and held it to his face. It gave him comfort, just feeling the warmth of it, just feeling her touch. David held her hand in his, with the back of it pressed against his cheek. He stared ahead and thought deeply. He had done this his entire life. Anytime he needed to think, to reflect, he would find a point in the room and just stare at it. It is how he would solve an equation in school, a situation at work, or a problem at home. He just stared at the small table that sat by the window and became lost in thought. How could this have happened? He thought about what the doctor said: "We can't explain what happened." David's mind began to methodically work on scenarios. Maybe the first doctor, the older woman, misdiagnosed her. Maybe with all the blood, the wounds just looked worse than they really were. He shook his head as he considered these and other possibilities. In the end, he had to admit he couldn't explain it either.

He pulled Ruth's hand to his cheek. As he rubbed the back of it against his cheek, he looked up and said aloud, "If you really did this, if you are really there, how could you leave me alone for so long? I have been alone my entire life. How could you sit there and just watch me and never help me, never show me you exist?" David shook his head slowly, looked straight ahead, and said, "Where have you been for so long?" His mind was so clouded, so full of questions.

Suddenly a hand appeared on this shoulder; it startled him. He spun his head around to see a young, African American woman. She had a flawless face and deep brown eyes. She said, "He is risen!" She walked behind him and went into the bathroom. David spun his head to follow her. She had grabbed a plastic container and took it into the bathroom and began to fill it with water.

As she came out of the bathroom, David looked at her and said, "What?"

She spoke as she sat the full container of water by the bed. She said, "The sun, it's almost risen."

David looked back toward Ruth and said, "Oh."

She walked around the room, straightened the sheets, and began moving a few things around the room. She checked the monitors and put her hand on Ruth's head and smiled. She looked at David and said, "Everyone is saying it's a miracle. What happened to her?"

David just stared ahead.

She asked, "Do you believe in miracles?"

David shrugged. She walked around the bed and began to leave the room. David began his stare again at the table. There was a red haze outside; the new day was just beginning to dawn. He noticed there was now a Bible on the table. The nurse must have put it there. He was certain it wasn't there earlier. As she pushed the door open, he said, "Nurse." She stopped in the door way. She didn't speak; she just turned back toward him with a smile. David asked, "That Bible. It wasn't there a minute ago. Did you put it there?"

She continued to smile. She looked at the Bible and then back at David. She said, "You mean God's word? It's always been there in front of you, hasn't it?" David stared at her blankly. She said, "Maybe you just never took the time to see it before." With that she wordlessly walked through the doorway and left the room.

David thought about it for another moment. She must have put it there. He hadn't seen her carry it in the room, but there was no other explanation. He wanted to talk with her more. He quickly went to the door and looked down the hall. There was no one there. He quickly looked in the opposite direction; no one there, either. He didn't know what to think. He stopped, turned, and immediately began to stare at the Bible. He didn't know why, but he was suddenly drawn to it. He decided to go and look at it. He had seen it a million times. He had read it cover to cover. There was nothing in it he hadn't seen before. He took slow steps toward it. He felt something coming over him the closer he got. He was so tired. He thought maybe he just needed some sleep. He finally got to the table. He reached down and picked up the Bible. He flipped through the pages; he wasn't sure what he was looking for. A piece of paper fell out and onto the table. While holding the Bible in his left hand, David reached down and picked it up with his right hand. It was a handwritten note. It was written in red ink, or what looked like red ink. As he read the words, he felt cold chills from head to toe. It said, "The question is: where have *you* been? For I have always been here, right beside you. If you needed me, you had only to reach out and take my hand…for it has always been there."

David dropped the note and the Bible and staggered backward in shock. He felt something. He didn't know what it was, but his entire body tingled. His knees buckled, and he fell to the floor. For an unexplainable reason, he began to cry again. It wasn't for Ruth this time. It wasn't for his mother or his brother. He didn't know what it was for, he just cried. As he cried, he lowered his head to the floor. Could this be real? Why would this person do anything for him? How could someone who he had ignored, thumbed his nose at for most of his life, still love him? How could he face him? He didn't deserve anything from him. What kind of love that must be? He thought about a parent, about the unconditional love a parent has for a child.

In that moment, David realized he was the child. This was his father. A father he had neglected. A father he had denied. A father he had never bothered to know. But when he needed him most, he was there; there, without hesitation. David's chest heaved as he cried now. How could he not have seen it? He had been so bad to him. When he raised his head again, with tears in his eyes, the morning sun was shining directly down on him, through the window and directly into his face. David felt like it was more than the sun. He felt a presence he had never felt before.

He said aloud, "I'm sorry, I'm so sorry." Now it was him who was apologizing; apologizing for a lifetime of denial, a lifetime of neglect. As he lay there on the floor, he went back upon his hands and knees and he sobbed. He felt a peace he had never felt. Something washed over him, something he could no longer explain away.

As he lay there, sobbing, he found himself. He found everything he was missing in his life. He felt as if something was touching him; like a hand was on him, comforting him. God was calling to him, telling him it was time; that he was forgiven, that He had missed him for so long. He didn't care about anything else. He didn't care about all the things he had done, all the things he had said, all the neglect, and all the times he had denied him. Somehow David knew none of it mattered now. The only thing that mattered to God is that one of His children had finally come home.

On a cold, concrete floor in a hospital in Sin City U.S.A, David, the atheist, discovered God.

Ruth awoke to David holding her hand. She was sore, but she was healing. David had not left her side for several days. She could see a Bible beside her bed. It was laying open, facing the table. She could see he was in need of a shave and a shower. He smiled at her. She asked, "How long have I been out?"

"Days," came the answer. "It doesn't matter," David said, smiling. "What's important is that you're okay." David had a lot to tell her. He knew now was not the time. He said, "I'll catch you up later. Now you just need rest."

Ruth smiled again, weakly. She put her hand on his face. She asked, "Can you tell me anything?"

David continued to smile. He said, "I love you."

She closed her eyes, still smiling, and said, "I meant something I didn't already know." She was so tired she was starting to doze again.

David said, "I promise when you get your strength back, I'll tell you everything you want to know."

As she drifted back to sleep, she said, "For now, how about your last name?" She smiled again with her eyes closed and said, "With all we have been through, I never got your last name."

David's expression went to surprise. He said, "How is that possible? You watched me, you knew Tim."

She replied, "Respect. We stay out of each other's lives; the lives we had before the anointing. I avoided knowing it out of respect for Tim and for his family. But I think I would like to know it now."

David took her hand in his and said, "It's Osborne...David Osborne."

She continued smiling as she went to sleep.

Beijing, China

High atop a sleek skyscraper was the headquarters of one of the largest, multi-national conglomerates in the world. The name of the company was not well-known; not among common people. Among the world's elite billionaires, however, it was very well-known. It controlled many of the most well-known companies in the world. While it raked in billions of dollars in revenue every year and was known for its extensive philanthropy, it was a very secretive company. Its CEO was reclusive and was rarely seen in public. She was rarely seen by anyone. She did most of her meetings by teleconference and almost never left the company headquarters. When she did, it was usually to go to one of their numerous offices around the world. The Grand Council rarely met. Usually she met with them a few at a time. She rarely brought them all together.

Today they were aware things were rapidly changing. They had just met a few days ago. She had impressed upon them the need to move vast resources to the United States. It was difficult. The U.S. had long ago been deemed one of their least important theaters, but she had done it. She had convinced them there was a need there and that they needed to react to it. Now, just a few days later, she was calling the Grand Council together again. This time she would have to brief them on recent events in America.

As she entered the room, they all stood. She was a very small woman. She was barely five feet tall. She dressed in traditional Asian attire. She always wore white. Her long, flowing, black hair was always pulled back tightly. Her appearance commanded respect among them. She was a workaholic. She was known to work all hours of the day and night. She rarely went home. Some said she sometimes worked through the night and then the next day again. While many outside this room didn't know it, she was arguably the most powerful woman in the world. With one command, she could kill anyone, erase anyone. No one in this room had to be reminded of that. She had initially hated being called the Chairman. She seriously considered having her title changed to Chairwoman, but she decided she would live with it. They all knew the title well.

She took her seat at the head of the vast table. They all sat. In this room were the representatives of over thirty nations. While their names were well-known, what wasn't well-known was that this was the largest front in history. This was the revenue producer that funded the worldwide Satanist movement, and these people were its leaders. She sat down and began. She had to remind herself to speak in English. Since 1522, English had been the universal language for them.

"Cain was defeated by the atheist." The room immediately exploded. She knew there would be a reaction. No one had defeated Cain, their most powerful soldier—ever. There was chatter and whispering among the many members. She let them talk for a moment and then cleared her throat. With this, they quieted and she started again. "Cain is alive. He has numerous broken bones and will be out of action for several months. The atheist is still under the protection of the Christians. We are not sure how he defeated Cain, but we will debrief him once he is out of America. Our soldier, Judas, was critically injured. He was burned severely in a fire and is recovering in a burn hospital in Los Angeles. I am told it is one of the best hospitals in the world. We will leave him there until he can travel, and then we will send in an extraction team to get him. We have been informed the Christian carrying the Testimonial was killed. We do not have it, and now that he is dead, we have to accept we may never find it."

She let that hang in the air for a moment and then continued, "It's clear that our master had his hands on our soldiers and saved them from Jehovah."

She was interrupted by the leader of their interests in the South American country of Argentina. He spoke in heavily accented Spanish. "Are we sure we are fighting against Jehovah? Do we really know where these powers come from?"

The chairman gave him a look that made him sit back in his chair. She did not like to be interrupted. She said, "We are always fighting against Jehovah. Don't ever forget that. He is our sworn enemy. We have pledged our souls to our master in the fight to defeat him."

She let that settle for a moment and then continued again, "I am slowing our movement of resources to America. In light of recent events, we have to be ready for our focus to shift. It could move to any point in the world now. We have to be ready for what is coming. We have to realize the time is upon us."

The man representing their interests in the U.K. spoke now. He slowly cleared his throat. He did not want to interrupt her. When he was sure it was safe to speak, he spoke in a heavy British accent, "Chairman, what *time* are you referring to?"

She said, "It's time for us to go to war with the Christians."

The room exploded in conversation again. There was lots of chatter, lots of talking. She let this continue. She was in her element now. She had learned to let them talk. She had learned the art of timing her remarks.

Just before she was ready to speak, the woman in charge of their interests in Australia said, "Chairman, we have been at war with the Christians for centuries. What exactly are you saying?"

She stood, looked around the table at each of them. She said, "Our master has sent us a sign. He is saying it is time to finish this. We have been slowly defeating them for over fifty years. He is telling us that it is time to end it. We will time our strike carefully. Soon we will launch a massive campaign against them. We will wipe them out. Completely.

Epilogue

The last few days had been like a whirlwind for David. He had stayed with Ruth until she was released. They were not allowed to leave the area until they were cleared by Detective Rigdon. David and Ruth explained to him they had no idea who the people were. They explained they went there looking for David's brother; that he had fallen in with some bad people and they had lost him. They told him they were both lucky to be alive. They discovered that one of the imps had survived, but was severely burned. Ruth had prayed for him. She hoped he would see this as an opportunity to give his heart to God.

When they got back to Salt Lake City, they discovered that Moses had recovered, although physically he would never be the same. David told Moses about the night in the hospital, about the miracle of Ruth's recovery. He told Moses he had decided he wanted to be trained as a soldier. Moses was happy to hear of David's acceptance of God. He told David he would have to pray about it and talk with some other people and get back with him.

David went back to the city he was from. Moses was opposed to this. He wanted to keep David close. David understood he could never go back to his life now. He understood he would have to forever change. He had to go back and put his affairs in order. Moses ordered Ruth to stay with him and continue to watch over him. He knew how close she and David were and, for now, he was going to allow them to stay together until something could be decided.

David went to see Rus. He explained that the vacation time had been an eye opener for him. He told Rus he was going to travel and find himself. Russ told him if he ever wanted a job, he would hire him again, in a minute.

David had to bury his brother. He had a simple, graveside service. David was happy he was able to secure a plot next to his mother. He felt at peace knowing they were together, and he was beginning to believe he could join them one day.

He took Ruth back to the church, back to where it all started for him. She wanted to know why they were going, but he told her it was a surprise. When they got there, the church was unlocked. No one was there. They walked up to the pulpit; David squatted down, and opened a small door at the bottom.

He removed some papers of sermons on which Isaac had been working. He removed some hymnals. Then he lifted the false bottom to reveal a secret compartment. In that compartment, wrapped in a simple cloth, was the Testimonial. He put everything back and stood up. As he straightened, he saw Moses and Ester at the back of the church. He wasn't sure what to say.

He asked, "What are you doing here?"

The attack left Moses in a wheel chair. David still couldn't get used to seeing him this way. He was told he may never walk again. Moses had taken it well. He had said that meant God still had some work for him to do. He said, "We wanted to pay our respects to Timothy's grave."

David nodded and then said, "Where is Jeremiah?"

Moses said, "Someone had to keep the recovery going back home."

David knew the recovery would still take several more weeks. The damage from the attack had been severe. They were re-fortifying the area, but it was a big job. David smiled now. He said, "I have a present for you." David placed the large book gently in his lap. He said, "From Tim."

Moses smiled broadly. David said, "Tim never took it. He said he didn't know who he could trust, so he hid it. He told me where it was and told me to get it to you."

Moses asked, "When did he tell you this?"

David said, "It was the last thing he said. As he was dying, he told me he had two things to tell me. This was the first thing. He died before he could tell me the second thing."

Moses said, "I'm sorry."

David said, "I think it was about Zeek. Tim said he discovered a horrible truth. I think he may have found out about Zeek before the rest of us did."

Moses noticed how he said, "us."

David said, "The important thing is that my brother never betrayed anyone. The Testimonial was always safe."

Moses nodded. He said, "David, I have been in touch with the Apostle."

"The Apostle?" David asked.

"Yes," Moses replied.

David looked confused. He said, "I thought you were the Apostle."

Moses laughed a little. "No, each country has an Apostolate, but our leader is at our world headquarters. That is also where we train our soldiers. We have decided to grant your request for training." Moses let David absorb that for a moment. He said, "Another reason I am here is because you won't be returning with us. It has been decided that you will go there to begin your training."

Moses looked at Ruth. He said, "You are temporarily being assigned to him. We don't know if they will try to get to him. He trusts you. You will be solely responsible for his safety until he completes his training."

Ruth beamed. She said, "Yes, sir."

Ester gave David and Ruth their plane tickets. Ester said, "The plane leaves this evening. We want you there and secure A.S.A.P." Ruth nodded. David had wondered where the world headquarters were located. He had given it a lot of thought lately. He had guessed Rome, London, or somewhere in the Southern U.S.

David opened the ticket. He had never guessed the destination on it. He looked up and said, "Tel Aviv…Israel?"

"Yes," Ester responded, "it's the most secure city in the world."

Moses chimed in, "And it's protected by one of the most powerful army's in the world. Not to mention God's chosen people."

Ester said, "You better get going; you don't want to miss your flight."

David and Ruth said their goodbyes. As they left the church, Ester and Moses both stared at the doors as David and Ruth went through them. Ester said, "This is dangerous. We don't know if he is going to be loyal. We don't know if his conversion is real."

Moses said, "Have faith."

Ester said, "Faith? Our entire worldwide mission could be destroyed by this man, and we are going to train him as a soldier?"

Moses said, "How do you explain the miracle that happened to Ruth? We verified his story. It was a miracle."

Ester said, "Maybe he did it himself. Maybe his power also allows him to heal people. I just think we trust him too much."

Moses said, "If he really joins us, it could make the difference in this war. We have to take that chance."

Ester said, "And Ruth. We know how wrong it is, but we let her go with him?"

Moses said, "The Apostle and I discussed it at length. It was his idea. He may not trust us either. We know it's dangerous to encourage the relationship, but right now we need him to trust us, and we need him to be focused. If we remove her, it could wreck everything we are trying to do."

Ester was quiet for a long moment. Then she asked, "Do you think he suspects Judas is his father?"

Moses shook his head slowly. "That is the only thing we haven't told him. We still don't know how Timothy found out."

"When will we tell him?" Ester asked.

"When he is ready to hear it," Moses replied.

They both kept staring at the doors, as if they were looking into the future but couldn't quite see it. There were so many different possibilities now. There was so much uncertainty. One thing they both knew for sure, though, was that now, more than ever, they needed to have faith in God.

CPSIA information can be obtained
at www.ICGtesting.com
Printed in the USA
LVOW01s1745150217
524374LV00010B/952/P

9 781480 911925